RUNAWAY
GIRL

EMMA TALLON

sphere

SPHERE

First published in 2018 by Bookouture, an imprint of Storyfire Ltd.
This paperback edition published in 2021 by Sphere

13 5 7 9 10 8 6 4 2

A CIP catalogue record for this book
is available from the British Library.

ISBN 978-0-7515-8143-0

Printed and bound in Great Britain by
Clays Ltd, Elcograf S.p.A.

Papers used by Sphere are from well-managed forests
and other responsible sources.

MIX
Paper from
responsible sources
FSC® C104740

Sphere
An imprint of
Little, Brown Book Group
Carmelite House
50 Victoria Embankment
London EC4Y 0DZ

An Hachette UK Company

www.hachette.co.uk
www.littlebrown.co.uk

Dedicated to my beautiful, wonderful son, Christian, who is the most powerful motivation the world could ever give me.

PROLOGUE

Anna ran as fast as her aching legs would carry her, her heart pounding so loud she was sure it could be heard for miles. She glanced over her shoulder as she ran and tripped over a stone. With a cry she fell, the two heavy bags on her back slipping and yanking her onto her side. A sharp pain shot up her calf and she stifled a yell. She looked down and saw blood begin to trickle out of a gash on her shin. She left it. If she stopped she would suffer much worse than this.

Terror took over and she ignored the searing pain, getting back up and moving forward at a pace almost as fast as she was going before.

This was it. This was the moment that would change everything, for better or for worse. If she made it there without being seen. If the car was where she had told Ellen to leave it, she might just escape and make it out of there alive.

If the car wasn't there though, then she was dead. That was a certainty. If one thing went wrong now, he would kill her.

Her lungs burned under the weight of the bags that carried her whole life, but she pushed through determinedly. She ran down the side of the house in which she had been held prisoner for so long. Brambles tore at her skin and clothes, and tree roots tried to trip her up again and again, but still she ran forward.

She could see the break in the bushes up ahead, at the back of the wall. It led to a dead-end street where hardly anyone went. It was here that her friend's car should be waiting, the keys on the front wheel. She prayed the keys were still there and that the engine didn't fail. It had been there for a week, while she waited for a small window of opportunity to get away.

Her heart leaped and her skin tingled in horror as she heard the unmistakable creak of the electric front gate behind her. He was back. She stifled the sob that escaped her mouth between unfit gasps of air and pushed forward for all she was worth, through the gap in the hedge and onto the street.

Branches scratched at her face and left a few small leaves in her dark hair, but all she cared about was the car parked across the road. She ran over and dumped the bags next to it, falling to her knees by the front tyre. She ran her hands over it and gasped. They weren't there. The keys weren't there.

'No, no, no this can't be happening,' she sobbed in panic.

Crawling quickly round to the other side, she grappled under the arch. Her hands knocked against something hard and cold, and the set of keys jangled to the tarmac. 'Thank God.' She grabbed them and quickly unlocked the car.

Glancing back for a second, she listened. She couldn't yet hear anyone running towards her, but that didn't mean they weren't looking for her. It wouldn't be long before he found her gone.

She hoisted the bags into the back of the car and jumped into the driver's seat. With shaking hands it took her a few precious seconds to get the key into the ignition. She turned it with bated breath and shouted in momentary elation as the car roared to life.

With one last terrified glance at the house, she put her foot down and with a screech pulled away down the road.

Her heart thundered in her chest as she stopped at a red light. She wasn't out of danger yet. If he found her, he'd torture and kill her. Frustrated, frightened tears filled her eyes as they flickered between the red traffic light and the rear-view mirror. She trembled more with every second that passed.

This was it. He was going to find her. She had come so far and it was all for nothing.

'Come on, come on, please…' she begged under her breath. A car came into view in the distance behind her. Was it him?

The lights turned amber and she slammed her foot onto the accelerator. She wasn't waiting to find out. She lurched forward and joined the fast crowd of cars on the main road. Pressing her foot down she sped away, overtaking everyone she could in the fast lane. As the minutes ticked past on her watch, the world rushed past her and the horrors of her previous life were left further and further behind. She slowly let it dawn on her. She had done it. She had actually done it.

She had escaped.

But he was still out there, and by now he would know she was gone. There was no way he would accept this. He wasn't made that way. He was evil to the core. Now that she had defied him and escaped his cruelty, he would never stop. He would hunt her down, and when he found her, he would kill her. There was no doubt about that.

She shivered. Yes, she had escaped him, and yes, she was alive. But for how long?

CHAPTER ONE

There she was again, that girl. She had moved in last week, renting a room in one of the buildings Freddie owned. He had watched her struggling along the path with her boxes, traipsing up and down on her own, from the back of the battered old Astra. It annoyed him that no one around had offered to help the girl. If he hadn't been in the middle of a business meeting in the café across the road, he would have helped her himself. That would soon have put the loitering bums surrounding her to shame and put a fire up their arses! It would be deep shame indeed for them to be seen by Freddie Tyler, doing nothing to help a young girl struggling on her own. Obviously they had no idea he was in the vicinity. But Freddie often preferred it like that. It was a good way to suss out what people were really about.

She had disappeared by the time he'd finished his meeting that day. He had scanned the high-rise building with a critical eye, wondering who exactly was subletting a room out. There wasn't much Freddie missed in his various businesses. His intelligent head was full of all the details, large and small, and he had a good firm of people in his employ to remember anything that he forgot. The flats were one of his less nefarious businesses, the paperwork all above board. There were too many dwellings to know who lived there exactly, but he would have been made aware of any new tenancy contracts being drawn up.

She was walking up the road towards the same building again now, arms full of shopping bags, barely able to peek over the top. She wasn't paying much attention to where she was going, her eyes unfocused as if in a daydream. She most certainly wasn't aware of the man standing just across the road appraising her. As he watched, one of the bulging bags tore a little at the side and a net of oranges fell out, along with a bag of flour, which promptly exploded on the pavement, covering her legs in a shock of white powder. Her eyes flew wide open and her mouth formed a little O of surprise as she stopped and bent over the bags to check her legs. She looked at the oranges and then back at the bags, trying to figure out how to get them without everything else spilling all over the road. Freddie stifled a grin at the comical scene and quickly jogged across the road to help.

'I think you'll have to put some of these down to roadkill,' Freddie said. The girl laughed, looked up and knocked Freddie Tyler for six. Her dark blue eyes sparkled as she laughed and were cloaked by a fringe of dark lashes. He felt himself hesitate, frozen for a second. It wasn't that he hadn't seen pretty girls before – he had. Of course he had. They were forever throwing themselves at him, desperate for the lifestyle and status that came with Freddie Tyler. But they all looked the same. The fake blonde hair, the fake orange skin, the fake plastic eyelashes and the fake plastic tits. This girl was different. She was natural.

'Thank you.' Her voice was quiet, melodic. She pushed a stray strand of thick, dark hair behind her ear and continued to pick up the oranges. The sparkle had gone from her face now, and though a smile remained, she looked sad. She looked vulnerable for a moment, but then that seemed to disappear and her expression became guarded. Freddie searched for something to say to her, but for once he really couldn't think of anything. This was a new sensation for him. He was never lost for words – it was one of the things that kept him on top in sticky situations. He laughed at himself slightly.

They stood up together as she dropped the last of the oranges in the bag and loitered for a moment, smiling, under an awkward silence.

'I'd… better…'

'Oh, yeah, of course! I'll carry these up for you.' He motioned towards the bags in his hand, but she shook her head.

'Oh no, really. Thank you for helping me though, I appreciate it. I've got it from here.' She smiled up at him again, tightly, and he realised she probably didn't want him to know where she lived. It was a sensible move really; he was a complete stranger after all. Single Girl Preservation Guide 101 – '*don't show strangers your home address*'. He decided he liked that about her. She seemed sensible, careful. The one and only thing he knew about her so far.

He smiled as he handed over the bags, realising he had assumed she was single. Maybe she was the bird of one of the men living in the building. That would explain why he didn't know about her. Birds didn't really count. He really hoped that wasn't the case. Not that it mattered, but she had something about her that the rest of the girls around here didn't. She spoke differently too, more gently somehow, like she'd been brought up with a bit of class. His eyes flickered over his surroundings. She definitely didn't grow up around this gaff. It showed, even in the cut of her clothes. They were decent, well made, fitted, skirt not too short, not showing too much cleavage. He realised that this was the biggest difference. She was so out of place. *What is she doing in an area like this?*

He watched her walk away and raised his hand as she glanced round to smile before walking through the front door of the building. It wasn't that he didn't like it round here – he wasn't ashamed of it or anything – but this area was for a different cut of people. Harder people. People used to a certain way of life. The kind of life a girl like that certainly would never have been introduced to. He shrugged and went back to the silver Mercedes parked across the road. It was parked on double yellow lines. That wasn't a problem. There wasn't a parking warden in the whole of East London who didn't know his car and who would have the bare-arsed stupidity to give him a ticket.

Maybe he was wrong about the girl; maybe appearances were deceiving. Either way, she was gone now and he was more than a little confused at the effect that a complete stranger was having on him.

He had to stop thinking about her. Tonight was a big night for him and he had important business to attend to.

CHAPTER TWO

Anna closed the front door of the tiny two-bed flat she now shared with a girl called Tanya and exhaled wearily. She called out to see if she was home and went through to the kitchen when there was no answer. It was small up here, but she had to admit it was cosy. And that was all she needed at the moment. In a way she really didn't care where she was. Just as long as it was somewhere that she could start again and forget everything. Well, perhaps not forget. She still had to be careful. But somewhere that she could at least stay lost and move on with her life.

Just over a week ago she had been in her car driving blindly for hours down roads she didn't know, with no idea where she was going or what she was doing. Her heart had been pounding and her eyes sporadically filled up with tears of anguish. That she had even got as far as getting lost was an unexpected achievement. She had expected to be dead already. Or at least expected to have been caught and then… well, she didn't want to think about what would have come next.

Somehow, through the twists and turns of traffic and fate, she had ended up here.

She had been at a petrol station and was walking back to her car when she'd heard a row going on between a young couple in the car next to hers. As she'd unlocked her door, she'd seen the woman jump out of the car and slam the door. The driver had screeched off as the woman yelled expletives at a pair of fading tail lights. Anna had paused, wondering if the girl was OK.

The stranded girl had stopped and felt her pockets, swearing again – to herself this time. 'Shit! My bag! Oh Christ…'

Anna had looked around worriedly, then, deciding she couldn't ignore the situation, walked over to the girl. 'Are you OK?'

The girl had glanced up at her, running her manicured hands through her long red hair, clearly agitated. 'Not really. That was my bloke – well, ex-bloke really. Stupid arse has buggered off with my handbag in his car. I ain't got my purse, phone, nothing!' She'd sighed heavily. 'It's gonna be a long bloody walk home!'

'Well…' Anna hadn't known the girl from Adam, but she couldn't just leave her there – she could've been attacked or anything. 'Do you live far?'

'Not really, only about ten minutes away. Driving that is – walking is another matter.' The girl's thick East End accent had shone through her irritated tone.

'Well, I'm not in a hurry to get anywhere. I could drop you off if you need a lift.'

The girl had looked her up and down warily.

'I'm not an axe murderer or anything,' Anna had said with a laugh, her eyes crinkling at the corners. 'I just feel bad leaving you here, and it's no skin off my nose driving an extra ten minutes.'

'Well, if you're sure you don't mind, that would be really helpful then, thanks, mate.' The girl had smiled, brightening up her face and showing small, white, even teeth behind her carefully applied lip gloss.

'I'm Tanya by the way.'

And that was where it had begun. Tanya had invited her in for a cuppa to say thank you for the lift. At first Anna had thought it best to refuse and continue her journey, but the thought of a comfortable seat and a hot drink was too tempting after being in the car for so long. The pair got chatting easily and before long, Anna had explained that she was looking to relocate.

'Where to?'

'Um… actually, I don't really know yet.' She'd stiffened up, worried that she had said too much. Tanya had seen the panic run across her face and rushed to calm her.

'It's OK – you don't have to tell me anything. We all have our secrets.' She'd smiled and busied herself tidying the coffee table, and Anna had immediately felt bad. This girl had been nothing but kind to her, and she must sound terribly rude.

'Sorry, it's not you; I just don't like to talk about certain things. It's silly really.'

'No, it's not, mate. Seriously, don't fret about it.'

Anna had relaxed a little and sipped at her tea.

'So forgetting all the previous crap, you must have somewhere in mind that you wanna go? Somewhere near family or friends?'

'No.' Her voice had come out a little too strong, so she'd softened it. 'No, I want to try somewhere new. Nowhere too special. Or expensive,' she'd added. 'Just somewhere I can be a little independent.'

'And you have absolutely nowhere in mind? Not even short term?' Tanya's face had looked comically appalled at the idea.

'No.' Anna had laughed. 'Not exactly the best-thought-out plan in history, is it?'

'Where's all your stuff?'

'In my car. You're lucky, another bagful of stuff and you'd have been walking home!'

They'd laughed together.

'Well, OK, then.' Tanya had paused and pursed her lips. After a moment she'd nodded to herself. 'I guess you're lucky too. My spare bedroom is, well, it's going spare. Can't let you sleep in your car. 'Specially not filled with all that junk.'

Anna had stopped and put her cup down on the newly cleared coffee table. 'Are you serious?'

'Yeah, why not? It's empty. And I need to rent it out really. My previous flatmate only went and got herself engaged and moved out, leaving me on me Jack Jones. Why don't you stay tonight, have a think on it and if you want the room, you can move your stuff in tomorrow.'

'Wow, Tanya, that's so generous of you—'

'No, not generous, mate, just sensible. You'll have to pay half the rent and bills – you are good for the money, aren't you?' she'd asked as it suddenly occurred to her.

'Yes, yes,' Anna had replied quickly, 'I have some savings so I'm fine for a while, but I will need to find a job at some point.'

'Well, that's not a problem.' Tanya had waved her hand dismissively. 'I can find you one of those easy. How about we go week-on-week to begin with, and then we'll see how it goes, yeah?'

Luckily for both of them, they had got on pretty well so far. Anna was the perfect housemate, and Tanya respected Anna's wish not to discuss *why* she had turned up in an unknown part of London, in the middle of the night, with nothing but a car full of clothes.

Anna busied herself putting the shopping away and started on making dinner as she checked the calendar on the kitchen wall. Yep, Tanya was working tonight, so it would just be her. She would leave a plate to warm in the oven for when her flatmate got home. Tanya was always ravenous when she got home and adored Anna's cooking. She was constantly remarking that she had never eaten so well in her life. This Anna had to believe, as within just a few days of eating her food, Tanya's wan complexion became rosier and her face less drawn.

Anna looked out the window nervously at her car. It worried her that it was in full view while it was parked, though she had gone to painstaking lengths to ensure he wouldn't be able to trace it to her.

Placing the slightly bruised oranges in the fruit bowl in the lounge, she grabbed her mug of tea and sat down in the comfy armchair, thinking about the man who'd helped her. He had swooped out of nowhere like a guardian angel – big, well dressed, handsome and ready to rescue her when she had no hands free. She knew she stuck out here. That's why she tried to keep herself to herself, not attracting any attention. She knew she was probably an easy target for anyone looking to take advantage. A 'greeny', as Tony and his men would say.

But that man seemed different. He talked just like everyone else around here, but he also looked different, like she did. He was wearing a sharply cut suit, his hair had been styled nicely and he'd had a quietly confident air about him. Odd for this area.

Well, whatever his story, it had been nice of him to help her. She couldn't help but remember how his easy smile had made little creases at the corner of those piercing, laughing eyes. It was a beautiful effect… She caught herself smiling and shook her head. She had no business thinking about men right now. She was definitely not in the right place in her own head for men of any kind. Especially after all she'd been through with the last one. It would be a long time before she could be convinced to trust anyone like that again.

Anna picked up her book and slowly but surely lost herself in the world of another, forgetting about Freddie Tyler completely. The dreams she had that night reflected nothing of her encounters that day.

CHAPTER THREE

Freddie slipped into the kitchen silently, through the back door. He pulled off the bloodied shirt and tutted in annoyance. He hadn't expected company tonight. Vince had been a man short on the ground and had asked Freddie to collect a large amount of money from one of the bookies under their protection. And for once, Freddie Tyler had been met with the sort of resistance that actually gave him a challenge. He smiled to himself. It had almost been fun really, after the initial surprise. Freddie was known as one of the hardest men in the East End. It wasn't often someone went up against him. If Benny had just paid up there would have been no unpleasantness at all. Now though, with the stunt he'd pulled tonight, Benny had practically signed his own death warrant, and the bookie was now safely tucked away in intensive care along with two of his men. Whether they had a chance at life or not, Freddie would decide later. Right now though, he had to clean up, get back to his club and sort the money out for Vince.

Freddie had got involved in this way of life when he was a kid. As a teenager, he was well built and ripped with muscles from various labour jobs he had picked up around school to bring a few quid home. He came from a big, loud and loving family, which rarely had two pennies to rub together. He had two younger brothers and a younger sister, all of whom hung on to every word he'd said back then. His father had died when he was just ten, leaving a gaping hole in all their hearts, but, as was the only way, his mum Mollie had carried on and done the best she could. It didn't matter how poor they were, she always made sure they had food in their bellies and a clean bed to sleep on. They had moved into a dingy two-bedroom flat with no windows at the back and cockroaches crawling in the corners. Mollie had waged war on the insects and managed to keep them to a minimum, but they were never gone completely. It had pained him deeply to see his poor old mum washing other people's clothes for a few measly quid each week, going out at the crack of dawn to scrub floors. It wasn't right. He knew it was his job to change things, to look after her like she had looked after them.

Big as he was, and hungry to better his family's way of life, at the age of eighteen he had been the perfect candidate for Vince to mould. He'd started out breaking a few arms or legs here and there, when money owed wasn't paid, and in return *he* got paid very well. He blocked his conscience about what he did: it was survival. It was how it had to be. After a while he didn't have to even think about it anymore. It was business.

In time, it became apparent that he not only had the strength and the mental capacity to do what he had to, he was also very intelligent. And he used that intelligence to the best of his abilities. Vince had watched him slowly make his way up through the ranks, never putting anyone's nose out of joint so much that he found himself on any big shit lists, but working damn hard and making himself valuable. He gave the boy different responsibilities, testing him out in different areas of the business. Each time, some way or another, the boy found a way to do it better, to make the work more lucrative, and eventually Freddie had taken his place as Vince's right-hand man.

Eleven years later and Freddie was one of the biggest East End barons in his own right. He had his own credentials, his own loyal group of men and his own businesses to run. These various businesses were all either created with the hard-earned money he'd made from Vince, or ones he had bought into alongside him, as equal partners.

As soon as he'd started bringing in a regular wedge he had moved his family out of the dingy slums and into a detached house on one of the nicer estates. It wasn't too posh – his mum wouldn't have liked that – but the houses were bigger, and there was lots of space and greenery around. It was a much better environment for his siblings to grow up in. As time went on he had refitted every room for her, no expense spared, so she had the best house in the street, and so that it was something she could be proud of. He knew this was important to her. He had paid for his brothers and sister to go to good schools and had made sure that his family never wanted for anything again.

He was splashing water over his face as Mollie came down the stairs quietly. She stood staring at her eldest son leaning over the sink and a rush of affection washed over her. She loved each of her children with all her heart, but Freddie… Freddie had done so much for the family, so much for her that she could never repay him. She would always try though, every day, in all the little things she could find to do for him.

Her smile faded slightly as she saw the bloodied shirt and, saying nothing, she went to the linen cupboard and brought a fresh one out, ironed only a few hours before. She knew enough about what he did from the rumours and from the utmost respect everyone gave her. She knew he was a face. She was grateful for everything he had done for her, so in return she didn't ask him about it, never tried to scold him about it. She knew he didn't want that. And she didn't want to know the details.

'Here you go, son,' she said, passing him the shirt.

He smiled. 'You don't miss much, do you?'

She winked jovially as she set about making some of the strong Italian coffee he liked so much. While everybody else was settling down for the evening, Freddie's night was only just beginning. They both knew that.

'Can I get you some cake, son? I made that fruit cake you like so much today – oh, or there's some angel cake too if you like. Thea made it earlier. She's getting to be alright at baking now.'

'I'll have some of that then, Mum, thanks.'

As he sat with his cake and coffee, he watched as Mollie turned up the fire on the huge Aga he'd had fitted in the kitchen. She bent over and peered in, making sure the flames were high, then picked up the bloodied shirt with the end of a wooden spoon and tossed it in. She unearthed a bottle of bleach spray from underneath the sink and scrubbed where it had sat on the side, though it hadn't really left any marks. That done, she checked there was nothing left of the shirt and turned the heat back down to low again.

'Another one bites the dust,' Freddie joked and got a disapproving look from his mother.

'I'll pick you up some more tomorrow. You're going through them like a baby does nappies!' She tutted and shook her head. 'Where are you off to tonight anyway? One of the clubs?'

'Yeah, got to get some graft in. These shirts don't pay for themselves!'

'Oh, go on with you.' She bustled him out the door with a kiss on his cheek as he shrugged his jacket back on.

'Thanks, Mum.' He hugged her and flashed her a winning smile. 'You're a diamond.' And then he was gone again.

CHAPTER FOUR

Leslie Davis sat down in her magnolia-coloured lounge and stared at the letter in her hand. It was Anna's handwriting. Relief hit her like a sledgehammer. She had been terrified he had killed her, and if he had, that they would never know.

Her darling Anna had left without a word. All these weeks waiting… But she had known in her heart that her daughter would get in touch. She'd known Anna would find a way to contact them. Anna thought Leslie didn't know what went on behind closed doors. But she did. Leslie always listened, never commented. Knowledge was power, and so she always sought it out. But the more she had found out, the more she had feared for her daughter. Then one day, she had disappeared. *He* had come around then, appearing grief-stricken. Such an extraordinary actor. She had played along, had comforted him even, outwardly keeping the peace while she waited to find out what was going on.

After agonising and thinking the worst for a few weeks, Leslie had thought over the last few times Anna had visited. She had been more emotional than usual each time she'd left. Like she'd known she wouldn't be back. Maybe she'd run away? Thinking logically, that might have been the only way out for her, and the more Leslie had thought about it, the more certain she had become. If he hadn't killed her, then she must have run away. And she mustn't have said anything to keep everyone else safe too. He wouldn't stop looking for her though, Leslie knew that much. He just wasn't built that way.

Smoothing her perfectly made-up, golden hair, she took a deep breath, then stopped as she turned the envelope over. It had been opened and resealed – this much was obvious. She went cold. It had been opened. It would only have been him. Which meant he was watching the house. Waiting for Anna to make her move.

Please, God, Anna, don't have said anything in here that you don't want him to know! She opened it with trembling hands and began reading, scanning the lines quickly to make sure there was nothing he could have used.

Hi Mum,

I'm so sorry to have disappeared as I did. I can't explain why, though I think you know a lot more than you let on anyway. I have to go away for a while, but I will come home to you one day. Hopefully not too far in the future.

Please don't worry about me; I'm safe. I've got money, and I'm renting a room in a nice flat with another girl. I'm OK.

I can't tell you where I am right now. I know that this must be so confusing for you, and I beg you, please don't be hurt. I'll tell you everything one day. Just know that I love you and Daddy more than anything, and that I really am safe and well and OK.

I will find a way to contact you again. Keep me in your heart. You're both in mine.

Your Anna xx

Her heart rate slowed down as she reread it, more slowly this time. Squinting, she tried to make out the postmark. God must have been on Anna's side the day she posted this letter. It was smudged beyond recognition. There was nothing in there he could use to find her.

She folded it neatly and put it back inside the envelope. Sitting back in the chair and absentmindedly biting one perfectly polished burgundy nail, she wondered what to do next. She had been right. Anna *had* run away from him. And had left no tracks by the looks of it, or he wouldn't be rifling through her parents' post. *Good girl*, she thought to herself. She let the ghost of a smile escape. The girl had a lot more strength than she gave herself credit for, and now she was using it. How to keep her safe though? That was the more pressing question. She couldn't go to the police. If the gossip was anything to go by, he had more of those on his payroll than off, so that would do her no good. Maybe a private investigator, but then he would know she was doing that, and what's to say he wouldn't just buy him off too? Then again, she couldn't do nothing, because that would be suspicious... *What to do?*

The phone rang shrilly and made her jump. She hadn't realised how quiet it was. She picked up the receiver quickly, half hoping and half dreading it was Anna.

'Hello?'

'Mrs Davis, how are you?' It was him. She swallowed a lump in her throat and tried to hold her voice as steady as she could.

'Tony, hello. How good of you to call.'

'Of course, Mrs Davis. I'll call every day until we find our Anna. I worry about you two, sitting there fretting... I'd like to think my parents would have people who care about them if anything happened to me.'

Oh, if only… she thought darkly.

'Really, we're both fine. Worried of course, but we're OK. Tougher than we look,' she added. She heard him hesitate on the line.

'Have you heard anything from her, Mrs Davis?' he asked politely. Too politely.

Damn him. Of course he knows – he went through my post. She sighed with resignation. She could either play along or be seen as the enemy. And anyway, there wasn't anything in the letter he could use.

'Actually, yes, sort of.' She perked up her voice in an attempt to sound eager. 'I was just about to call you actually. I've just finished reading a letter she's sent home.'

'Really? A letter?' his fake astonishment came down the line.

'Yes, isn't that good news? She's safe!'

'That's fantastic news, Mrs Davis. So where is she, did she say?'

Leslie rolled her eyes. 'No, that's the sad part of it, Tony. She says that she's safe, but it sounds like she doesn't want to be found right now.'

'Oh right, I see. Well, I don't agree. I'm worried. I think it's too dangerous out there for a girl all alone, with no family or friends around her. I worry about her mental state too, going off like that for no reason. Anything could happen to her. It's not safe.'

Safer than anywhere near you, she thought, but said nothing.

'If you don't mind, I'll send one of my boys to come and collect it. We have people working on finding her, perhaps it will help.'

Leslie stayed quiet for a moment, wondering what to say, searching the letter over frantically for anything she might have missed.

'Not at all. That's fine. Any time tomorrow morning before eleven is good for me.'

'They'll be over around ten then. Bye, Mrs Davis.'

His silken voice made her want to tear his face off. But her own voice betrayed nothing. 'Goodbye.'

Leslie hung up the phone and let the tears fall silently down her face. She walked wearily up the stairs and opened the door to her only daughter's childhood bedroom. Rocking back and forth in the chair, holding Anna's favourite teddy bear, she sat staring into the distance for the rest of the day, until her husband came home from work and led her away.

CHAPTER FIVE

'And then the idiot tells me he doesn't feel like paying anymore, that he's decided to *go another way*,' Freddie said, rolling his eyes. 'Starts playing Billy-big-balls because he's got his two mates in there with baseball bats.'

'Baseball bats?' Vince asked in disbelief.

'Yes, baseball bats.'

'That stupid twat. He was on to a good thing there. We put a stop to all the skimming in his gaff, all the robberies, all the nitpicky stuff; we got him better security and this is how he repays us? He never had a better ally than us in there. He was taking home almost double what he was before we started.'

'I know,' Freddie said quietly. 'He got greedy.'

Vince sat back in his chair and played absentmindedly with the tumbler of whisky in his hand. 'Where is he now?'

'Lying in a nice cosy hospital bed. Along with his mates.'

'And the damage?'

'Nothing but the best. ICU.'

'OK.' Vince nodded his agreement.

They sat in companionable silence for a few minutes. Freddie had many offices in his various places of business, but this was his favourite. The furniture was dark oak, antique and expensive. There were four safes hidden away behind pictures that held assorted weaponry, money and fake papers, should he ever need them. Always better to be safe than sorry. It was also virtually soundproof, so even though it was just two doors away from the noise and hubbub of his largest club, you could only hear a soft droning, which was almost soothing.

'Perhaps we should buy him out. Take this, erm, obviously very stressful place of work off his hands.' Vince smiled a slow predatory smile, and Freddie laughed.

'Looks like he just nailed his own coffin shut, didn't he?'

'You'll get someone to take care of the paperwork, Freddie.' Vince waved his hand. 'Get it valued, offer him half. If he's difficult, we'll cut that to a third, got it?'

'Got it. By the way, I'm going after that money Scottish George got collared with.'

'Really?' Vince seemed surprised. 'Where they holding it again?'

'Romford Road station.'

Vince raised his eyebrows and whistled. 'It's a bold move, but they won't see it coming.'

'Exactly. Got enough of their officers on payroll – they can start actually working for it.'

A few months back, one of Freddie's men had been given a tug while transporting profits from a job back to Freddie. They had confiscated it, just over half a million pounds. A small amount Freddie would have let go – it was one of the risks you took in this business. But that was too much to swallow. He wanted it back.

'Hm. Who are you taking on for this? Sammy? Bill?' Vince asked.

'Yeah, pretty much. Need a few more but want to just run the plans by Sammy first, make sure he's up for it. It's a risky play – he might turn it down.'

'Nah, long as it's well planned, which I have no doubt it will be, he'll be up for it. He's smart but game, that boy. Anyway, I must get going.' Vince stood up to leave.

'OK – oh, don't forget this.' Freddie chucked a bundle of notes at him. 'Got our brass out of them after all. Seems they had a change of heart once they saw James and Scot behind them. And an even bigger change of heart once they were on the floor.'

Vince paused and then chuckled. 'You'll never stop surprising me, Freddie.'

*

Tony growled under his breath in rage as he paced up and down beside the small side gate outside the kitchen door. It led out of the long garden to an overgrown scrub area, the other side of the high walls that bordered the house and grounds. Aside from the large, electric front gates, it was the only exit out of the property, and he kept it locked. He had thought this to be enough to keep that stupid bitch in, where she belonged. His lip curled into an ugly expression as he thought of Anna.

The house was practically a fortress; a necessity in his line of work, and of course he enjoyed keeping her locked up as well. As a boy, he had often trapped small animals and kept them in tiny cages that he made himself. Birds, mice, whatever he could get his hands on. He would watch them for hours, days, weeks as they struggled and despaired. Eventually the light would dull behind their eyes and they would become still. Their spirits would be broken. It made him feel big – powerful.

When he looked at Anna he saw those same dull eyes. It excited him, that feeling of power. It turned him on. He watched her wilt in front of him. He took pleasure in demeaning her and pushing her spirits lower every day.

She was his personal possession. The thing he eagerly came home to every night. Abusing her body while watching the despair in her eyes made him feel good. Having someone there to serve him food, clean his house, satiate him in bed and do whatever else he needed worked perfectly for him. In his mind, this was exactly how things should be. He thought those men who treated their women like equals were idiots.

He wasn't bad to Anna, he reasoned. He allowed her to live in this big, expensive house and bought her designer clothes and shoes. After all, he needed her to look good, to reflect well on him. She should have been fucking grateful. Where would she ever get better than this? She didn't even need to work for it. Not that he allowed her to. He didn't need her swanning around getting airs and graces again, thinking she was something special. She had everything she needed already, without that. And what does the ungrateful bitch do? She steals his money and runs away!

Frustrated, he turned and flounced back into the house.

When she hadn't answered his calls that day, he had gone looking for her. The house had been empty and half her clothes had gone. He had quickly checked all of his many stash holes and realised that there was money missing. It had taken a while to sort through what should have been there and what had gone, but he worked out that she must have made off with around fifty grand in total. He had torn the house apart in rage.

Fifty grand wasn't a lot of money to him, not really. But the fact that she had stolen from him made him angry. That money, just like everything else here, belonged to him. Just as she did. He owned her.

He leaned forward on the marble worktop of the kitchen and stared blankly out of the window with dead, dark eyes. He would find Anna, and when he did he was going to torture her in every way possible until her weak, pathetic body gave out.

And he was going to savour every second.

CHAPTER SIX

Anna smoothed down the front of her new bright-blue dress. It was a fitted, high-necked number, down to the knee. Figure-hugging enough to show off her curves but modest enough to not stand out too much.

The taxi was pulling up outside the club. After weeks of staying in the flat and never going anywhere, Tanya had finally convinced her to go on a night out. Anna had been reluctant, but her fiery friend had decided she wasn't taking no for an answer this time, so Anna had finally given in. She had to get back out there sometime, after all.

Her hair was smooth and her eyes were bright under the subtle layer of make-up she had applied. A stark contrast to Tanya's smouldering look, with her ruby lips and dramatically volumised red curls.

As she walked into the club she almost felt like her old confidence was beginning to creep in again. Although that was probably just the Prosecco they had drunk while getting ready. This was her first time properly out in public since… She didn't let herself finish that thought. She had avoided going to places where there were crowds. Tony would have people out looking for her everywhere. This she was certain of. Only his closest men though, not the whole army he had at his disposal. It wouldn't be widespread knowledge that she had escaped, not yet. Tony was a man driven by a darkly twisted ego; the fact she had defied him and shamed him by leaving would not be something he would share easily. Pride was everything to men like him.

If she knew him at all, he would be working on getting her back before anyone knew. Then he would punish her. A very painful, calculated punishment before he finally killed her. He would enjoy every second of it too. She shivered and pushed the thoughts away.

Tanya strode confidently over to the bar with Anna in tow, all male eyes sticking to her as she passed by. She was incredibly impressive, Anna had to give her that. With her striking colouring and plunging red dress to match, she was a walking sex bomb. Anna paled into the background beside her, but this she was happy about. The less attention she got, the better.

'I'll get the drinks, what do you want?' Anna said.

'You sure?' Tanya replied, studying her thoughtfully.

Anna knew Tanya was trying to work her financial situation out. They'd known each other almost two months now and apart from going to the supermarket, or to post the one letter she had sent, she hadn't left the house.

She didn't need to get a job just yet. The rent and bills had been cheaper than she had thought they would be, and the cash she had managed to take away with her had stretched a long way. Anna had much more too, in her bank account. Tony had no idea how much was there. It was all dirty money from his various scams and businesses. She had siphoned off large wads of cash here and there and slipped them into her account unnoticed.

Anna had felt a pang of guilt each time she did it. It was against her nature to act deceitfully. But then she would remind herself of her situation. Tony had kept her in that house against her will for years as an unwilling and unpaid housekeeper. She reasoned that she had more than earned the money she was taking. Perhaps if she had other options it would be different, but she didn't. It had been the only way.

She knew now though that Tony would be watching any activity on her account. He had someone in the bank that kept tabs on certain accounts for him. He had never bothered checking hers before. Why would he? He would now though, and she couldn't risk him finding out where she was drawing money from. So the cash she had stuffed in her bag when she fled would have to stretch.

While they stood deliberating, two glasses of Prosecco appeared, compliments of a man at the other end of the bar blinded by Tanya's curves. She waved her hand and rewarded him with a smile before grasping Anna's arm and pulling her to a nearby table. Anna felt sorry for him as his face dropped, sorry to see his siren go.

'Right. Now. Let's enjoy these drinks then head on out to the dance floor, shall we?'

Anna grinned at her and nodded. She hadn't danced in so long.

An hour later, Anna sat back down at the table with another drink. She needed to cool down. She happily sat watching Tanya enjoy herself, surrounded by all the best-looking men, and smiled. She liked to see Tanya happy. She deserved to be, especially after everything the girl had done for her.

She looked around, admiring the place, then squinted, barely able to make out the silhouette of the man who slipped behind a door as she looked up. She couldn't see much in the dark.

Just then, someone bumped into her from behind, causing some of her drink to spill down her dress.

'Oh!' she exclaimed, jumping up and brushing off as much as she could.

He moved round to face her. 'So sorry, didn't mean to do that, darlin'… Let me get you another one, yeah?'

'No, no, really, it's fine. I'm fine, no harm done,' she said, looking over his shoulder, still wondering who had been watching her.

The man tried to focus his gaze on her, obviously the worse for wear from his night out.

'Well, how about I buy you one anyway, gorgeous? You ain't bad looking! How about it, eh?' He pushed himself closer to her, so close she could smell the stale alcohol on his breath. She cringed as she was trapped, the chair and table behind her and him in front. She put her hands flat against his chest and pushed him away with all her strength.

'I said, no thank you!'

The man toppled backward and fell into a table full of people, knocking more drinks flying. Anna's hands flew to her mouth. He straightened up with some difficulty, then, face red with anger, he lunged towards her, swearing loudly at the same time.

'You cheeky fucking bitch, think you can get away wit—'
And at that moment, the bouncers, who had seen the whole
episode unfold, stopped him in his tracks and dragged him
outside, still shouting abuse.

Tanya ran over when she saw the commotion. 'God, are
you alright?' She leaned down, looking into her friend's face
and checking for any damage.

'Yes, I'm fine. He just scared me a bit, but I'm fine now.
I promise.' She smiled reassuringly at Tanya, embarrassed at
the spectacle she'd created and nervous at the attention it had
drawn.

'Are you sure?' Tanya bit her lip, torn between staying with
her friend and going back to the crowd of fans waiting for her
on the dance floor.

'Yes, honestly, go dance, Tan. I'm happy here.' She urged
her friend back to the floor and, after a moment's deliberation,
Tanya sashayed off, a smile forming again on her pretty face.

Anna sat down awkwardly and forced herself to smile and
sit still. Her heart was thumping inside her chest. She felt very
exposed. The other clubbers kept looking at her, glancing over.
Were they just gossiping about what had happened, or did they
recognise her? People were getting up, moving. Was one of
them on their way to make a phone call to Tony right now, to
let him know where she was? Did he have people everywhere
in the East End too, like he did in North London? Even if he
didn't, she wasn't exactly a million miles away – there were
bound to be people here who knew him. And if he had sent
the word out, and maybe even her picture… She felt herself
sweating, picturing Tony on his way here, thunder in his eyes.

Her rushing blood began to roar loudly through her ears. She couldn't breathe; she had to get away from all these people. Get away from this place where she was boxed in, where there would be no escape if he entered. There was only one way in and out. She needed to leave. Get somewhere that no one could see her. She picked up her bag and jacket and headed over to where Tanya was still dancing away, not a care in the world.

'Tan, I don't feel very well, I'm going to go home.'

'What?' Tanya clasped her arm before she could slip away. 'You're not upset about that guy, are you?'

'No, no, it's not that – I really don't feel well. I just need some fresh air and to go home.' Anna's throat began to feel like it was closing. She was on the verge of a full-on panic attack; she had to hurry.

'OK, then I'll come with you.' Tanya started guiding her back to the table, but Anna stopped her.

'No, Tan, please stay. You're having a great time, you don't need me here and I'll be fine. I don't feel like I'm good company right now. I just want to slip off quietly.'

'But, Anna, I can't just let you go on your own.'

'I'll get a cab! I promise. Just go back. I don't want to ruin your night. I'll see you in the morning.' Her eyes darted desperately to the door.

'I'd rather you didn't go alone.' Tanya looked at Anna's pale complexion and pushed the hair back from her face. 'OK. But do get a cab. I'll bring you breakfast in the morning. I'll play nurse for the day. Well… depending on the size of my hangover.' She winked. 'Get home safe, babe. Emergency numbers are by the phone.'

Anna smiled fleetingly, then fled from the club as fast as she could. She got outside and it was still too crowded, so she turned towards the darkest route out and began to run.

Halfway down the road, she stopped to catch her breath. Her sides were beginning to hurt. Then she heard the sound of running footsteps behind her. Soft, heavy thumps, like those of a man rather than the click-clack of a woman's heels. She heard herself draw in a high-pitched breath, almost a shriek, and silently cursed herself. The adrenaline hit her and she began to run for all she was worth. She couldn't believe it – she was right to be scared, all that time she had been in there… She'd probably only just made it out. He had probably seen her as she started running off. Fear seeped into every pore. Of course someone recognised her. Tears began to sting her eyes. She should have stayed; why did she run off alone? She was done for. Whether he killed her or made her go back, her life was over.

She began to sob as the footsteps caught up behind her and she cried out as two big hands grasped her shoulders.

'No!' She tried to pull away as the man grabbed her closer.

'Stop, wait! It's OK! It's just me!' The man steadied her and she looked up in terror.

It was him – the man who had helped her pick up the oranges. She sobbed again, this time in pure relief.

'It's OK, calm down, nobody's after you.' He looked in amazement at the wreck the girl in front of him had turned into. 'Who did you think it was? That bloke from the club?'

Anna quickly processed this in her head as she tried to catch her breath. If he thought she was scared of the drunk guy from the club, he couldn't know who she was. He couldn't be working for Tony. She tried to be calm, suddenly aware of the spectacle she was making of herself.

'Yes. No. I don't know. I just – I heard someone chasing me and panicked.'

Freddie took off his jacket and put it round her shoulders. She was shaking.

'You shouldn't run off like that on your own in the dark. It's bloody dangerous around here at night.'

'I know, it was stupid.' She cursed herself for getting into such a precarious position. Even if he wasn't one of Tony's henchmen, he still could have been someone else with bad intentions.

'Why did you run off anyway? Are you OK?' Freddie's voice was tinged with concern, and Anna suddenly felt grateful that he was there.

'I'm sorry. I didn't feel well. I just needed to get away. Needed some fresh air. I was on my way home.'

Freddie looked confused and glanced down the street. 'What, this way?'

Anna suddenly realised she had no idea where she even was. She could have been running anywhere.

'Well, I…'

'You don't know where you are, do you? Your gaff is in the opposite direction.' He stared at her for a few moments. 'Come on, I'll walk you home. You do look like you need some fresh air.'

They started walking back the way they had come and Anna, her fear subsiding, felt a fresh wave of embarrassment wash over her. How pathetic she must have looked. And she must have torn him away from all his friends. It was funny, she hadn't noticed him at the club, but he must have been there. She said as much and he grinned at her through the darkness.

'Nah, you didn't spoil my night. I wasn't out for pleasure. I own the club, along with a couple of others.'

'Really?' she asked. That would explain why he dressed so well: he was a businessman.

'Yeah, get more work done here in the evenings. Plus, I like to keep an eye on the place, make sure things run smoothly. No hassle.'

They passed the club again and kept walking on. The bouncers nodded their respect to him, and he acknowledged them with a slight incline of the head.

'I saw you earlier on in the evening. I saw that guy come up to you and was about to come down, but you seemed to be doing alright on your own.' He chuckled to himself. 'Right little spitfire you were in there.'

Anna laughed. 'Yes, well... I don't like people backing me into a corner. I get claustrophobic.'

'Seems like you don't like people getting within ten feet of you.'

Anna looked up, worried she had offended him. 'It wasn't you. I just got scared.'

'I know, I'm only messing.' He put his arm around her, rubbing her shoulder, then dropped it, not wanting to frighten her away. For a second there was a part of Anna that wanted him to keep his arm around her. Then she banished the thought. She had no place thinking about any man right now, let alone trusting one again.

'So that's twice you've saved me now. I'm beginning to think I have my own personal knight in shining armour,' she joked.

'Here to protect and serve,' he replied, flourishing a mock salute. He cringed internally at himself. What a stupid line. He was becoming soft. What was it about this girl that made him act so daft? He looked down at her out of the corner of his eye as they walked in companionable silence. She looked so small, so fragile, and so… so haunted. That was the only word that could describe it. He'd presumed it was sadness, and maybe that was part of it. But it was more than that. She had looked utterly terrified when he finally caught up with her tonight. Like she had been running from more than just the man from the club.

She looked stunning in that blue dress. It wasn't a statement; it just fitted her right. It showed off her figure without leaving her semi-naked, as seemed to be the fashion. Her hair was glossy and her face needed no help, it was perfect as it was. To most of the men in his clubs, she would probably fade into the background amongst all the heaving bosoms, cherry-red lips and platinum, glittery artworks that made up the bulk of his female customers' appearances. He had been interested in that once too. But unlike the other men, he'd grown tired of the fakeness. He'd grown tired of waking up in the morning to someone completely different from the bronzed, heavy-eyed woman he'd gone to bed with. None of it was real and therefore he could never conjure up any real feelings. Those girls fell in love – and into bed – more often than they had hot dinners, and typically the love they felt was for the credit cards, fast cars and status. He couldn't muster any respect for those girls. But this girl seemed different.

He mentally shook his head and frowned. He didn't know the first thing about her, not really. She was just some bird who seemed not only accident-prone but a nightmare in the making, walking herself into danger everywhere she could. No, he definitely did not have time for this puzzle. It would have to solve itself.

'It's Anna, by the way.'

'Hm?' He snapped out of his daze as she spoke.

'It's Anna. My name,' she said, a little awkwardly. He realised he must've seemed rude, spacing out like that.

'Sorry, world of my own. I'm Freddie.'

'Well, Freddie, thank you for walking me home tonight. I owe you one. Well, two actually.' She smiled.

Freddie looked up and realised they were outside her building, and he felt a pang of regret at having to let her go.

'Oh. Right. No problem. Glad I could help.'

'Goodnight then, Freddie.' Anna headed to the front door.

She had the key in her hand when Freddie blurted out, 'Tomorrow…'

'Sorry?'

'Tomorrow afternoon. Are you around?'

'Um, yes, I guess so. Why?'

'Well, you can start paying me back that one you owe me. Well, two.'

Anna debated it for a minute, wondering if it was really wise. It couldn't hurt, she supposed. It wasn't like a date or anything. 'OK then. Come by when you want. I'm at number twenty-two.'

'Great, see you then.' He turned and walked away quickly, cursing himself. What had he gone and said that for? Now he would have to come up with ideas for tomorrow that made it look like he'd already had something in mind! *Pay him back the one she owed him? For God's sake, Freddie,* he thought. *Smooth.*

CHAPTER SEVEN

Anna slept badly that night. She tossed and turned as she dreamed about Tony.

She was in the car trying to keep her face completely blank, but she knew it was futile. It didn't matter how compliant she was, if he was in a black mood she would be made to bear the brunt of it. She hadn't seen him since the night before, and she had thanked God for the short but sweet respite. Then he'd come home like this. She shifted her weight and took a deeper breath, aware that she was hardly breathing. Wrong move.

'What's that sigh about? Eh? You're in that mood again, aren't you? Well, don't even think about it – not today.'

Tony started playing with his phone, texting a reply to one of his employees.

'Tony, look out!' Anna shouted, natural instincts kicking in and making her cry out, alerting Tony to look up just in time to avoid hitting the parked car he was heading straight for. 'Jesus!' She let out the breath she'd been holding.

'Oh shut up, I wasn't even close.' He carried on texting away as he drove dangerously close to cars and other objects. His driving was scaring her. She tensed and bit her lip in silence,

but eventually her fear of a painful death by car crash overrode her fear of upsetting Tony.

'Tony, please! Please can you put the phone down? It's not safe.'

'What the fuck are you talking about? Just shut the fuck up, Anna. I knew you'd be nothing but trouble today, I fucking knew it. Stupid bitch.'

Anna bit her lip again. She'd done it now – whatever she said, she would be in the shit for it. She glanced into the back of the car, where Tony's daughter from a previous relationship sat quietly. She had learned from the word go to stay quiet and invisible. But the car was veering into the middle of the road and Anna had to call out again.

'Tony! I'm not trying to be difficult, please, but this is unsafe. You're all over the road, you have me and Alexis in the car—'

'I told you to SHUT THE FUCK UP.' The thump to the side of her head came in hard and fast as he savagely yelled in her face. She froze. The pain was strong, and she begged silently for the tears not to fall.

Two and half days of abuse had followed that incident. She had repeatedly apologised and grovelled to him to forgive her for what she had done. For everything she had not done, for everything she was not.

She hated herself for bowing so easily to a bully. But not half as much as she hated him right now for what he was doing to her. She had worshipped him when he'd first shown interest in her. She had been in such a vulnerable place and he so strong and caring. She'd thought he had such a big heart. She knew about him and what he did, and she accepted that. Not everything was perfect. He had managed to convince her all the rumours about how evil-tempered and fucked-up he was were untrue. She had felt for him, wanted to be the one to understand him. But things had changed. She felt helpless; she felt like she was drowning.

He came at her again, the curses falling thick and fast, the vein in his temple throbbing as his anger built up inside him, ready to explode.

'You fucking bitch, you dirty, lowlife fucking bitch, you think you can take me for a mug, do ya? Eh?'

She just sat there. There was nothing she could do but take it.

*

Anna gasped for air as she woke up, panting, crying, half with terror and half with relief that it had just been a dream. He wasn't here; he couldn't do that to her anymore.

Her bedclothes and linen were soaked through with sweat. Rubbing her tired eyes, she turned the light on and went to the closet to get a clean nightie. She shuffled to the bathroom and quickly jumped under the shower to wash away the last of her nightmare and rid herself of the cloying, sticky feeling of her own sweat. Anna hated feeling sticky now. Dirty in any way. It just reminded her of him, of how their relationship had been.

Feeling better, she looked at the bed, which was still damp. She was too tired to change her bedding now and she needed some proper sleep. Grabbing one of the warm blankets from under the bed and switching the heating on as she passed, she headed out to the couch and settled herself down there, finally falling into a peaceful sleep.

*

It was the smell and the popping and sizzling of bacon that roused Anna from her slumber. Looking through half-asleep, half-open eyes at the sunlight shining in the window, she guessed it was probably late morning. She yawned and stretched, then propped herself up against the cushions so she could see Tanya.

'Morning, sunshine!' Tanya chirped and handed her a glass of orange juice. 'You haven't got a hangover, have you? I didn't think you knocked back that much last night?'

Anna took the orange juice gratefully and sipped at it, recollecting the previous night's happenings. The nightmares always took it out of her. She ran her fingers through her long dark hair, massaging her head as if trying to clear it.

'No, not hungover. I was a bit tipsy, but not hammered. Did you have fun after I left?'

'Yeah, it was a good laugh. Didn't stay that long though, there wasn't much happening.' Tanya flipped the bacon onto the plates and scraped the scrambled eggs out of the pan next to them. Chucking the ready-prepared bread and butter on top, she passed one of the plates over to Anna on a tray then sat down next to her and tucked into her own breakfast. Both sat in silence for a few moments, enjoying their food.

'Are you feeling OK today?' Tanya asked between mouthfuls.

'What? Oh, yes,' Anna added hastily, 'much better this morning. Don't know what was wrong with me, maybe something I ate yesterday.'

'Hardly likely. You cook nearly everything in this gaff and you're more anal than a Sunday-school nun about your cooking,' Tanya said sceptically, munching another mouthful of crispy bacon. 'Though I have to say, you've been tossing and turning all night, and you were quite hot to the touch when I came in to check on you. Maybe it was a sort of fever or something.'

Anna relaxed. Her nightmares had one positive to them: it didn't look like she had just been ducking out last night after all.

'When did you check on me? I didn't hear you come in.'

'No, you were dead to the world, but you were mumbling in your sleep. I thought you were talking to me – that's why I came in.'

Anna started to feel a little coldness creeping in on her again.

'What was I saying?' she said calmly.

Tanya laughed. 'Oh, I don't know, mate. Just a load of old boot really.' Tanya's smile faltered and she looked at Anna sideways. 'I think you were having a bad dream though. You kept saying "no" and "please stop"… and when I put my hand to your forehead to check how hot you were, you pushed me away like you'd been burned.' Tanya went quiet and waited for Anna to answer. It was silent for a moment.

'Well. Like you said, sounds like a bad dream.' Anna carried on with her breakfast, the conversation obviously over.

Tanya slowly followed suit. 'Yes, from the fever,' she said quietly. She hadn't told Anna everything she had heard. If truth be told, she had initially gone in to check that her friend and flatmate was alright, but what she'd heard had made her sit down in the dark and listen.

She had watched Anna struggle with her demons and heard her begging for the torture to stop. She heard Anna despair that the man she called Tony had found her, heard the utter terror in her voice as she begged him to leave her alone. She had recognised the defeat, and the submission elicited by the fear he instilled in her, even just in the dream, and had prayed that in reality, Anna's past had not been as horrific as what was playing out in her dreams. Though looking at Anna's secrecy so far, along with her reaction to what she had just said, Tanya realised that it was probably all of that and more. But Tanya respected Anna's privacy. She believed everyone was entitled to their secrets.

Tanya shrugged mentally and took her plate over to the sink. She had too much on today to think about anything else. Trying to save up as much money as she could in order to open her own business someday, Tanya was pulling as many long or double shifts at the club as she could.

She moved herself towards the bedroom to get ready for work. 'I'm on a double again today, so I won't be back till the early hours. Will you be OK?'

'Yes, I'll be fine. I actually have plans today.' Anna smiled to herself and Tanya stopped in her tracks.

'You? Really? I thought you didn't like going out in the day?'

'Well, I've sort of made a friend. Just this guy I've bumped into a couple of times. Nice guy. He saw me home last night.'

'Well, you sly dog!' Tanya exclaimed, a big grin stretching over her face. 'What's he like?'

'It's not like that. We only really talked last night, and it was purely a friendly chat—'

'OK, whatever,' Tanya joked. 'You're going to have to tell me all about him later because I really do have to get ready now, but seriously – I want to know all the details.' She winked saucily and swept out of the room. Anna rolled her eyes and smiled.

CHAPTER EIGHT

Tanya had had a turbulent upbringing. Being the only girl with three older brothers, she had been left to play by herself most of her younger life. Her mother, Rosie, had been an alcoholic who had despised her for her pretty face, being deeply jealous of anything that took her boys' or husband's attention away from her. Rosie's husband was a wastrel who came home only when he wasn't living off whatever piece of skirt he had managed to shack himself up with. Rosie, loving him and wanting him still, always welcomed him back with open arms, convincing herself that he had changed. He, for his part, was a good actor, flashing his handsome smile and promising the world to her each time. But it never lasted. Sometimes he would stay a month, but he always went on his merry way once something better came along.

For all his fake promises, he'd always had a true soft spot for his daughter. And for that, Tanya suffered. Between beatings, verbal lashings and cruel punishments, Tanya lived only for the times when he would be home and bring some happiness into her dismal life again. When she was allowed outside of the house, Tanya would sit on the small bit of grass at the corner of the road, wishing that her daddy would come home to save her from her dark existence.

To make her life even more miserable, Tanya's mother only ever dressed her in grey, shapeless garments; the cheapest, oldest items she could gather from the rag markets and pawn shops, telling her that she didn't deserve to have pretty clothes. The whole world could see what a bad girl she was. She didn't need to be showing her figure off as well – she was already going to the devil.

With her brothers off married with families of their own to worry about, and her father returning less and less, no one was there to see or intervene. Between her mother ensuring she had no friends at school due to the way she looked, and not ever being allowed out in the street to play and interact with the other children as her brothers had once done, Tanya had no one to turn to in her lonely life and nothing to do but comply with what she was told.

Once she was old enough to get a job, she had gone out and found one straight away, hoping to earn enough to buy her own clothes in future. Her mother had put paid to this immediately, collecting Tanya's wages herself. She had reacted viciously when she'd asked her mother why she couldn't keep any of the money she earned. Rosie told her that she deserved none of it, seeing as it was her who'd put a roof over her head, clothes on her back and food in her mouth all these years. Tanya didn't fight her – she never did, knowing she could never win.

There was one good thing about the new job though. Her employer at the corner store said that if she was to work there, she would have to dress smartly and fashionably, so as to attract the right sort of customer. Although this had raged a fierce internal battle in Rosie's head, she had grudgingly allowed Tanya to buy one outfit, not wanting to part with the regular extra money coming in. Her alcohol supply had taken a boost since her daughter had been working, and she had no plans to let her stock run low again.

Tanya had gone running to the shops in glee, so excited to be able to buy something pretty, something to make her feel better about herself. Something she could finally feel entirely unashamed in. She had spent two hours trying on almost everything in the shop, looking at herself in wonder as the different styles gave her shape, while the colours transformed her. When she finally went home in a high-waisted beige skirt and fitted emerald-green satin shirt, with pretty beige court shoes to match, she was so elated that for a second she thought her mother might look at her and realise how nice she looked. For the first time in her life she felt like she was floating down the street towards her home, walking on air. That feeling was short-lived, however, when she was dragged into the front room by her hair and told repeatedly that she was nothing but a whore. That people would look at her in that outfit and see her for what she really was. Tanya had been crushed yet again.

When news came that her father had passed away, Tanya's heart finally died once and for all. He had been the only person she cared about and now he was gone. Her mother had dragged her by the hair down the stairs as revenge. Blaming her for every time he had gone away, blaming her for his death. Tanya had known then that although she had nowhere to go and no one else in her life, there was nothing here for her either. Worse than nothing – here was a place filled with hate and cruelty.

The next day, heading off to work as usual, Tanya hid the only other decent outfit she now had in her shopping bag. She had begged a second outfit after a year at the shop so as to not wear the first one out completely. Working up the courage, she explained to her employers that her father had died and that she needed to go away for a while. She asked politely if she could have her wages early and up-to-date, as if it was the most natural thing in the world. The man she worked for was a kindly old soul who, privately, disliked Tanya's mother immensely for the suffering he could see she inflicted on her only daughter. Tanya had been a good worker and proved to be a bright and friendly girl. He'd be sad to see her go, but at the same time, he was elated that she had finally upped and done it. Sealing the envelope, he had grasped her into a big bear hug and wished her well.

'Now that lot in there is right, lovey. You earned every penny, alright? Go on out of it now, and maybe come visit sometime if you're back passing through.'

Later, standing at the train station, not sure where to go, Tanya opened the envelope. Her eyes swam with tears as she counted more than double what she had earned. That small pay packet had set her on her way towards a new and better life, and for that she would never forget the kindness shown to her by that lovely old man.

Two months on, she'd found herself in East London, and having secured herself a job as a waitress, she could just about afford a flatshare. It was a complete eye-opener, finally being free of the restrictions she had lived with for so long. Her appearance became the most important thing to Tanya now, after years of being dressed as an ugly duckling. She felt like the proverbial swan, blossoming into the colourful creature she now had the freedom to be. As long as she looked good, she was happy.

There were two lessons Tanya had learned in life. Firstly, and most recently, that her looks gained her almost anything she wanted or needed, so she used that to her advantage. Secondly, she never, ever wanted to end up like her mother. Her mother had married for love and had ended up with nothing. Without the man she loved, without support and without money. If she ever got married, it would be on her terms, so that whatever happened she would never be left to rot.

As time went on and Tanya settled into her new life, she became unhappy with the meagre amount of money she was bringing in. To be able to turn heads she needed more, but to get her lifestyle paid for and the attention she craved, she had to first turn those heads. Her flatmate, Karen, always seemed to have ample amounts of money, able to get whatever she wanted, but Tanya suspected that she carried out some dark deeds for it, and despite her rebellious love for freedom, she wasn't up for going to that level just yet.

Karen had laughed when Tanya voiced this. 'Love, what do you think it is we do? It's not like the horror stories you hear out on the street, you know. We work in the club. Yeah, we wear our scanties, but we don't ever sleep with any of the punters. All we do is walk around showing off, spend a bit of time chatting them up and dancing. It's as simple as that. And we take home more in one night than you bring home in a week, including your tips!'

'I'm not so sure, Kal…'

'Look, why don't you come along with me tonight and just have a look, see for yourself. I know the owner would be more than happy to take you on. You've got all the necessary bits and bobs.'

Tanya went red. 'And you don't do anything sexual with them?'

Karen had paused and lit a cigarette. 'It's up to you, to be honest. No, you're not *expected* to, and no, it isn't on the offer at the door. But if you want to and they're offering you a good price, there is somewhere you can go discreetly.' Karen started moisturising her legs with shimmery lotion. 'But you don't ever have to do that if you don't want to. Plenty of the girls don't – they're just there to dance.'

So she had gone. She had been quite surprised at how normal it all seemed, how relaxed and warm, and had spent the evening being charmed by the club's owner. Within a week she had given up her waitressing job. With her creamy skin, heavy breasts and vivid red hair, Tanya immediately became one of the main attractions in the busiest gentlemen's club in East London. An underworld starlet had been born.

CHAPTER NINE

Pulling the brush through her long, sleek hair, Anna gave herself a little nod of approval. She had changed several times, not knowing what sort of outfit she should be wearing. Jeans, dresses, heels and flats were strewn across the usually tidy bedroom as she deliberated. In the end, she settled for a casual wrap dress with low heels that she thought would be a flexible compromise, whatever they ended up doing. She bit her thumbnail absent-mindedly as she appraised herself. Yes, it would do. She looked at the clock and checked she had everything in her handbag one more time. It was almost 12.30 p.m. She'd realised after Tanya had left for work that Freddie hadn't actually mentioned a time. Not wanting to be dithering around when he arrived, she had hurried to get ready. Now though, the excitement of that was gone, and she had nothing to do but wait.

Feeling antsy, she set about cleaning the kitchen. It was as she was setting the duster down that there was a knock on the door. It made her jump.

She shook her head in annoyance at herself. *What a stupid thing to jump at when you were expecting company*. But she was expecting the outside door to buzz, not the door to her flat.

Slowly she opened the door and found herself faced with a huge bunch of flowers. Freddie's face appeared from around the side and registered her shock. 'Sorry, I didn't mean to startle you! Actually, to be honest, I thought this would have slightly better results than my approach last night. Obviously got that one wrong...' He trailed off and gave her a large grin. Anna laughed and apologised immediately.

'Sorry, I don't know what's wrong with me these days. They're lovely.' She took them from him and blushed, feeling a little shy.

Taking this as embarrassment, Freddie said, 'Well, you know, it's not a big deal, I just know you haven't been in here long, so it's just a little housewarming gift... sort of thing...' *Oh, Freddie, you bloody prat*, he kicked himself mentally. *What are you doing making excuses like some awkward little prick in the playground?* Before he could think of something better to say, or backtrack, she had thanked him and gone to the kitchen to put them in water.

'Please, make yourself comfortable while I sort these out.'

Seated in her small but cosy lounge, Freddie was deliberating where to take Anna on their date. He'd even visited Vince last night to get his advice.

She came through and looked at him expectantly. 'So what are we doing today?' she asked with a smile.

He smiled back. 'Well, that's what I wanted to ask you. I was thinking we could maybe get out of the city for the afternoon – there are a couple of nice places I know. Or if there's something you want to do, we could do that.'

He cringed inside. It went completely against the grain for him to talk like this. Usually he would tell his dates when he'd pick them up, where they were going, what they were doing and even sometimes what they should wear. Now he was sitting here like a little boy, just trying to find something to please her. It was new and uncomfortable ground.

She gazed off into the distance as though she was somewhere else. After a long moment, just as Freddie was beginning to think she wouldn't answer, she turned to look at him.

'Do you know what I'd like to do?' she asked softly.

'Tell me…'

'I'd like to get lost.'

'Lost?' Freddie asked, unsure if he'd heard her correctly.

'Yes, lost,' she said and laughed. 'Let's get out of the city like you said, but let's just go somewhere we don't know. Go down roads we've never seen before and end up somewhere completely new.'

Freddie smiled. It was the first time he'd seen her animated since he had met her. No nervous smile or glances over her shoulder.

'Don't you ever do that?' she asked him as he tuned back into what she was saying. 'Just go somewhere, disappear off the map?'

Disappearing off the map means something entirely different in my world, he wanted to say, but didn't. He doubted she had any clue that a world like his existed, and he didn't want to spoil that. Not yet.

She paused, waiting for him to answer her, suddenly not sure if she should have said anything.

'Come on then,' he said, laughing. 'Let's get well and truly lost then!'

CHAPTER TEN

Anna felt happier than she could ever remember. She had quickly changed into a warm jumper and jeans and then they'd run down the stairs together like children, past the gawping neighbours, who watched their descent incredulously. This made Anna laugh even harder. They had looked at Freddie like he was some kind of ghost. Had they never seen two people happy before?

She slowed down when they got to the front door. As much as she wanted to feel carefree, in reality she wasn't, so she proceeded with caution towards the silver Mercedes parked across the road, checking over everyone in sight for any old face she might recognise.

Freddie opened the passenger door for her like a real gentleman. He said nothing but noted the sudden change in her.

'Right, wait there a second while I get the top down…'

'No!' She softened her voice. 'I mean, why don't we save it until we're out of London? Don't fancy the sooty air so much,' she added with a smile.

'OK.' Freddie blanked his face, unsure what it was that was scaring her. Did she not want to be seen with him? He doubted it; she didn't know him well enough to want to keep him a secret yet. He was hoping to suss her out more today.

'So where to then?' He looked at her expectantly as he slid into the cool leather driver's seat. 'North, south, east or west?'

'South,' she replied. 'South-east.'

He put the car into gear and they swept out of the street.

As soon as they reached the smaller roads and quietness of the countryside, Anna relaxed once more. She pointed out little twists and turns, directing him right into the middle of nowhere. They sat comfortably with each other, Anna enjoying the feeling of complete escape and Freddie surprisingly taking immense pleasure in being part of an innocent adventure for once.

'Take that one! The road on your left.'

Freddie turned as requested and carried on down the windy road.

'How far do you want to go today?' he said with a smile, watching her face as she took in the countryside.

'I don't know really. We can stop if you want to… sorry, I didn't really think of you doing all this driving or whether you have plans. You probably do need to get back, don't you?' The worried look returned to her face and he quickly tried to banish it again.

'No, no, it's not that; I'm enjoying this as much as you are,' he said, surprised at how truthful his words were. 'We can go all day if you want.'

'Really?' she asked, still a little worried.

'Honestly,' he said seriously, looking into her eyes.

A little while later Anna turned in her seat to face him. 'I suppose it wasn't entirely sensible to come out here with you when I know nothing about you…' she began cautiously. Freddie didn't say anything, waiting for her to continue. 'But the few times I've seen you, you've helped me, so I guess I trust you, even if I don't yet really know you…' She trailed off, not knowing why she'd just voiced her thoughts so openly. After a minute Freddie answered.

'What would you like to know about me? We have time on our hands – ask what you like.' He hoped she wouldn't ask too many things that he didn't want to answer.

'Well…' She thought about it. Better to stick to things she didn't mind answering in return, as this opened her up for questioning too. 'How about your family? Tell me about them.'

Freddie smiled. 'Two brothers, one sister – all younger – and me mum. We're very close. No dad, so it's just been me to look after them for the last few years. I guess that's what makes us so close.' He turned a corner. 'What about you?'

'Well…' It wouldn't hurt if she gave him no details. 'It was just me; I have no brothers or sisters. My mum and dad and I were always a tight unit. We did a lot together. They really wanted kids and they tried for years without luck, then just as they gave up, I came along, so they tried to make the most of every second.' She smiled, remembering. 'We did everything and anything that we could, every weekend. I suppose some people think I was spoilt, but it wasn't like that. They just appreciated every moment we had as a family.' Anna compressed the pangs of homesickness that appeared with her memories.

'You're speaking about them in past tense, are they not around anymore?' Freddie asked. *Is that what you're running from?* he wanted to say, but he didn't for fear of overstepping the mark.

'No, they… I just haven't seen them in a while.'

'Why don't you go visit?'

'Because I… well, it's difficult.' Anna shifted awkwardly in her seat and stared out at the passing scenery. Her body language clearly demonstrated her reluctance to discuss it further. Freddie frowned. It was hard to get to know her when she clammed up so often. He decided he needed a little patience so he let it go.

When they came across a sign for the beach, he turned off and sped down the road towards it.

'Oh, it's beautiful! Let's go walk on the sand!' Anna said, looking at the sea as it turned pink under the early-evening sun.

Freddie parked up next to an old couple eating ice cream, watching the sea together. Immersed in their own thoughts, they both envied the old couple for a second. Anna, in her excitement, took Freddie's hand absentmindedly and led him eagerly down to the beach. Careful not to show his surprise, Freddie glanced down. It was the first time she had voluntarily touched him since they'd met. He had put his arm around her that night, spun her round her living room earlier today, but she had so far kept a cautious distance. It came across as an unconscious habit. But now she'd grabbed his hand and was still clasping it as they tripped down the sand dune towards the waves.

Anna kicked her shoes off and motioned for Freddie to do the same, then she laughed and ran down the beach. She breathed in deeply and closed her eyes. Suddenly she felt so free. There was nothing but the sound of the waves and the seagulls. She forgot everything. She forgot who she was, what had happened, where she was, Freddie. The muscles in her legs awakened joyfully from a long hibernation, and she flexed them as she ran faster.

Freddie's breath caught in his throat as he watched her, spellbound. Her long dark hair glinted auburn in the light and danced around her playfully in the wind. She spun around, her arms in the air and her eyes closed in rapture. He had never seen such a beautiful sight. He walked towards her slowly, not wanting to break the spell she seemed to be under, but when she opened her eyes, he stopped in his tracks.

Leaving his shoes and jacket on the ground beside hers, Freddie unfastened the top buttons of his shirt and rolled up the bottom of his trousers to give himself more freedom of movement. Anna was dancing around with her arms up, eyes closed again. He started running silently, trying to take her by surprise, but she opened her eyes and saw him. He grinned and picked up speed, heading straight for her.

'Ha ha!' Anna pushed off again. 'You won't catch me!'

'I'll bet you my grandmother I do!' he answered, laughing and pushing his hard muscles into action.

'You'd best get her packed then!' Anna shouted over her shoulder.

'Ha!' He grinned. She would never outrun him.

A few metres later though, Freddie started to get alarmed. Anna was incredibly fast, and as much as he appreciated the view of her lithe figure streaking ahead of him, he couldn't believe she was actually giving him a run for his money! Or more technically, his grandmother. He switched his head into competition mode and focused on getting closer, slowly but surely now catching her up.

'No!' she squealed as she checked behind her to see how far away he was. She put one final push into her game, but Freddie could see she was beginning to tire. He smiled. Now he had her. She was fast off the mark, but she was no endurance artist. And endurance was an area in which Freddie had trained himself religiously over the years. He was only just warming up.

Anna was out of breath, but she was determined to try to win. She hadn't had this much fun, or exercise come to think of it, in ages. She turned to check just in time to see Freddie reach out to her. He wrapped his arms around her and tackled her to the ground, protecting her from the impact with his body.

He quickly looked up at her to see if she was hurt. He'd got carried away with winning; he shouldn't have tackled her. But Anna was laughing. She laughed so hard that tears came out of the corner of her eyes. He laughed with her, partly in relief and then looked at her lovely face as they lay, still touching, in the sand. There was a wisp of hair coming out over her face that he ached to push back behind her ear, but he restrained himself, still scared she might retreat into her wary state.

Anna wiped the tears from her eyes and looked up into the face looking down at hers. God, he had beautiful eyes. As he looked at her, she felt like they were going through her, seeing right into her soul. Usually this would have sent her running, but somehow today, away from it all, it felt so good. The early sunset behind him framed his head like a halo. Each was acutely aware of the warmth where the other's body touched their own. Anna thought that if she could have stayed in this moment forever, she would have done.

They lay unmoving for what seemed like both hours and just seconds, until a shiver through Anna's body from the cold, damp sand below awoke them both from their trance.

'You're cold,' Freddie tutted, annoyed at himself. 'Come on, back to the car.'

Anna hid her disappointment.

He helped her to her feet and she dusted off the sand, straightening her jumper. They walked back to the car slowly, enjoying watching the sunset glinting on the waves. Freddie looked at his watch and frowned.

'It's getting late; I didn't realise the time.' He glanced at Anna. 'How would you feel about finding somewhere here to stay tonight?'

Anna blushed a little, unsure of how to answer. Her heart raced a little.

'Not like that,' he rushed to assure her, taking her reaction as a negative one. 'I'll get us separate rooms – you don't need to worry. I just mean it's late to be driving back. We could just make an evening of it, then drive back in the morning... if you were up for that?' *And I just want to spend more time with you*, he added silently in his head.

Anna's heart dropped. *Of course he doesn't look at you like that*, she thought. *He's incredibly good-looking, obviously well off and probably has every pretty, single girl in the city after him.* Anna still wasn't sure what it was that kept him in her company, whether it was pity for her obvious helplessness whenever he was around, or perhaps he saw her as someone to be a friend or a sister figure. Either way, it definitely wasn't for the same reason that *she* wanted to be around *him*.

'Um, yes, OK. That sounds nice,' she answered, with a falsely bright smile. 'I didn't bring any stuff with me though.'

'Nah, don't worry about that.' He shook his head as he dusted off his jacket. 'I have a couple of clean tracksuits in the back for when I go to the gym. You can borrow one of my T-shirts if you don't mind roughing it?' He grinned.

'I'm sure I can cope with that,' Anna replied, and they set off to try to find somewhere nearby.

CHAPTER ELEVEN

Tony rolled up the crisp, fifty-pound note and leaned forward. He snorted the line of fluffy white powder up his nose and sat up again.

'That's better,' he said to himself, after a few moments. He sniffed a few more times and cut another line. He wasn't sleeping well lately, enraging thoughts of Anna swimming round and round in his head. The coke was helping him get through the day. He snorted the second line quickly and placed his stash back into the box in his desk drawer. The drugs began to kick in and he felt a rush of energy hit him.

Someone knocked at the door and he told them to come in. It was Stefan, one of his men who worked at the bank.

'About time. Come on, I ain't got all day,' Tony said irritably.

'Yes, sorry, traffic was a nightmare. Right,' he responded, sitting in the seat opposite Tony and getting straight down to business. He could already see it wasn't wise to linger today. 'That account, there's still no activity. Card's not been used at all.'

Tony made an exasperated sound but let Stefan continue.

'As for the new system at the bank, I've found a way of getting all the information now, without leaving a footprint.'

'Oh?' Tony perked up.

'Yeah.' Stefan looked excited. 'So I can get name, address, number, balance and credit-card limit in ghost mode.' Stefan was part of the IT team who worked on the internal systems.

'Perfect.' Tony banged his hand down on the table, a gleam in his eye. 'That's everything we need. How many can you get per day?'

'Not sure yet. I'll start with five and then up that gradually to be on the safe side.'

'OK, good. So you pick five high-limit low balances, get that information to Mike via burner then he'll ring up and pretend to be the bank. He can feed them back their own info as fake security, tell them their card has been compromised and that a courier will pick it up and deliver them a new one.' Tony stood up and started pacing excitedly, the cocaine coursing through him. He loved getting stuck into new scams. It kept things fresh, and right now that was exactly what he needed – something other than Anna to focus on. 'Chris will then print off a dummy card with their details, deliver that and get the real one. Then he can siphon the money off into the fake offshore accounts and I'll distribute it from there. It's genius.'

'Yes,' Stefan continued, 'then the customer complains about the new card and it hits the fraud system. Insurance pay out to the customer and the case never gets anywhere, as they won't have the correct details of the offshore accounts to investigate with. It's foolproof. And the only losers are the banks.'

'Which they can afford, the rich fuckers,' Tony replied. 'Yeah, I like it. Tell everyone to gear up, start the ball rolling

Monday. I want you to check over the dummy cards to make sure they're good copies before the first one goes out.'

'No problem.'

'Get this running smoothly and I'll see about cutting you in on some of the gold scams.'

Stefan nodded eagerly. The gold scams were huge earners. He was desperate to rise up in the ranks with Tony. He didn't want to have to keep going to his nine-to-five at the bank for the rest of his life.

'Yes, boss. I'll make sure everything is perfect.'

'Good.' Tony sat down and opened the top desk drawer again. 'Now fuck off.'

*

'I'm sorry, sir, but I'm afraid we have no single rooms available at all. There's a conference on this week – we only have two rooms left in the entire hotel.'

'Right.' Agitated, Freddie ran his hands through his hair, worrying that Anna might be getting uncomfortable. He looked over at her. Her face betrayed nothing, but at least she didn't look worried.

'We do have one twin room, sir, a very nice suite overlooking the bay. It's one of our premium suites, so slightly larger than normal.'

'What do you reckon? We can check out some of the other gaffs around here if you'd prefer?' He looked at her expectantly.

'It's fine with me; I don't mind.'

'If you're sure… Alright then, mate, we'll take it.'

'Wonderful choice, sir. If you will just allow me to take some details, I'll book you in and take you through to your suite.'

A couple of hours and several glasses of wine later, Freddie and a very tipsy Anna were walking back to their room. She laughed as she tripped up the last step and he reached out and caught her. They had talked and laughed animatedly all evening, though Anna had skilfully skirted around anything to do with her past or where she came from. Short of asking her outright why she wouldn't answer, there wasn't much more Freddie could have done to try to find out. She obviously had something to hide. Or something to hide *from*. Freddie could understand that better than anyone, and he had done his fair share of topic dodging tonight as well. Unlike a lot of other people, Anna had not pushed, respecting his privacy, which was the main reason he had extended her the same courtesy.

Freddie kept hold of her while he found the key card and opened the door, then carefully manoeuvred her into the room. Once they were inside there was an awkward moment as they both looked towards the beds.

'Oh, here you go.' Freddie rummaged in his gym bag and pulled out a big, plain white T-shirt. 'This should fit you to sleep in. Might be a bit big, but…' He shrugged, unsure how to finish his sentence.

Anna thanked him and walked into the bathroom to get changed. She closed the door and leaned on the marble top by the sink, looking into the mirror. Her face was flushed and her eyes bright. *Probably all that wine*, she thought, smiling to herself. It had been an amazing night. And day too. She hadn't felt this happy and relaxed and carefree in such a long time.

She shrugged off her jumper, then shimmied out of her jeans and let them fall to the floor. The soft lighting in the bathroom made her skin look even creamier than usual. She unhooked her bra and let that fall too. Slowly pulling back her hair, she exposed herself completely to the mirror and looked at the big fluffy robe on the back of the door. She could leave the T-shirt off and just put the robe on. Exit the bathroom and slowly walk up to him, wrap her arms around his neck and put her lips to his… undo the robe and let it melt away…

She snapped back and shook the thought out of her head. What was she thinking? She'd clearly drunk too much wine. He would likely push her away, and then she would have ruined a perfectly lovely trip, not to mention causing herself untold embarrassment and, most probably, the loss of a friend.

In the next room, Freddie had got changed and was waiting for Anna to appear. Usually he slept naked or just in boxers, but he was in a very unusual situation, a novelty to be exact, and for the first time he could remember, he felt self-conscious, so he'd thrown on his other gym T-shirt.

'Everything OK?' he called tentatively.

Inside the bathroom Anna jumped at the sound, as it jogged an unpleasant memory. 'I'm fine!' she called. 'Just getting changed, won't be long.' She sat down on the side of the bath and waited, unable to stop the wave of memories flooding her mind.

*

Anna stood looking in the mirror in the en suite of the master bedroom at their grand sprawling house. She hated this room. She hated this whole house. It was far too big, furnished with expensive things and protected by large, impregnable gates. It was her gilded cage.

Alexis lived with them full-time, and she had just finished putting her to bed. Tony had taken Alexis from her mother when she was just a baby and had set about making sure she had no claim, planting drugs in her house and reporting her. He had even arranged for her drink to be spiked the night before she was due to be drug tested and had paid a witness to say that she had hit Alexis repeatedly while drinking. She had next to no chance of seeing her baby again by the time he was through with her. Now Alexis lived a barren life, only doing what her father thought was acceptable.

And now Anna was pretty sure she was pregnant. She hadn't been able to get a test for fear he would find it, but two months had gone with no sign of her period, and she had started being sick. Feeling her stomach, she shivered. It would show soon and then what? The minute he found out he had fathered another child that would be it. There wouldn't be a safe place for her.

Anna bit down on her fist, stifling the sob. Tears streamed down her cheeks. She didn't know what to do. She would rather die than let her baby go through that.

'What are you doing in there?' A low, calm tone floated through the door and she jumped in fright. Calm tones were always the most dangerous. Most of the time it meant that there was a calculated anger bubbling under the surface. He would watch her, waiting for her to give him any excuse, and then he would *pounce. She saw it coming a mile off every time, but there was nothing she could do.*

'Nothing, sorry. I'm coming now.' She quickly splashed water over her face and then wrapped the see-through silk robe around her naked body. This was the only thing she was allowed to wear to bed.

'What's wrong with you? Are you sick?' he demanded as she walked out into the bedroom.

'I don't know, perhaps something I ate — nothing serious.'

'You look like shit.' He curled his lip. 'I work all day, hard graft to give you everything and I come home to this? What's the point?'

Then let me go, she pleaded silently.

'I'm sorry,' she said, lowering her eyes.

She stroked his face and knelt down, knowing this was her final attempt at peace. He would either allow her to grovel and make it up to him or he would rip her to shreds, dependent on his mood. He grabbed her jaw with his hand and forced her to look up at him.

''S'alright… you can make it up to me with that pretty little mouth of yours, can't you?' he said, laughing. As he pulled her to him roughly, Anna closed her eyes, switched off and resigned herself to Tony's demands. It was pure survival.

CHAPTER TWELVE

Anna snapped back to reality. Splashing her face with water again, she pinched her cheeks to get back the colour that had drained from them, then walked briskly into the bedroom, pulling the robe tightly around her. Freddie was seated in the armchair with a brandy in his hand, his suit folded neatly over the back. She averted her eyes but not before she had clocked the tanned skin on his muscular arms and legs. He was watching her as she walked. She probably looked about five years old in his oversized top. She shrugged mentally. Wouldn't change anything anyway. She lay the robe over the back of the sofa.

Freddie kept watching her, swilling the brandy round in the glass. She didn't wear a lot of make-up anyway, that much he could already tell, but now, completely barefaced and in nothing but his top, she was just as beautiful. Naturally, quietly beautiful. He looked away as she slid onto the sofa, curling her legs beside her. His T-shirt rode up to the top of her thigh, exposing her smooth skin. He couldn't watch or his arousal would start to show. He looked out the window instead.

'Would you like a nightcap?' His voice was soft and relaxed as he unwound.

'No, thank you.' Anna smiled warmly. 'I think I'm ready for bed – I'm tired out.'

'OK.' Freddie put his glass down and slipped on the bathrobe that was twin to hers. 'I just need to step out to make a couple of calls and I'll be back. I'll take the key, you settle down and I'll see you in the morning.' He fished in his jacket pocket for his phone, which he'd switched off earlier in the day. He had wanted just one completely uninterrupted day with Anna.

'OK.' Anna walked to the bed. 'Oh, and Freddie?'

'Yeah?'

'Thank you.' Her eyes met his. 'Thank you for everything today. It's been the best day I can remember in… a very long time.'

'You're welcome. But the pleasure's been all mine.'

'Freddie! Where the fuck have you been?'

'Off, Vince, just off radar today.'

'Off the radar or off the fucking planet, Fred? Haven't you heard?'

'Heard what? Vince, what's happened? I switched my phone off. I'm not in London. You're my first call.' Freddie's pulse quickened. It was unusual for Vince to be anything other than cool and entirely in control; he must have missed something pretty big.

'Ahh, you got away with that pretty little bird you was on about then… S'pose an old man can't really blame you for turning your phone off for a few hours—'

Freddie interrupted him, worried now. 'Vince, will you just fucking enlighten me, mate?'

There was a silence on the other end as Vince tried to decide how to proceed. Freddie waited impatiently.

'Big Dom's dead.'

There was another long silence as Freddie tried to take this in. Big Dom was one of the elite few faces that had been part of the East End underworld going back years; he was practically royalty. Vince's age, they had moved up the ranks together. They were business partners in many ventures, as well as close friends. Most of the East End and Soho massage parlours, the majority of which were a business front for prostitution, were owned by those two. They were run well and fairly, and the girls worked through choice and in fair conditions. The pair of them had a big stake in the cocaine and cannabis that came into the country from the east. Half of the clubs they ran masked their various weapons' trades, and like the proper old-school faces that they were, they still had a big hand in the protection of other businesses. All of this they did together. Vince had to be devastated. Not only would he have lost his best friend, but his business partner too. This would leave the back gate ajar for trouble and everyone would know that by now.

'I'm so sorry, Vince. I don't know what to say—'

Vince cut him off. The last thing he wanted was pity; he couldn't stand it. 'I don't need you to start spouting like me mum's best bloody teapot. I need you to do something.'

Freddie bit his tongue and listened.

'It was a hit.' Vince lit another cigar before continuing. 'Who it was, I don't yet know. It won't have been any estab-lished firms, not around our gaff anyway. As much as they would like to get their hands on some of our assets, they definitely wouldn't want the fallout.' He took a long puff as Freddie stood listening, silently. 'Could have been someone we ticked off in the past, biding their time… but I doubt it. Our reputation precedes us – always has. My guess would be that it's some young hot bloods betting on us being soft, betting on us being practically dead because we seem so old to them.' His voice rose towards the end in anger. He inhaled deeply to calm himself before continuing. 'Whoever it is, the fact they managed to get that close to Big Dom means they've got some sort of connection in the first place, which means that someone, somewhere, knows something.'

Freddie took this in and ran his free hand through his hair in agitation. 'Right. So as of now we must assume that we and our joint firms are both on someone's hit list. We're all connected, all work together on the majority…' He paused. 'Give me the gories.'

'Shot. Close range. Looks like there was a struggle. He had two of his men posted in the vicinity. He was at his gaff in Soho – he'd been sorting something out at one of the clubs to do with a shipment. The other two are brown bread too. Paul found them.'

'Fuck.' His younger brother Paul was champing at the bit trying to follow in Freddie's footsteps. At first, he'd fought against it, but recently Freddie had been trying to give him work that involved him in his life, but not enough to land him in any real danger. Vince had humoured him on this, referring to it as a babysitting job. Freddie had been grateful, but knowing Paul had discovered the stiffs worried him greatly. Now he'd be wanting to get more involved, and that was something that Freddie definitely didn't want.

'I sent him on an errand. It was just to pick up a package,' Vince started.

'OK. Right.' He straightened up from where he'd been leaning against the wall. 'I'll be back tomorrow. Start rounding up the usual suspects, so to speak.' He tried to organise his thoughts, get back into work mode. 'I won't miss anyone out. If there's information to be got, I'll get it.'

'Good man. I'll be at Ruby Ten tomorrow night if you've got anything of interest.'

'Gotcha, and Vince? I'm sorry... He was a good man.'

There was a pause before Vince spoke again in a hard voice. 'He was one of the fucking best. And I'll unleash hell on the fucker that did this because of it.'

Vince cut the call, and Freddie stared at the blank wall for several minutes before picking up the phone again. It rang to voicemail.

'Paul? Why the fuck do I not have any messages from you? You'd best be at home tomorrow. Twelve sharp, ready to go.' He snapped the phone shut and composed himself before walking back to the hotel room.

By the time he opened the door Anna was fast asleep. He crept in and sat down in the armchair. Picking up his brandy, he watched her, peaceful in her escape. What was she dreaming of? *Who* was she dreaming of?

He watched her small chest rise and fall slowly with her breath. How nice it must be to sleep easy at night. He looked out the window at the sea, noting a vast change in its temperament from earlier in the day. The calm, still, glittering waters were now churning, deep and dark, as though unspeakable things lurked beneath the waves. If only he could see himself, he'd find the change mirrored in his face.

CHAPTER THIRTEEN

Tony walked in through the back door of the Greek restaurant in Wood Green. It was a family business, one of his cousin's places. They often conducted their less-than-legal business meetings here. Angelo stepped across and closed the door behind him.

The room was full of Tony's closest men, most of them family of some sort. Cousins, second cousins, husbands of female relations who had been allowed to marry in. Like most Greek families, theirs was a large one, and they were particularly close. There were a few men who were not family but who were loyal to a fault.

Everyone waited in silence for Tony to begin talking. They sensed his irritation and all knew better than to draw any attention to themselves. Tony was known for his violent mood swings.

'Go get me a whisky.'

One of the younger men quickly scarpered through the doors to do as he was bid. Tony took a deep breath and addressed the rest of the waiting men. 'What I tell you now does not leave this room. It is not to be discussed, even between yourselves. I won't have you gossiping like fucking women.' He pulled a cigarette packet out from his inside jacket pocket.

One of the men to his right stepped forward and lit it for him. Tony took a deep drag and continued speaking, the smoke escaping his mouth and nose with each word.

'Anna has been unwell recently, mentally. She ain't quite the full ticket at the moment. Anyway, she's disappeared. No one's taken her – she's gone off by herself. It's her mind, it's playing tricks on her.' Tony made a screwing motion with his hand against the side of his head. 'She don't know what she's doing.' Tony's face twisted as he tried to contain his rage. He hated that he had to sit here in front of his men and admit that his missus had done a runner. He stared at each man defiantly, as if daring them to question his thin excuse. There was silence for a few moments. He took another deep drag on the cigarette in his hand.

The door from the kitchen opened and the man who had gone to get the whisky returned. Tony took the glass and gulped gracelessly at the deep amber liquid.

'Whatcha want us to do, boss?' a deep voice asked.

Tony turned to answer but stopped as the crashing noise of a bin falling over sounded just outside. Tony stood up, immediately alert, and his eyes shot to the small window near the back door. A thin, pale, panic-stricken face stared back at him before the lanky youth backed up and bolted back down the side alley.

'Get that little fucker now!' Tony bellowed. The men around him swarmed out of the doors, both to the front and back. A minute later they frogmarched the boy back in. Tony looked him up and down. He was no more than eighteen. His trainers were scuffed and dirty, and he wore a thick, black-

and-white-chequered apron. His face was as white as a sheet as he was pushed in front of the red-faced, angry-looking man he knew to be Tony Christou. He shook and stammered as he tried to explain.

'I-I-I d-didn't mean—'

'You didn't mean to what?' Tony roared at him, spittle flying out of his mouth and onto the boy's face.

'I didn't mean to in-interrupt. I'm sorry.'

'Waiting outside the door of a private conversation – you think that's acceptable?' He held his hands out and shook his head in exaggerated disbelief. 'Do you know who I am?'

'Yes, y-yes.' The boy nodded hurriedly. Tony curled his lip.

'Yet you were still out there listening to my private conversation, sneaking about, spying through the fucking window.' Tony's voice got louder and shook more and more with all the pent-up rage that was inside of him, needing a release. His hands began to shake and his eyes went vacant. The boy cringed away, terrified.

'You're a spy. You're a fucking spy, trying to find a weakness to exploit.'

'No, please, I just work here. It's my shift.' The boy screamed as Tony finally boiled over and lunged forward, grabbing him by the throat.

'Do you know what I do with people who spy on me? Do you know?' Tony bellowed.

His black, dead eyes swept the perimeter and landed on a dull kitchen knife that had been left out to be sharpened. Grabbing a handful of the boy's hair with one hand, the other still firmly locked around his throat, he dragged the boy across the room towards the knife. The boy tried to scream again, but all that came out were desperate gurgles as Tony squeezed his windpipe shut.

None of the men moved. Most looked away. All of them knew there was nothing that they could – or should – do. It would be their own funeral being planned if they got involved now. Tony was unstoppable when he reached this point. Reason and logic no longer played any part. Tony needed blood.

In one quick movement, and with a manic expression on his face, Tony grasped the large knife and pulled the boy towards him, holding him against his own body, facing away. He inhaled in anticipation and then pulled the knife hard and fast across the boy's throat. He gave an exultant cry as thick, dark blood sprayed the room. The warm liquid gushed out over Tony's hands, and he closed his eyes, feeling the relief and calm that came over him with every kill. He breathed in deeply, savouring the feel of his prey and the metallic scent in the air. It made him feel good. It cleared out his previously overstressed, pounding head.

Opening his eyes with a relaxed expression, he dropped the body to the floor unceremoniously. He sighed as he looked at his bloodied hands before walking to the large sink in the corner of the room. Leaving a red smear on the tap handle, he turned on the water and began washing his arms down as calmly as if he were just washing off some dirt. Without turning around he spoke to his men.

'Get that cleaned up, then wash this place down diamond standard after closing. Andreas, bag him up and get rid of him somewhere he won't be found. I don't care where. Oh and tell Paul he'll need another kitchen hand. This one didn't work out.'

Looking at his blood-soaked clothes, he turned to one of his men. 'I'll have to go clean up at home. Angelo, you drive me.'

Angelo nodded. Tony went to walk out but turned back to the room of men at the last second.

'Oh, going back to what we was talking about, not one word about it to anyone. I want all of you out looking her up, but dead quiet. You don't mention what you're doing to no one. You just sniff her out and get her back here where she belongs. Got it?'

As he sat in his car, he closed his eyes and thought about what he would do to Anna when he found her. The sound of her future screams resounded in his head, like the perfect melody.

Not long now, he thought. With the underground skills his men possessed, it would only be a matter of time before they found her.

'Tick tock, Anna,' he whispered to the night lights of London outside the car window. 'Tick tock.'

CHAPTER FOURTEEN

Freddie walked through the back door of the house into the kitchen. His mother greeted him with a big smile and a hug. 'Paul said you'd be home. I 'ope you have time to eat. I've just taken a lovely joint of beef out of the oven, Yorkshires and all, just how you like 'em.'

He sat down and silently glared at Paul, who was seated in a similar fashion at the other end of the table. He shrugged and widened his eyes as if to say '*What?*', and Freddie just shook his head in frustration. Now was not the time for family dinners – now was the time for taking action. They had neither time nor the element of surprise on their side. Mollie, sharp as a pin, caught the interaction.

'Now don't be getting mad at Paul. He told me same as you probably want to, that you're busy today, but you can make time for food, the pair of you. I won't be having you out eating trashy crap when you can have a decent meal here at home.' She folded her arms across her generous bosom and shook a wooden spoon in their direction as she berated them. Freddie smiled. She was a good old girl, his mum. She was the only person within a hundred-mile radius who would dare to have a go at him. The only one he would let try.

'Just make it quick, Mum, yeah? Things are looking a bit dark today. Got to see a man about a dog pretty sharpish.'

Mollie nodded and hurried to dish up. She wouldn't ask, he knew that. But she understood.

'Where were you off last night anyway? Thought I'd see a peep of you coming in to change or grab a bite.' It wasn't a nosy question, Freddie knew – she just cared. She liked to know where her boys were; it made her feel more secure, like when they were young. Old habits die hard.

'I went to the beach.' He smiled through a mouthful of potatoes, waiting for her reaction to this random statement. Paul laughed and choked on his food.

'The beach? In this weather?' Mollie's face was incredulous. 'Are you 'aving me on, son? Why on earth would you do that?'

Paul, having recovered, chipped in. 'Yeah, seriously, what made you go to the beach? A bird?' He winked, teasing.

Freddie didn't laugh.

'Is that it, Fred?' Mollie prompted, interested. 'Were you with a girl?'

'Mum!' Freddie protested, wanting them to drop it. He felt like he was a kid again.

'I'm just asking, love. You've never once brought a nice girl back here. I'm your mother, it's natural that I'd take an interest.'

'You met Sally, Mum,' Paul put in wickedly, ducking as Freddie threw a piece of bread at his head.

'Yes, well…' Mollie pursed her lips, no longer smiling. 'Like I said, you've never bought a *nice* girl back here. The least said about that dirty piece, the better,' she sniffed.

Freddie rolled his eyes. Sally had been his high-school girlfriend. She'd come from the estate where they'd grown up and had seen Freddie as her ticket out of there. When they were eighteen, she'd faked a pregnancy to get him to marry her. He eventually found out the truth and dumped her.

After Sally, Freddie had changed. All the girls whose eyes gleamed when they took in his smart suit and his nice car, they only wanted to use him. So *he* used *them* instead. The only women he had really respected, until now, were his mother and sister. His mother was a survivor the way she'd held it together and raised them. And his sister was sharp and intelligent. She didn't miss a thing, which helped Freddie out no end with keeping tabs on his brothers.

Freddie finished his food quickly and in silence as his mother and brother discussed his youngest brother, Michael, who was currently away at a private boarding school, which Freddie paid for. He was coming home soon, and Mollie wanted to arrange a big get-together to welcome him back.

'Thanks, Mum, that was blindin'. Paul, get moving.'

Paul quickly shovelled in the last mouthful and gave his mum a peck on the cheek before joining Freddie. They both waved goodbye with fixed smiles on their faces before turning to the car.

'Now, what the fuck happened?'

*

Tony paced the small office, listening to the youth seated in front of him with his oversized suit and high-pitched voice. Angelo had that look about him, like butter wouldn't melt, and he appeared at least five years younger than he really was. He was known internally as Angel Face. It was something he regularly used to his advantage. People talked in front of him – saw him as a bit green and easily led. What they didn't know was that underneath his sweet and harmless exterior, there lurked a psychotic and truly dangerous young man with no moral compass and a hunger for money. Tony had him on the payroll for a good number of little jobs, most often the ones involving the dirty work. He had spotted him young and, realising his potential, had won his loyalty, ensuring he was never without a good wedge. Dangerous little fuckers were always better onside. Right now though, he was on the scout team for Anna with the rest of them. It had been weeks since he had set his men to task.

'So there's still no sign of her anywhere?' he said quietly, more to himself than to Angelo, who nodded slowly. Tony's voice began to rise. 'There has to be some fucking sign of her somewhere. What is she, a fucking ice cube? She didn't melt!'

'No, boss.' Angelo didn't know how he was supposed to answer that, but Tony's face throbbed with thunder, glaring at him like he should have some miraculous answer.

'No, of course she didn't. She's around here somewhere.' He bit at his nails as he went over it all again. 'She isn't abroad, she isn't working and she hasn't used her bank card. She didn't even take her car. So where is she? She can't have gone fucking far.' He said this last bit to himself, looking out of the window onto the busy high street.

Angelo watched him. Tony had always been possessive to a degree, liked to own things and people, but this was an obsession. He definitely wouldn't want to be in Anna's shoes when the boss finally caught up with her. And catch her he would, there was no doubt about it. Tony Christou always accomplished his goal, no matter what or who it was. He wouldn't stop until he did. That was what made him so good at what he did. That was what made Tony such a feared and successful face.

CHAPTER FIFTEEN

Tanya wrapped her coat firmly around her waist. It was freezing and her breath was lingering white on the air in front of her face. She couldn't wait to be home, with a huge mug of steaming tea warming her hands. It had been a long night in the club; she'd pulled a double shift again. Nights like these were lucrative. She was being honest with Anna when she'd explained that it could just be dancing. You stripped off, give them a good eyeful and sat with them for the evening in your scanties. It was a technically respectable club to the outside world. There was, however, the underground option of offering more private services. Back in the old days this was up to the individual women to sort out, slinking off to seedy hotels late into the night with one of the punters, but that had resulted in too many beatings and the girls frequently getting mugged off. The manager of the club Tanya worked for, Ellen, decided to adapt the way they worked to avoid this. Rearranging her own living space, she turned two of the upstairs rooms into bedrooms where the girls could take the punters quietly and discreetly, and hired a minder to stand within earshot at the top of the stairs. This afforded the girls much more safety, and in return, Ellen and the club took a cut of the money. It worked well for everyone.

Walking down the dark streets, Tanya felt the tight pull of her thigh muscles. She would run a bath, she decided – take away the ache. Not all of the girls went up into the back rooms with the punters. Some nights, depending on who was working alongside her, Tanya would be one of only two or three on that sort of work. Tonight had been one of those nights. Having spent an hour with a large table of men on a stag do, eager to spend their money, Tanya had been quietly asked the golden question.

'Well…' she purred, 'everything is available for the right price.' She ran her long, manicured nails down the top of the fat, sweaty man's thigh. He was short and round, ugly as sin, not to mention the incredibly bad breath that was assaulting her senses. But she would ignore all that. All she cared about was his money. She ran the price list off to him and awaited his response. He licked his podgy lips eagerly.

'OK then. Me first though, then the others. I want a suck and fuck and no time restraints either.'

Tanya swallowed but her smile remained, not portraying her surprise. 'That price is for each twenty minutes.' She gave a discreet hand signal to Ellen, who immediately sent one of the free girls to check the room was ready.

'No problem at all, darlin' – I've got money to burn and an appetite to feed!' He licked his lips again and then turned back to the table of equally fat and unattractive men. 'Then, as a present to the stag and my friends, one for each of them too.' He grinned from ear to ear as they whistled and applauded his generosity. Tanya paled slightly but said nothing. This was what she did at the end of the day. Every second lying on her back was another second towards building a better life. So she would grin and bear it.

Five minutes later she was stripping off her already skimpy clothing in the dark red bedroom, trying not to curl her lip in disgust at the man in front of her. He was rubbing his hands together, his beady little eyes raking up and down her body.

'Oh yeah… you'll do,' he grunted as he stood massaging his flaccid red penis in nothing but his socks. 'I'll just get this nice and hard for you, wouldn't want to disappoint, eh?' He laughed and motioned for her to sit on the bed. 'Oh… yeah…' He grunted some more and closed his eyes. At this close range, she could smell his unwashed body and see how sticky with sweat he was underneath his boxers. She fought the urge to vomit. He opened his eyes and guided her head, forcing himself into her mouth and started grinding. After several minutes he pushed her back and pulled her legs apart.

'Pull them back,' he ordered. 'Right back, as far as you can go. Go on, open that up for me.' He ran his calloused fingers over her most sensitive parts, ogling away. Finally, he entered her and fucked her hard for just over an hour. When he was finally spent, Tanya sat there shocked at how much stamina he had for such an overweight man; her body was exhausted. Unfortunately though, this was only the beginning of a very long night, and there were still seven more of them waiting for her. Each of them ensured they took full advantage of their friend's generosity, spending time and as much energy as they could muster pumping away at her in the large double bed.

Wincing, she had pulled her clothes back on and made her way slowly down the stairs. She nearly lost her balance at the top and Marvin, the minder, had quickly steadied her. He caught her eye for a moment, and she saw a quick flash of concern for her before he looked away. He had been aware of every second of what had happened in that room, and she knew he probably felt sorry for her. Nothing was said though. It just wasn't done in their world. She had to be hard to get by in this game. It was her own choice. He would never admit to feeling sorry for her either. She was just another tom.

As she walked through the cold, the pain started to wear off. She wondered to herself whether Anna would be home yet. She hadn't made it back last night. *Must have been a good night,* Tanya thought, smiling to herself. She thought perhaps she ought to worry about her, but Tanya wasn't the type to worry, and her mind quickly moved onto a conversation she'd had with Anna before she'd left for her date.

'Have you ever been in love, Tanya?' Anna had been curled up on the end of her bed. Tanya had thought about how to answer this, concentrating on applying thick liquid eyeliner along the top of her eyelids.

'Yes. Once.'

'When?'

Tanya coloured her lips a bright blood red. Her warpaint. Her daily mask. She pressed some tissue to her lips, blotting the excess colour.

'Oh, a while ago now.'

'Not the guy who left you in the petrol station then?'

Tanya laughed. 'Oh God no, not that worthless piece of shit! He was a bleedin' nightmare from start to finish. No, not him.' She smiled at Anna, amused by her suggestion. Anna smiled back questioningly.

'No one you'd know. Just this guy I had a very short but sweet thing with.' She glanced at Anna, not wanting to look daft in front of her. 'It was a couple of years back, way before you showed up all carpet-bag looking, with your house-car.' She chuckled at the memory. 'He was amazing…' Her eyes glazed over as she continued. 'He was something special. Had an air about him, you know? He just had that… thing. Made me weak at the knees, he did. Had the gift of the gab alright. Could sell ice to an Eskimo.'

'What happened between you? Where is he now?'

Tanya frowned at Anna's sudden interest. She wasn't used to spilling her heart out. She continued though, the memory bringing a sad smile to her face.

'He's around, I guess. He ain't gone anywhere. I just didn't mean the same to him as he did to me. So he ended it before it could go someplace.' She looked down; the words hurt her as she said them, even though she tried to act nonchalant. 'I was just another piece of skirt, not serious material to him. I still fell for him though… stupid, really. A girl like me should know better. We don't get nice men.' She shrugged.

'Oh, Tan, I'm so sorry…' Anna leaned forward towards her friend.

'Nah, it's OK.' Tanya brushed her off, embarrassed by the heart to heart. 'Anyway, I plan on showing him what's what one day,' she continued brightly. 'One day I'll be up there living it large, all rich and important, and I'll bump into him and *show him what he could have had,' she said, nodding to herself in the mirror determinedly.*

'That's not true, Tan, you are *good enough.'*

'I'm an exotic dancer and that's putting it really politely—' Anna winced but Tanya continued '—no, I've got to be somebody, be able to offer someone something. It's the way the world works. That's why I'm pulling shifts night and day and saving every penny. I want to start up my own place one day. Become a real businesswoman. I'll show him.' She swivelled round and shone a brilliant smile at Anna. 'I'll show everyone.'

Snapping back to the present Tanya walked gingerly up the stairs and to her flat. Opening the door she saw the light on and she was relieved that Anna was back. Things had changed in the house since Anna had moved in. It felt like a home, like they were a family. She missed her when she wasn't in.

Anna popped her head round the bedroom door at the sound of Tanya's arrival and took in her friend's weary and dishevelled appearance. They never really talked about what Tanya did at work. Anna knew, and Tanya knew that she knew, but neither of them wanted to discuss it. Home was home.

Anna saw the bruises on Tanya's legs as she hung up her coat and averted her eyes as Tanya turned round.

'Come on, go get out of those clothes and I'll run you a bath. Your fluffy dressing gown's in the pile of clean washing on your bed.'

Tanya almost cried as she squeezed Anna's arm gratefully.

CHAPTER SIXTEEN

The next morning over breakfast, Anna looked over her cup of tea at Tanya and smiled. After a minute or so, Tanya started laughing at her.

'What do you 'ave to be grinning about then, eh? That bloke, I'll bet.'

'Well, yes, but no, not that.' Anna dismissed her comment with a wave of her hand and sat forward animatedly, her eyes dancing. 'I've had an idea. A brilliant one.'

'OK. Go on then,' Tanya answered warily. She noted silently that for once Anna had not brushed the man comment under the rug like she was ashamed of something.

'You want to make something of yourself, right? Build up a business, get out of the club, etc., etc.'

'Yeah, so what?' She shrugged. 'I barely have half of what I need to even begin thinking about starting something up.'

Anna chewed on her toast slowly before continuing.

'Well, what if you had someone going into business with you? A partner, someone who'll also put up money for the venture… What would you think about that?'

'A partner? Who would do that though? Who has that kind of money?' She pondered on this for a second. 'You certainly don't. I've seen you being all careful and that lately. You ain't even working.'

Tanya reached over and picked up another couple of bacon rashers from the serving plate Anna had laid in the middle of the table and stared at them glumly. Anna finished her corner of toast and wiped the crumbs off her hands.

'What if I said I *did*? What then?'

Anna had sat up for hours after Tanya had fallen asleep, contemplating the idea. She wanted to help her friend achieve the life she so desperately craved; each bruise and haunted look that passed across her friend's face broke her heart. It was also time to do something for herself – she had been mulling this over for a while.

Tanya frowned at her but didn't say anything. Anna pressed further.

'I know roughly how much you have saved, and I can match it. I can actually even put a little bit more in if I needed to. So I'm putting the offer to you. I'll go into business with you if that's something you're happy with. My only stipulation is that we don't open a club with "back-room services", like the one you work in. We would have to work out something we're both happy with.'

Tanya was stunned. It wasn't often she was knocked speech-less, but it looked like this was one of those rare times.

'Anna, I don't know what to say.' Her mouth wavered open for a few seconds until she broke into a surprised smile. 'Yes! That would be perfect, yes!' Tanya gave a little shriek and jumped up, and the two of them laughed and danced round the living room.

'There's just one other small thing.'

'What?' answered Tanya, worried.

'Do you have a wig?'

*

Two days later Tony was watching the CCTV footage from a bank in Swindon. What on earth was she doing here, of all places? She didn't know anyone in Swindon, did she? The manager hovered nervously next to him, obviously uncomfortable with the situation. He was, however, being paid an awful lot of money just to let this man watch the cameras, and as the police weren't involved, there didn't seem to be much that could go wrong.

'Do you remember her coming in?' Tony asked.

'There are a lot of people in and out of here all the time, sir. Unless she's a regular client at this branch, we would have no reason to recognise her.'

'OK, so 2.34 p.m., you say?'

'Yes, sir, that's when the transaction took place, as you told me.'

Tony had someone in the bank watching Anna's accounts, knowing she would have to access money at some point. She couldn't live on thin air forever. He had jumped for joy upon noticing she'd taken money out and had got his men on the case quick-fast. She had withdrawn a large sum, so he knew this would be the only chance he would have in a long time, if she was careful. His heart had lit up at the thought of getting close to catching her when he thought back to what she'd done.

'Here we are, sir.' The manager leaned over and paused the image on the screen. Tony exhaled, his breath hissing out like a snake when he saw her. Well, he thought, she'd certainly gone to great lengths to change her appearance. Her hair was short and blonde and her face heavily made-up. He shook his head in disgust. She looked like a common whore. He would beat that out of her soon enough.

*

'What's happenin', Sammy?' Freddie closed the door to the bookies behind him and turned the lock. Dressed in a dark grey suit and shirt, his face betrayed nothing under its cool and collected exterior.

'Freddie! Long time no see, mate, how've you been?' Sammy greeted him warmly. The two men walked through the back door into an office and Sammy immediately took out two tumblers from the cabinet underneath his desk. He fished out a bottle of whisky and motioned for Freddie to join him in the two comfortable chairs by the coffee table.

The bookies wasn't particularly big, looking at it from the outside. A few TVs, a couple of tables. Sammy's uncle had built it up and run it until a few years ago, when Sammy took over. Until then it had been a straight shooter, earning their family enough to be comfortable on but not much more. Sammy had seen the potential almost as soon as he'd started working there, and when his uncle wanted to retire, Sammy was quick to take on the family business. Having nowhere near the capital needed to fund such an investment, he'd approached Freddie with a business proposition. Freddie had put up the money for the venture, taking back part of it once Sammy was earning and becoming part-shareholder with the rest. Sammy had moved into the flat upstairs and modified the back rooms into high-stake, illegal gambling dens, which was where most of their income now came from. He ruled his roost with an iron rod and stood for no nonsense. Freddie's input had been invaluable, and word of his protection ensured that Sammy received only minimal trouble, usually from an upset client with empty pockets at the end of the night.

Over the years, the two men had built a solid friendship, and although Freddie no longer spent much time there, he knew it was in safe hands.

Sammy knew why his business partner was visiting. Word on the street travelled fast in their game. Sammy eased his large frame down into the chair opposite Freddie and poured two generous helpings of whisky.

'Get that down you, mate; I reckon you need it.'

'I certainly need something, Sammy,' Freddie answered. 'What've you heard?'

'Nothing of interest, I'm sad to say. I liked Big Dom – he was a good old boy. It's a real shame. But I guess that's the occupational hazard, ain't it.' He shook his head.

'I asked around, knew you'd be in, but no one knows anything. It's strange; there's been no whisper. It don't look like it's no one we know.'

This was the same answer Freddie had been getting every-where. Friend or foe, everyone he had visited was completely stumped. Stumped and worried. No one knew this guy's motive or who was next on his list – and Freddie was sure there *would* be a next. You didn't just gun down one of London's most prominent faces without a detailed plan and end goal.

'Have you been round the docks yet?'

'Yeah, Sam, nothing there neither.'

They both sat contemplating this. It was a weird situation, that was for sure. Freddie changed the subject, as there was obviously nothing left to discuss.

'How are things here? Everything running OK?'

'Yeah, things are ticking over nicely since you last came. Willy Wanker's been trying to cause hag since we won't tick him anymore, but I gave him a little talking-to a couple of days ago, which seems to have shut his trap.'

Freddie nodded. He had every faith that Sammy had efficiently dealt with it.

'Have a look over these, Sammy. Strictly between us. If you want in, you're in.'

Sammy took the plain beige folder and pulled out the file. There were blueprints and schedules. It took his professional eye less than a minute to work out what Freddie was planning.

'Blindin' hell, Freddie! Where did you get all this? You got someone inside?'

'Bent filth with a bad habit. Do you get where I'm trying to go with this?'

'Well, yeah.' Sammy's eyes flicked over the pages as he took it in and worked it all through in his head. It was a good set-up as far as he could see, but he'd have to go over it in more detail before he was convinced.

'Can I keep these?'

'For tonight you can; I need them back tomorrow. That's the only copy.'

Sammy nodded his understanding. You didn't want stuff like this all over the place. One copy was dangerous enough if it fell into the wrong hands. Especially when Lily Law came sniffing round.

Sammy pushed himself up from the chair and walked round to the back of his large pine desk. On the wall, he moved a small photo of his aunt and uncle when they were younger and punched in a code on the security pad hidden behind. Across the room one of the cream raised-wood panels made a soft clicking sound and popped out. Repositioning the photograph, Sammy walked across the room, his gait unusually graceful for such a large man. He opened the door and slid the file into the steel safe and pushed the door closed, sealing it inside. From the outside, you would never guess it to be anything but a wall. Once the simple carved panel was shut, it sealed flush against the rest of the unraised panelling, and even on close inspection you wouldn't be able to tell they were two separate pieces of wood.

'I haven't put anyone else onto this yet. We've got time. If you want in, we'll figure out the right team together. We'll partner up on it.'

Rubbing his hands, Freddie headed towards the door. 'I've gotta go, mate. It's cold enough to freeze the Pope's bollocks off, this place. Don't know how you stand it!'

Sammy laughed. 'I'll come back on this tomorrow after I've had a proper look. Where will you be?'

'At the club in Dean Street. I'll be there late though, come after ten.' He walked out the door and the cold October air hit him like a sunny day in Spain.

CHAPTER SEVENTEEN

Anna flicked through the post, as she did every morning. This was more out of habit than anything else; no one knew she was there to send her anything. But she did glance over the mail to check there were no red bills coming through, or anything that looked too urgent. She hummed to herself as she climbed the stairs, then stopped dead as she saw a handwritten envelope with her name on. No address. No postmark. It had been dropped in by hand. She tried to get control of her breathing as the familiar panic set in. *Come on, Anna. Just get up the stairs and into the flat!*

Urging herself forward, she mounted the stairs, shaking. She stopped. The door was open. Did she leave it open? Yes, of course she did; she'd only run downstairs to get the post. But if whoever had posted that letter was still here, they might have slipped in while she was preoccupied downstairs. Her blood ran cold, and her heart turned to ice. She bit her lip, trying to decide what to do. Cautiously, she retreated backward down the stairs, being careful not to make any sound. At the bottom step she let out the breath she didn't know she had been holding. Looking down at her feet she silently cursed. *Damn it, I haven't got any shoes on.* Wrapping her cardigan around her small frame, she took a seat on the top step just outside the front door, shuffling to the side so that her back was against the wall and she couldn't be seen from inside. Trembling slightly, she opened the letter.

A minute later, she burst out laughing, startling two children playing nearby.

She put her hand to her chest as her heart finally slowed and slumped back against the wall, rolling her eyes to the heavens. *Stupid girl... why on earth did I not think of Freddie?*

Pulling herself up, she tripped up the stairs and was careful to lock the door behind her when she was back inside. She sat on the side of her bed and read the short letter again.

Anna,

Had an amazing day with you. Are you free Saturday? I have a party to go to, would love to take you. You've got my number – let me know.

Freddie x

Smiling, she hugged the piece of paper to herself. Grabbing her phone, she left a voicemail for Freddie confirming that yes, she would go, then filed the letter away in a shoebox under her bed. As she went to replace the lid, her eye caught the end of a pink satin ribbon poking out the side. She trailed the end of her finger over it gently, then sat down and pulled it slowly out of the box and into her lap. A little girl had given it to her in hospital. That simple act of kindness had brought forth the realisation of what her life had become. What she had lost. She stroked the ribbon sadly and allowed the memories to overcome her once more.

*

Anna sat in the hospital wheelchair, shaking as Tony wheeled her out, roughly enough that she felt every bump and the wrath that radiated from him, but slowly enough to give the impression he was caring for her. He hissed at her as soon as there was no one around to hear.

'You scheming little bitch. Three months pregnant and you kept it to yourself? I bet you're blaming me for this mess, aren't you? I bet you have the fucking cheek to blame the loss of our child on me. Well, let me tell you this, you fucking whore – you weren't fit to carry my child. You murdered my child. You just wait till I get you home. You won't know what's fucking hit you.'

Her body convulsed and her head swayed. She wasn't even supposed to be out yet; he had discharged her against the doctors' orders. An icy chill descended on her heart. This was it. This was when she was going to die.

The day before, Tony had lost a lot of money on a bad business decision. She knew she was in for it the second he'd walked through the door. Her mothering instinct had cut in and at the last minute, just as he went for her, she had bolted. She might have made it to the front door if she hadn't tripped. Falling over the edge of the rug, she had gone down and before she knew it, hard blows were raining down on her along with a torrent of abuse. She'd tried to curl up, to protect her baby, but he'd dragged her up by the wrist and delivered one last horrific kick to her stomach. She'd screamed out in agony as the miscarriage violently started. Blood seeped out onto the cream carpet from under her pale blue dress, and she writhed as he stood back, observing her with wide eyes.

'Anna?' he faltered, as if seeing her for the first time, 'what's happening? What's the matter with ya?'

He scooped her up and ran out to the car. He put her in the back seat and strapped her in, wiping the tears of agony from her cheeks. 'I didn't mean it – you know I didn't. I didn't mean it.'

The concern hadn't lasted though. He'd turned back into his dark and vicious self as soon as he realised she had been pregnant.

Once he'd got her home, back behind the solid gates and big thick doors, he had beaten her to a bruised and bloody pulp, with no regard for the fragile state she was in. He executed his punishment calmly and calculatedly and beat her within an inch of her life, only avoiding her stomach to ensure she didn't actually bleed to death. Only once she'd passed out, her skin turned ashen, did he finally take her back to hospital with the explanation that an ex-boyfriend was responsible. In his version of events he had stepped in and saved the day. The story was thorough and his lies silken. He was labelled a hero.

It was three days later, as she lay on the hospital bed, that a little girl had wandered into her room.

'Why are you so sad, lady?'

Anna turned her head painfully and tried to talk through her swollen lips.

'I just am, princess.' She tried to smile but couldn't quite make it reach her eyes. The little girl bit her bottom lip as her eyes swept over Anna's wounds.

'I think you're sad because you're hurt.'

'I think you're right.'

They stayed there in silence for a moment, contemplating each other.

'I was poorly with chicken pox a little while ago. That made me sad.' She chewed her lip and looked around the room. 'But my friends bought me some pretty things to look at, which made me cheer up a bit. Don't you have any friends?' she asked.

'My friends are a long way away now,' Anna answered softly.

'Well, then I'll be your friend today and you can have this, because this is pretty. Maybe you could put it in your hair or maybe around your wrist so you can see it.' She pulled one of the pink ribbons from her hair and placed it in Anna's hand. Her chubby little pink hands were warm against Anna's thin lifeless ones.

Tears sprang to Anna's eyes at the innocent gesture.

'Thank you,' she whispered emotionally.

A woman's voice wafted through into the room and the little girl turned.

'That's my mummy,' she whispered conspiratorially, 'I'd better go.' She walked towards the door and then turned. 'I hope you feel better soon.'

Anna fell asleep that night with tears wet on her cheeks, clutching the pale pink ribbon and yearning for a child that she knew was better off now in heaven.

CHAPTER EIGHTEEN

Tony sat at the desk barely listening to his cousin, Cos. His mind was still on the recording of Anna in Swindon. There had to be something more to it.

'So we have to pull them back slightly. It's raising eyebrows.'

'What? Pull back what?'

Cos sighed, frustrated. 'You ain't listening to me, Tony. Why are you wasting my time?'

Tony's eyes narrowed but he held his temper. Cos was the head of the largest Greek firm in North London and as such had to be shown respect. Unlike a lot of set-ups, they were all closely connected up here and worked side by side. Tony resented this, but he wasn't stupid. He had to play by the rules.

'Please, go on.'

Cos took a sip of brandy and his annoyed expression smoothed.

'Our sharks. They're pushing down too far towards the centre. We need to pull them back a little, remind them of the perimeter they were set to work in.'

Tony stared at him steadily. 'Why? Why shouldn't we take some more ground? It's not like they use it.' He shrugged. 'They aren't lending in the West at all. Only East and South.'

'That's not the point. You know as well as I do, you don't push into other territories. It isn't done. And it is not worth the hassle either. We don't want to start a war.'

Tony threw his hand up in the air in annoyance. 'You're too soft. You let these English idiots treat us like third-rate citizens. We get left up here in the North to rot, told to stay put like some fucking dog that has to obey its master.'

Cos frowned. If truth be told, he didn't like Tony at all, but as he was family and a business partner of sorts, he had no choice but to put up with him. The constant chip on his shoulder was getting on his nerves a lot more lately though.

'It is nothing to do with English versus Greek. There is no competition. They were there before us, they built their empire, they earned their place. We have done the same here and they respect that. What, do you want to take on the Jews too? Or what about the Yardies down South? You start trouble with one firm, none of them will trust you.' Cos shook his head wearily.

Tony frowned in disagreement but took a deep breath and changed the subject.

'I've bought a warehouse in Hackney. It's an old antique place, full of old vases and furniture and shit. Got word that the old boy was selling it and wanted rid quickly. He's past it now, got no kids and just got told he had cancer, so he wants to live out his days on a beach somewhere. Left me the stock.' Tony lit another cigarette. His hands felt too empty without one on the go lately. 'I'm going to keep it running as a front, but the beauty of this place is that it has a series of hidden rooms behind a fake wall that's set up tighter than Fort Knox.

Apparently in his day he dealt with a lot of high-value goods – needed somewhere to keep them safe at night.'

'Wow, sounds like a real gem.' Cos was impressed. 'What are you thinking?'

'The rooms link up by a long corridor, and they're not bad size-wise. I'm going to set up another brown factory there. You remember our operation up near Stevenage was closed down a couple of months back by the filth? Should be big enough to replace the gap that created.'

'Good thinking. We've been hard pushed to meet the demand since then. Some of the dealers are getting pissed off. They've already started looking elsewhere. This should put a stop to that.'

One of their main enterprises was dealing heroin. Small factories were dotted around all over the place. This ensured that when one was discovered and shut down, it only dented their flow of product until they set up another, rather than pausing their business completely.

Cos shifted his considerable weight in his chair. 'That reminds me, the foreman who took the stretch for that, you sorted his family out?'

''Course. His missus got a wedge upfront and knows she'll be getting a regular pay cheque till he's out. Probably piss it all up the wall while she shags every bum in Stevenage, now her husband ain't there to keep an eye on her.'

Cos frowned. Tony's warped view of women was unhealthy. He'd met the foreman's wife once; she was a nice, respectable girl.

Haroula, Cos's wife, couldn't stand to be near Tony. Although careful not to cross a line with Cos, Tony treated her as an inferior creature whenever he came to the house. It was something that got her back up significantly. Cos showed his wife respect and love and treated her like the hard-working partner that she was. They were a team.

Cos gave a short cough and sat up straighter in his seat. Their business was conducted for the day, and he was eager to get home. He switched to small talk, to indicate as much.

'How's Anna? Haroula sends her regards.'

He noted the sudden tension in Tony at his question.

'She's fine, mate.' Tony's reply was curt and a dark look crossed his face before he masked it in a tight smile.

'OK, well, I'll be off. Let me know who you want down the new place and when. I can get Donnie to pull most of the equipment together by tomorrow afternoon if that suits.'

'Yeah, I'm gonna need suspended heat lamps too – big ones. There ain't anywhere outside to dry the bricks, but there's a room I can use for that if you can sort lamps.' The process of making heroin was long, exact and methodical. One of the steps along the way was drying out the clay-like bricks of morphine base. In some of their factories they had glass-roofed or open areas in the summer to allow for the bricks to dry naturally in the sunlight. In this new one though, they had no such area.

'No problem.' Cos nodded. He stood up and smiled tightly as he left the room. 'Later.'

'Later.' Tony watched his cousin leave. He shook his head. Cos was too small-minded. He couldn't see the bigger picture. But he soon would. He nodded to himself. Cos would soon see things differently after Tony had shaken things up.

CHAPTER NINETEEN

Saturday came around surprisingly quick for Freddie. He wasn't any closer to finding out who did the hit on Big Dom. It definitely wasn't anyone they had regular connections with. It wasn't any of the Southend firms that they dealt with; he had gone through all the usual channels at that end. They certainly wouldn't want to upset the natural order of things anyway: they made a hefty wedge each week dealing with Freddie and Vince, and they wouldn't want to deal with any of the hag that came with taking on further ground.

He lit a cigarette as he sat on the low brick wall outside his mother's front garden. Paul came out and joined him.

'So let's go over what there is left then.'

'Hundreds of small-timers and the civilians, Paul. We could spend a decade sifting through that shit pile and not get anywhere.' He flicked his cigarette butt away in disgust.

'Yes. But it don't look like we have a lot of choice. So where do we start?'

Freddie smiled sadly to himself. Paul was getting more and more involved every day. In a way this was perfect. There was no one he could trust more than his own brother to be his number two; blood always came up on top. But it was also saddening to know that it was his fault alone that Paul was now only really fit for a life of heavy crime.

'We start looking at the firms that deal in other lines of work, first off. Maybe they know something. Though they've always stuck to their side of things before.'

'Like who? What other lines of work are there?' Paul looked genuinely confused, and Freddie rolled his eyes.

'Seriously, Paul?' He shook his head. His brother never used his common sense. 'Look around you. We supply the girls, the clubs, the spirits, the recreational drugs to various businesses and the general public. We import weapons; we supply protection. We own property for various purposes. But we also only stick to the East and West.'

'Well, yeah, but we also have the bookies, the yards—'

'Yes, Paul, I could stand here all bleedin' day running off all the pies we have our fingers in. But what about all the rest of it?'

'The rest of what, Fred?'

'How about the other stuff on the street that we don't touch, like brown, crack, meth?'

'Oh.'

'What about loan-sharking? What about the European girls that get shipped here and get tom'd unwillingly? What about protection outside of our area? There's loads of things going on, Paul – I could be here all day naming them.' He lit another cigarette and Paul followed suit. 'Most of it is stuff we wouldn't touch with a barge pole, which is why we live in peace with the guys that do.' He blew out his smoke. 'They don't piss on our cornflakes; we don't shit on theirs. Some of it they had fair and square – before we wanted it, so—' he shrugged '—we aren't unfair.'

'Right. OK.' Paul took this in and nodded to himself. He probably should have realised that without Freddie having to point it out. Whereas Freddie always knew what to say and could read deeper into any situation, Paul could only ever see the black-and-white picture that was put in front of him. He wasn't as sharp as his older brother. Despite this, he ran around doing everything they asked of him, determined that one day he would at least become a valuable asset and make his brother proud.

'There are the Yardies down South who run the hot dogs, ice creams and also act as one of our weed outlets,' Freddie was saying, when Paul zoned back into the conversation.

Paul snorted. 'Hot dogs and ice creams?'

'Yes,' Freddie snapped, looking him in the eye. 'Don't laugh at things you know nothing about. It might sound soft but the set-up is a bloody good one by all accounts. It's actually a good little earner. Let's just say you would think twice before attempting to turn that one over.'

'Oh, OK.' Paul mentally shrugged. If Freddie said so…

'The Jews over in the West End – technically our ground, but we let them trade on it. Their game is some money laundering, scrap, blood diamonds and hot jewellery. Then there are the Turks, who deal mainly in heroin and crack. They have some toms lurking, but nothing major – that's more the scraggy end of the market. The Albanians, their business is the girls they bring over from Europe. They get pimped out. Unfortunately it's not their choice. They have a few good hitmen, but then all of us do…' he trailed off, lost in thought for a moment. 'Then you have the Greeks in the North. They hold the monopoly up there on gambling dens, laundering and loan-sharking. They have a pretty big hand in chemicals too, but their preference is always set-ups to do with hard brass. A few bank jobs too – they bankroll a lot of the insiders, deal with a lot of large fraud set-ups.'

They stopped talking as Thea tripped up to the front gate on her way home.

'What are you two brooding over? You look like a pair of slapped arse cheeks.' She stooped and gave both her brothers a hug and a kiss on the cheek. She loved her brothers as much as they loved her.

'Nothing, you cheeky mare.' Freddie laughed. 'Go help Mum, she's preparing to feed the five thousand.'

Thea rolled her eyes.

Thea had privately been looking after the financial side of things for Freddie for a while now. She had been nosing around in his room once – which she had been strictly told never to do – and found his barely legible books. Thea was already well aware of Freddie's profession – she was sharp like her brother and fast on the uptake. Open ears, closed mouth. That was how she grew up. By the time Freddie came home, she had gone through the books and had written notes suggesting ways he could make them look more legit, should he ever need to prove anything.

At first, Freddie had been livid, but after a while he had come into her room and she'd frozen, wary, scared that he was going to go crazy again. Instead he had given her a stern talking-to, reminding her never to delve into his personal things again uninvited, but then he had asked her to go over her work with him in the confines of her room. And from that day, Thea had had a hand in making the books look legit.

Up to now, this strange business alliance had been kept between the two of them; Freddie was sure their mother wouldn't approve, and he didn't want anyone else in his world to know who Thea really was. Civilians were untouchable, out of bounds to anyone looking to take out any grievances. While Thea was seen as a civilian she was relatively safe.

He watched as she went into the house. 'Come on, Paul, we've got business to attend to.'

*

'There you are! Could you give us a hand, love?' Mollie flustered around the kitchen, her round face reddened from the heat of the Aga. As Mollie took a tray of scones out of the oven, Thea tried to grab one. Mollie swatted Thea's hand away and grinned.

'Oh, go on, Mum, just one…'

'Just one. These are my Michael's favourite; I want there to be plenty left for him later on.' Mollie's face lit up as she talked about her youngest son. She was fit to burst with pride at the fact her son was at such a prestigious school, but Thea knew her mum missed having him here at home. The last time they had seen him was in the summer holidays and he had come home, bursting with animated tales of his new life. At first he'd written a letter home every week, but for the last couple of months that had trailed off. Mollie had just shrugged it off and put on a brave face. 'Well,' she said, 'he must be busy having fun and learning all these new things; you can't blame him for not finding time to write. Young boys don't want to do that these days.'

Personally, Thea thought it was out of order, that he was being ungrateful for the charmed life he had been handed. Though, she reasoned with herself, he hadn't really known how bad they used to have it. He had been blissfully unaware while he was an infant, and then Freddie had dragged them all out from the gutter way before he was old enough to understand. He didn't really realise what they had been through as a family. Hunger and desperation were a driving force. It was a darkness that, once touched, you ran from for the rest of your life.

'When is he getting here?' Thea asked through a mouthful of scone.

'In a few hours. Paul's picking him up from the station. Everyone needs to be here for six. I hope he likes the spread; I've done all the things he likes.' Mollie looked around at the food, excitement marred with anxiety on her face.

'Mum, he'll love it,' Thea said gently.

'I hope so, love.'

CHAPTER TWENTY

Freddie and Paul pulled up outside a block of dingy grey flats. The desperation of this place seemed to seep out of its every pore. They locked the car and walked up the stairs to a shabby front door. Freddie nodded and Paul booted the door in easily, the wood rotten and brittle. The stagnant smell of bodily odours and chemicals hit them as they crossed the threshold. They walked into the lounge where a greasy young man with a twitch now cowered into a corner. He just stared at them, mouth gaping, revealing a set of yellowing teeth.

Freddie took an exaggerated look around the room. 'Lovely gaff you've got here, David. Love what you've done to the place.'

The man seemed to find his voice as he stood up, warily eying the two well-dressed men in front of him.

'Well, I wasn't really expecting company—'

'Really?' Freddie cut in, a cold smile on his face. 'That surprises me. If I were you, I would have been expecting visitors, wouldn't you, Paul?' He turned to his brother.

'Oh yes,' Paul answered immediately, no emotion crossing his hardened features. 'I would definitely have expected visitors, Fred.'

'Hm.' They looked at him expectantly, waiting.

'Look, guys, I can explain—'

'Explain what exactly, David? Explain why you are treating Vince, therefore me, therefore my brother here, like cunts?'

David flinched. 'It weren't like that, Freddie. I'm getting it; I just need a bit of time—'

'You've had time, David. You've had time, you've had money and you've had trust. Three things that we expect to be respected, and all three of which you have badly *dis*respected.'

Freddie paced slowly across the room and studied the cheap, faded print hanging on the wall. The only picture in the sparse, depressing room.

'Do you like boats, David?'

'W-what?'

'The picture.' He pointed at it. 'Do you like boats?'

'Um, n-no, not really…'

'Oh, why's that then?'

'I d-don't like water. Can't swim.'

Freddie turned and beamed at him, feigning interest. 'No, really?'

'Um, yeah, I never learned.' David leaned on the side of the armchair, not really sure where this was going.

'Would you say the thought of drowning scares you, David?'

David shrank back and started to hyperventilate.

'Oh, David, I'm not going to drown you!' Freddie laughed. 'Would you look at that, Paul? The geezer thinks I'm going to drown him!'

'I don't know why he would think that, Fred. Why would you want to drown him?'

'I don't know, Paul. Why would you think I want to drown you, David?' Freddie's laughter died, and his eyes glinted like steel as he stared at the trembling man.

'I asked you a question, David. Why would you think I want to drown you?'

David tried to swallow the lump gathering in his throat as his eyes darted from one to the other.

'I-I know that I-I haven't delivered, F-Freddie.'

'No. You haven't. But you are going to, David. And I am going to tell you how. But first of all, I wanted to show you something new I learned.'

He pulled a pair of leather gloves out of his pocket and put them on, pressing them into the creases of his fingers with care. Paul followed suit.

'Did you watch that film the other night, Paul? That one with the rogue FBI guy they had to sort out?'

Paul looked up to the ceiling as he considered. 'Nope, can't say I did, Fred.' He shook his head.

'Aw, you should have, mate, it was blindin'. You learn all sorts of things from these films. For example—' he moved one of the least broken, old wooden dining chairs into the middle of the room '—did you know you can make a man feel like he's drowning without actually doing it?' He looked expectantly at his brother as David started moaning in fear.

'Nope, didn't know that, Fred. How's that then?'

'Well…' He walked into the kitchen and rummaged in the cupboards until he found a large bucket, then started filling it up from the grimy sink. 'I'll show you. Tie him to the chair. Arms back.'

David cried out and Paul silenced him with a resounding slap around the face.

'Shut it, Dave. You give us shit and you'll come out worse, you got that?'

Paul pushed his face into that of his unwilling ward and David nodded, tears now making track marks down the dirt on his face. Paul grimaced.

Freddie came back into the room as Paul finished tightening the cable ties that now bound David's wrists and arms to the chair. He was lugging a bucket full of water and spilled some down the front of his trousers as he set it down.

'Aw shit, look what you made me do, David! Now I'm going to have to change before my brother's party tonight and I really like this suit.'

'That's a good point actually, Fred.' Paul pulled back his glove to steal a glance at his watch, a titanium contraption that had cost him an arm and a leg, but of which he was incredibly proud. 'I haven't got long before I have to go get Mickey from the station.'

Freddie frowned his annoyance at Paul, who immediately shut his trap.

'So!' Freddie clapped his hands together as if performing to an audience. 'What we do now is this…' He dunked an old towel that had seen better days in the water a couple of times until it was sodden. David's eyes were agog, watching the slow, deliberate action.

'Hold the chair back so he can see the ceiling, Paul.'

Paul did as he was told, and David tried to hold back the guttural moans that were coming from his throat.

He was terrified. He'd fucked up big time. He kicked himself mentally as he tried to keep quiet. What on earth had he been thinking, messing around with the business of people like this? He had hidden his problem with cocaine and gambling pretty well, keeping his lines of access well away from his own doorstep.

There had been a large cocaine shipment in and once the usual outlets had been stocked, there was some left over. Needing to move the goods on, they'd offered David an in. The instructions had been sent to him along with a large amount of the illicit product. All he had to do was cut it, sell some of it off and keep the rest of it hidden until they sent someone round to get it, which would happen once one of their usual suppliers ran out. Instead, David had got high. Very fucking high indeed.

After a week-long bender, he thought he could get away with cutting it more than usual to pad it out. And when he'd started selling it, he couldn't believe how much money he was making! As with all their dealers, he was told to keep a certain percentage and put the rest away, ready for collection. Somehow in a haze of chemicals, gambling dens and girls who suddenly found him incredibly attractive, David had spanked the lot.

Waking up one morning sober, ill and cleaned out of every penny he had taken, he realised exactly what he had done. He was brown bread, of that he had been sure. When the brothers had walked through the living-room door, he thought he was a goner.

Freddie put the wet towel over his head and held it taut at the neck. David couldn't breathe.

'And now, Paul, put your hands where mine are—' David felt the change of pressure and squeezed his eyes closed '—and we do this…' Freddie poured the water over David's head, and Paul shifted position to stop the chair from toppling over completely as their victim struggled.

After what seemed like an eternity, which in reality was only fifteen seconds, Freddie stopped and whipped the towel off a now hysterical David.

'Sit him up.'

Paul pushed the chair up unceremoniously, and David started crying like a baby.

'Shut up!' Freddie slapped him hard around the face, and David struggled to contain his reactions.

Freddie could see Paul wasn't convinced by the method of punishment. 'The trick is in the towel. Apparently if you do that and then pour water, it tricks the body into thinking it's actually drowning. They use it as a torture method in the special forces.'

'Oh, OK, does it actually work?'

'I don't know, first time I've tried it. Let's ask dickhead here. Did you feel like you were drowning?'

All David could manage was a nod. The experience had been horrific.

'I don't think he's sure, Paul; let's do it again.'

'Please. No—' They stifled his cries with the towel and repeated the process.

Three goes later, they appraised the quivering, barely conscious wreck in front of them. Freddie sighed loudly to himself and looked out the window.

'Best get on with the finale then, Paul. I'll meet you at the car.'

'What?' Paul frowned at him, annoyed to be asked to leave.

'Car, please, Paul. Get the engine started; I won't be long,' Freddie commanded quietly and turned on the steely glare that had made many a grown man's blood run cold. Paul nodded his acceptance and turned towards the door without another word. They all knew who was boss in this firm, blood relation or not.

David convulsed, still tied to the chair. Freddie set his mouth in a grim line and turned back towards him.

'You know, in most countries they kill traitors.' He sauntered to the kitchen and rifled through the drawers until he came across a steak knife, blunt and dull from years of use. 'And we were all for killing you too, David. We would be within our rights to. Street law, of course. But you fucked off a nice little wedge of our hard-earned brass, not to mention our product, and we want compensation. So here is what's going to happen.' He turned the chair towards him so that they were face to face. 'I'm leaving you with this lesson, along with a reminder that you never, *ever*, even begin to think about mugging us off like that again. Do you understand me?'

David nodded as hard as he could.

'Good. Now. You are going on a little trip. A little holiday, let's say. You're smuggling a load of gear across one of the European borders I'm having a little trouble with. In fact, you're going to be going on several little holidays, doing the same thing.'

David's face paled even more.

'You'll be watched, so you can't pull any fucked-up stunts again. Trust is not something you are being handed back.

When you've done what I want, you'll be brought back. You won't be paid, and you won't be employed this side of London again.' He looked him up and down in disgust. 'But you won't be dead either. You can call it payback.'

Picking up another tea towel from where he had left it on the sofa in anticipation, Freddie stuffed it into David's mouth.

'Now. The lesson you've had. The reminder is about to come. Vince didn't want you losing your memory any time soon.' He looked at the knife before putting it against David's cheek. 'We thought a "T" on your ugly mug would perhaps remind you not to be such a treacherous little cunt in future.'

The end of the knife bit into David's skin, held taut by the gag in his now screaming mouth. Freddie cut deeply and quickly, before throwing the chair back against the sofa. Cutting the cable ties off David's hands, he pushed him onto the cushioned surface. He threw the knife into a corner and walked towards the door.

'You'll want to get that seen to, mate. Your knife was rusty. God knows what infections you'll get from that. Oh, and don't bother running. You'll be off on your holidays next week, give that time to heal. We'll be in touch.'

As he walked out of the building Freddie took a minute to breathe in and closed his eyes. It was all part of the life; he knew that – it had to be done. Mostly, he ruled his empire on respect and fear. He found that threats worked wonders if the need arose. But every so often someone took the piss and when that happened, everyone watched to see what they were going to do about it. If nothing was done, the firm would look soft, and it would be an invitation for any Tom, Dick or Harry to have a go at taking over.

Squeezing the bridge of his nose, Freddie took another deep breath and headed for the car. As he closed the door, he turned to Paul.

'I'll drop you home; get changed and go get Mickey. I'll be round for six.'

'Where you off?'

'Seeing a man about a dog. I'll be there for six,' he repeated in a clipped tone.

CHAPTER TWENTY-ONE

Anna's jaw dropped when she saw Freddie walking up to the building. His crisp white shirt fitted his sculpted body perfectly and accentuated his classic good looks.

Freddie explained on the way over to his mother's house that it was a welcome home and belated birthday bash for his youngest brother, who was back from boarding school.

Freddie approached the door and automatically reached for Anna's hand. He pulled away at the last minute, cursing to himself. He was forgetting himself. Apart from that one time at the beach, where all her defences and cautions had blown away in the wind, she naturally shied away from him. He didn't take offence at this; it seemed she was like that with everyone. But he didn't want to scare her away. He knew without having to be told that Anna had been damaged somehow. She hid it well for the most part. But he could see it. And until such a time as she was willing to invite him in, he wouldn't push her.

Registering his gesture, Anna lifted her hand to meet his, but just before her fingers reached his he pulled them back. She looked up at the side of his face and saw him curse silently to himself. Her heart dropped through the bottom of her stomach. Swallowing her disappointment, she forced a smile onto her face and walked forward into the house.

Mollie eyed Anna excitedly across the room. She was thrilled to see her son with a pretty young woman. She couldn't wait to be introduced. She waited while Freddie was greeted respectfully by each of the guests as he made his way through the throng towards her. The young woman looked slightly puzzled at the attention Freddie was getting but stayed one step behind him and kept her own counsel. That was a good thing, Mollie thought. The last thing Freddie needed was some loudmouth Suzie drawing attention to herself. By the time the pair actually got to her in the kitchen, she had already decided to like Anna, very much.

'Mum, this is Anna, a friend of mine. Anna, this is my infamous mother, Mollie.' He flashed a big roguish grin and put his arm around her. Mollie laughed and pushed him off.

'Oh, get on with yer! Infamous indeed.' But she blushed just the same, secretly pleased at the comment.

'Just don't get on the wrong side of her when she's got hold of a rolling pin – I'm telling you, she's scarier than Freddy Krueger on steroids!'

Anna burst out laughing with the rest of the room, as Mollie hit out at him with the tea towel she was carrying. Freddie backed away with his hands up in mock fear.

'Oh you!' Mollie narrowed her eyes, attempting a murderous glance and failing to hide her grin before turning her attention back to Anna.

'It's lovely to meet you, Mrs Tyler.' She held her hand out, but Mollie batted it aside.

'None of that, love. Come here and give me a hug.'

Anna's eyes widened in shock as Mollie pulled her into a hug. It had been so long since she'd had a cuddle with her own mother. She felt tears begin to prick her eyes and forced them back, not willing to make a spectacle of herself in front of all these people.

Mollie noticed the change. After a stiff start, Anna had gripped her tightly, as if she were a lifeboat. She waited until Anna let go first. Bless the poor girl.

Across the small space, leaning against the table, Freddie noticed the exchange. He had watched as, after her initial surprise, Anna had melted into his mother and hugged her back fiercely. He saw her sadness. He guessed that she missed her own mother and that the heartfelt embrace with his mum had just accentuated that. Her eyes opened and she blinked rapidly. She was close to tears.

Suddenly she pulled back and smiled widely at Mollie.

'It's so lovely to meet you; thank you so much for having me,' she said brightly.

'Don't be silly, love. It's nice to have my Freddie bring someone over that isn't six foot, surly and dodgier than a jammy biscuit!'

Freddie shook his head. The change in Anna was so swift that he wasn't sure for a minute if he hadn't just imagined it all. She smiled at him. Then Freddie's phone rang and he shouted over the mixture of conversations to get everyone's attention.

'He's coming into the road now, guys. Everyone quiet and get ready to scare the shit out of him.' They all laughed and then quieted quickly as Mollie rushed to turn the light off.

*

Paul racked his brains to find something to say to the young man sitting next to him in the car. He was like a stranger. At sixteen, he had shot up and seemed like a completely different person to the young, pink-cheeked lad they had sent off less than a year ago.

'I guess you probably missed all this, didn't you?' There was no answer. He wasn't sure Mickey had heard. Probably just lost in thought. 'Well,' he said awkwardly, 'we all missed you. It's nice to have you home, mate.'

Mickey didn't answer him but headed towards the door. Paul was puzzled but just shrugged. *Kids.*

Opening the door now, he gently pushed Mickey through it. The lights flicked on and there was a roar as everyone yelled *'Surprise!'* in unison. Party poppers went off everywhere, covering Mickey and Paul too in the process. The music came on from somewhere and everyone rushed forward towards the shocked young man, Mollie front and centre. She clasped her youngest son to her bosom, tears in her eyes, talking ten to the dozen. Freddie eventually prised him away and ruffled his hair, happy to see him too.

'Come on, Mum, share him with the rest of us! Hello, mate, how have you been?' He appraised the young man before him and grasped his shoulders. 'Crikey, you've grown, Mick! You're almost as tall as me! Dressing pretty sharply too – good man.'

Mickey smiled tightly up at Freddie before turning towards the crowd of people and scanning their faces to see if he recognised anyone. There were a few he knew. He twisted gently out of Freddie's grasp and moved through the group slowly, stopping as people hugged and talked loudly at him, excited by his presence. Freddie observed his youngest brother. Something was wrong with Mickey – badly wrong.

Paul sidled up to Freddie and followed his eyes. He scratched his head and squinted, trying to figure out how to voice his own confusion. Freddie glanced across to him, then back to the figures now in the kitchen.

''S'OK, mate. Spotted.'

'Ah, 'K.' Paul blew out a relieved breath. Freddie would deal with it.

Just a little too late, Freddie saw Thea swoop in on Anna. She had been standing to the side, watching everybody greeting Mickey. Thea started chatting animatedly to Anna and led her by the arm through to the back of the kitchen. Freddie cursed under his breath. He had no need to worry about Thea discussing his business. No one in his family would willingly volunteer information about his life in the underworld to anyone without good reason. But he was a little worried for Anna, knowing how private she was and how inquisitive his sister could be. He began to make his way towards them when Bill signalled him with a slight incline of the head.

Thea passed a plate to Anna. She moved close to Anna's ear and whispered conspiratorially, 'Anything you don't like, just tell Mum you've already tried it and it was perfect, but that you're full and couldn't eat anything more. Otherwise she'll make you try it. Trust me.'

Mollie made her way over to them. 'Anna, let's get you some food – anything you can't eat? Not vegetarian are you?' She waited expectantly.

Anna smiled warmly. 'No, nothing I can't eat.'

'Right then, love, you just help yourself now. You look like you could do with a bit of feeding up – you ain't got an inch to pinch.'

'Mum!' Thea protested, laughing.

'Well, she doesn't!' Mollie replied. In Mollie's eyes a girl should have some solid meat on her and a pair of decent birthing hips. How else was she going to work through all the struggles women faced? That life had changed drastically for women since she was a young girl did not register in Mollie's mind.

'Just ignore her,' Thea said, linking arms with Anna. 'You're fine as you are.'

The two young women started filling their plates while Mollie moved on to accost someone else.

'Now, Harold, have you tried some of that roast lamb yet?'

'I don't eat lamb, Molls – never liked the stuff.'

'But you haven't tried mine, have you! I slow-roasted that all morning with garlic and rosemary, it's absolutely pukka. Come on, let me put some on your plate. I won't take no until you've at least tried a bit…'

Thea threw a smirk at Anna and rolled her eyes. Anna couldn't help but laugh, though she stifled it enough that Mollie wouldn't hear. Thea was lovely, larger than life, as was all the family, each in their own ways. Although her own home and family were not quite as loud as this one, the obvious love and happy, carefree laughter reminded her of her parents and the life they used to have together. Before she had made the biggest mistake of her life…

'So where are you from? You ain't from around here, that much is obvious.' Thea bit into a mini beef Wellington and smiled.

Anna froze. She stumbled mentally for a moment. What should she say? She couldn't tell the truth, but she didn't want to tell an outright lie. She desperately wanted to run away.

CHAPTER TWENTY-TWO

Freddie slipped back in through the front door and saw Anna freeze, a look that he was now getting very familiar with. His eyes switched to Thea, who had a mouthful of food and an expectant expression on her face. He didn't need to have heard the conversation to understand the scenario that had just played out. *Well, that didn't take long.*

'There you are! Was wondering where I'd left you. I'm stealing her, Thee. You can have her back later on.'

He steered Anna off into the crowd and led her out into the garden. They sat down together, now slightly set back from everyone else and Freddie lit a cigarette.

'Are you OK?'

Anna smiled at him. 'I'm perfect! Your family are absolutely lovely, so friendly and welcoming…' She trailed off, looking over at the warmth inside the patio doors. 'Thank you for bringing me here.'

Freddie watched her face, the light from the door bathing her features in a soft glow. He fought the urge to stroke her cheek. Her deep blue eyes were hypnotising and he shook his head to clear the effect.

'Don't thank me; I wanted you to come.' Her eyes moved back to him and widened slightly. He continued, not wanting to scare her off. 'I mean, I know you don't know many people here, thought I'd introduce you around a bit,' he finished lamely, kicking himself at his cowardly excuse.

'Fred—' they were interrupted as Bill Hanlon approached the table. He nodded to Freddie and smiled politely at Anna.

'Bill, this is Anna; Anna, Bill – a work colleague.' He didn't give her a title, which was usually expected, because he didn't know what she was exactly. They weren't together, which is what people were now assuming, and he didn't want to introduce her as just his friend.

Bill paused a minute before offering her his hand. 'Nice to meet you, Anna.'

'And you,' she replied warmly.

Bill Hanlon was nearing forty, mostly bald and with a pug-like face. He had carved himself out a solid career in bank robbery, having pulled and got away with some of the most outrageous robberies the country had ever seen. The first couple of big jobs he had pulled off had people calling him 'lucky' or 'jammy', but years down the line, and with a past dotted with successful pulls, he had one of the most respected careers in criminal history. His specific set of skills had earned him the nickname Billy the Banker, which he rather liked. Like most people in their game, he had spent a long stretch in a Category A prison, but instead of retiring from a life on the edge when he came out, he just learned from his mistakes and improved his game.

Bill turned back to Freddie. 'That phone call – all went as planned. I'll pop by the club later, twelvish, if you'll be in?'

Freddie looked at his watch. 'Should be fine. I'll grab Sammy on my way in. He should be expecting me.'

'OK, see you later then, mate.' He glanced back at Anna, his gaze lingering on her face for a second before he continued. She didn't notice, having reached back to the table for her drink. 'Pleasure meeting you. See you again perhaps.'

Anna smiled and sipped her drink. Freddie had noticed the hesitation and was surprised. Anna was beautiful, of that there was no doubt, but in all his years he had never seen Bill even glance in the general direction of another woman. His wife, 'his Amy' as he referred to her often, was his whole world. They were almost sickeningly happy and would have run for Olympic gold in World's Most Perfect Couple had it not been for their sadness at never being able to have children. So it was out of the ordinary to see Bill study the pretty face of another woman, even for that split second.

Bill turned his attention back to Freddie, smiled briefly and then disappeared into the throng once again, heading towards the front door. Freddie shrugged and turned towards Anna and his family. Didn't matter. Maybe Bill was only human after all.

*

Bill made his way to his car and leaned against the bonnet while he took a deep drag on his cigarette. His eyes strayed to the lights of Freddie's house. He hadn't recognised her at first but knew he'd seen her before. It was only as he was leaving that it had dawned on him. It was her without doubt – she had a definitive air about her that he'd clocked the first time around, though it had been more subdued back then. She hadn't recognised him, that was for certain, though she wouldn't, because she used to be very careful never to lock

eyes with someone in Tony's presence. It was well known
that he guarded her with the determination of a Rottweiler.
It had been by chance that he had even caught that glimpse,
an emergency meeting at Tony's home. He had witnessed that
day just how terrified she was of him.

It hadn't been broadcast that Anna had gone on the
missing list, and it wouldn't be either. Bill knew it was seen
as disrespectful for a woman to leave her man in the Greek
culture and that that man would be seen as weak and therefore
avoided in business by other Greeks. Tony would not want
that information leaking out. Bill only knew about Anna's
disappearance because he had overheard a phone conversation
between Angel Face and Tony.

And now it seemed she was here. Half of London was being
quietly turned upside down in Tony's ferocious search for
her and she was sitting quietly in Freddie Tyler's house in the
East End. Well, good luck to her, Bill thought. He certainly
wouldn't be telling anyone where she was; he didn't want to be
the one responsible for leading that lamb back to the slaughter.

He wondered if Freddie knew who she was. He didn't
think so. If he had done, he would've either left well alone or
been much more guarded in who he introduced her to. He
shrugged to himself. It wasn't his business.

CHAPTER TWENTY-THREE

Leslie turned towards the hallway with a frown as the door went. She wasn't expecting anyone.

'Laura, I have to go, there's someone at the door. Give my love to Roger. OK, bye for now.' Leslie pressed the red button and it beeped as the call ended. The doorbell chimed again. It was barely nine on a Sunday morning. Arthur was still in bed. She untucked her legs from underneath her and stood up, pulling her dressing gown tight. She padded barefoot through the otherwise silent house to the door and peered through the eyehole.

'Eugh,' she breathed quietly, rolling her eyes. It was him. Why was he here? She opened the door, barring entrance with her body to stop him walking in.

'Hello, Tony. This is a surprise.'

'Good morning, Mrs Davis. How are you?'

'OK, thank you. It's quite early. Is something wrong?'

'No, no, not at all. I just wanted to speak with you. Check in on any contact Anna might have had with you.'

Tony's eyes were sunken in his face. His usually warm complexion was looking a little grey and his hair was an unstyled mess. Leslie noted all of this along with his tight, edgy stance. He stared at her, with hollow, empty eyes and she shivered.

'Let's get you back inside, Mrs Davis. You're getting cold.' She couldn't help but shrink back as he reached his hand out to her and he used the opportunity to step forward into the house. She cursed mentally. Her eyes flickered to the stairs, in the hope Arthur had heard and was on his way down, but there was no sign of him.

Tony stepped through to the large kitchen-diner and sat down at the table expectantly. His eyes bored into her as he sat in silence, waiting.

'I'll get the kettle on then, shall I?' Leslie found herself saying.

'Black coffee, thank you. So,' Tony looked around, not hiding his scrutiny, 'she been back yet?' His words were clipped, as though he suspected her of something. Leslie felt a prickle of fear run over her skin.

'No, Tony,' she replied, equally clipped, 'she hasn't been back here.' Remembering who she was talking to and the position Anna was in, she softened her voice. 'I would have rung you to let you know of any changes, of course. I know how worried you are.' It grated to have to speak to him sympathetically, but she played the game like she knew she had to.

She poured the coffee into two mugs and placed one on the table in front of him. She sat opposite and nursed the other steaming cup between her cold hands.

Standing up slowly, he walked round the table to Leslie. She tensed but forced herself to stay still. Her heart pounded as he leaned over her and placed his hand on her shoulder, squeezing hard, and spoke quietly in her ear, his voice deadly sweet.

'Don't worry, Mrs Davis. I have a small army out there looking for her. They will turn over every stone from here to

Timbuktu until we find her. And we will find her. There is nowhere in this world that she can hide. It's just a matter of time.' Leslie winced as the squeeze on her shoulder became more intense and pain shot through her. His voice darkened, the pretence of care running very thin. 'I will get her back, you know. Don't you worry your little head. You can be sure of it.'

Leslie's breath quickened as she tried to dampen her fear. She bit her lip instead of crying out as he cruelly dug his thumb into her collarbone. Keeping up the pretence that he was holding her kindly, he pulled her to him in a brief hug before releasing her.

'I'll be seeing you soon, Mrs Davis. Thanks for the coffee.'

With a light smile and a nod, Tony let himself out. As the door slammed shut, Leslie let out a sob. Her tears dropped as her body shook in frightened shock. Anger coursed through her as the tears flowed. How dare he come into her house and threaten her like that? How dare he touch her?

Walking to the mirror in the hall she stared at herself. She wiped the tears from her face and took some deep breaths. She wouldn't tell Arthur. He would be angry too, but there was nothing he could do about it. She might as well save him the frustration.

Gingerly she pulled back the dressing gown. Her shoulder was red where he had squeezed, and she could already see the beginnings of a bruise.

Tony wasn't going to be patient much longer, and she had no doubt he would be round to terrorise them again. But it was Anna she was worried for.

Oh Anna, she thought desperately, *please stay hidden*.

CHAPTER TWENTY-FOUR

It was Monday morning and Anna woke up to the cold wintry sun shining in through her window. She showered and dressed quickly before going through to the lounge-kitchenette area to join her housemate. Today was an exciting day for both of them – they had plans to shop around for the right premises. They'd gone through a few options together and had eventually come up with an idea that they both liked. Tanya wanted to stay in the club scene – it was all she knew. Anna had conceded. After all, at least one of them needed to know what they were doing. Anna was well aware that although she was smart, she still had a lot to learn and currently didn't have expertise in any area that could become lucrative.

Tanya poured them both some coffee. 'Morning, sunshine! Excited to get started?'

'God yes!' Anna grinned.

'Me too, can't wait to get going now,' Tanya replied enthusiastically.

'The club will be amazing if we pull off the plan. Amazing acts, sexy girls, but classy. With none of that back-room stuff,' Anna added. She glanced at Tanya. 'I know you do what you do through necessity, and I don't judge you or anyone else who does it one bit. It's life. But I just mean that this is different.

This is our club – we want it all above board, don't we? Straight as a die. All the girls clean and classy.'

Tanya fought back her natural defensiveness. She knew Anna wasn't having a dig; she was genuine when she said she didn't judge her. 'Of course. We'll get a better class of girls anyway if we aren't hiring the ones who are flogging their clouts.'

Anna saw her friend blush as she said this and realised she was referring to herself. 'It's nothing to do with class,' she said quietly, squeezing Tanya's arm. 'It's to do with survival. Now, come on, let's go find our club.'

Anna had always wanted her own business. Perhaps it came from spending too much time among the Greeks, in whose culture it was important to work for yourself, or perhaps it was her hunger for freedom. Tony had never allowed her to work – she was only allowed to stay at home cooking and cleaning. That was a woman's place in life, Tony had said.

Hours later, they tripped back up the stairs, laughing hysterically.

'Did you scc his face?' Tears of laughter streamed down Anna's face as they recalled the afternoon.

'Ha ha, oh God, I can't stop laughing!' Tanya doubled over, clutching her stomach. After several minutes and several curious glances from neighbours walking down the stairs, they got hold of themselves and made it, still giggling quietly, through the front door.

'Well…' Anna collapsed onto the sofa. 'I think it's safe to say that those premises are ours if we want them. And for not too high a price either. Oh, Tan, you are funny!' She giggled again, pushing her forehead against Tanya's arm; Tanya had collapsed beside her after grabbing a bottle of open wine from the fridge and two glasses.

'I know! Here, take this,' she said, offering Anna a glass of wine. 'It worked. I can't believe his panic when he thought I was going to walk out.'

'Oh, his face was a picture!' Anna replayed the afternoon in her head. The poor guy hadn't stood a chance.

The pair had walked into the estate agent's and asked for a viewing. The only person free had been Robert, a young twenty-something man in a suit that was obviously a size or two too big. Tanya had worked her magic, practically purring at him as he nervously stuttered through the details. On their way to the property, Tanya had linked her arm through his, chatting away animatedly about how she hoped to achieve her dream and perhaps, if she was lucky enough, even find a nice, stable young man to share it all with one day. Red in the face, he had nearly burst with pride at being seen with Tanya on his arm.

The first property had been a dud. The place was just shy of being located on the edge of the buzzing West End nightlife.

By the third one, they were becoming disheartened. Eager to please the red-haired angel that had fallen into his life, Robert had practically begged them to go and see another property that had just come onto the books.

'It's not up on the boards yet. We've only just received instruction on it today.' He'd pushed his glasses further up the bridge of his nose again and blushed as Tanya giggled and smiled adoringly at the action. 'I was going to put it up this afternoon, but perhaps if you ladies…?'

'OK, where is it?'

Robert had torn his eyes away from Tanya to answer Anna's question. 'It's just around the corner, on Greek Street, so great location. Used to be a karaoke bar or something, but it got run down and the son raided the vaults and went on the trot. Old man couldn't get this place up and running properly again, up to his eyeballs in debt. Can't even sell it, needs to get it rented out pronto, get some money coming in to try to cover the mortgage. Gambling problem or something. Really stupid if you ask me…'

'Oh, I completely agree, Rob – may I call you Rob? I'm sure your friends must call you that.'

'Oh, well, uh, yes. They don't, but, erm, yes, if you want to.' He blushed as she beamed at him.

Anna had raised her eyebrows, though it was at the location rather than Tanya's role-playing. Greek Street. Of course it was. Sod's law it would probably end up being perfect too. Well, it was certainly ironic if nothing else.

The outside had been shabby, but nothing some elbow grease wouldn't fix. The inside was run down, there was a lot of work to be done. Anna tutted to herself. What a waste of such a good size building in such a busy area. After walking round twice and mentally checking off everything they needed, Anna gave Tanya the nod, and she set about discussing money. In fairness to the poor boy, he did start off on a fair price, obviously trying to win Tanya over. But Tanya's face had fallen theatrically, all huge stricken eyes and colour-drained cheeks. Anna distractedly wondered how she was able to do that on cue, go pale like that. She really was a very good actress; she'd missed her calling in life.

'Oh dear… And I was so hoping we could get something agreed and then go to lunch together and celebrate. But never mind, we've got other agents to see.' She lowered her gaze to the floor as she slowly turned to gather up her things from where she'd left them at the bar.

'No wait! Wait! Perhaps… perhaps I can talk to the owner, see if there's any wiggle room on that price.'

Tanya, after a dramatic pause, asked hesitantly, 'Really? You could?'

Anna rolled her eyes and fought the urge to laugh. It had taken less than an hour for him to finally get them to a price that made the building an absolute steal. Tanya had wheedled her way to almost half the amount they had initially started out at. The owner must have truly been in dire straits to have agreed to such a drop, and Anna was surprised at Tanya's tenacity. There was a steely businesswoman hiding under that exterior, which was exactly what the venture needed.

They had handed over the deposit and signed a contract that day, not wanting to give the owner any time to find a better offer.

Anna knew it was a risk putting her name to a business in London, or anywhere in England, to be honest. It was a stumbling block that she had deliberated over for a while. She still hadn't told Tanya much about her past but had confided in her enough to explain that she was trying to stay on the missing list. That she didn't want to be found, with good reason. In the end, after some fiddling around with the contract, the premises and the business were put under Tanya's name, with Anna down as a silent partner. Anna was gambling on this being enough to keep her whereabouts under the radar. She doubted Tony would think to look for her name under a new bar opening in the West End. He would still be underestimating her, assume she was cowering away in submissive terror. But, like a phoenix, she would rise again from the ashes of her old self and grow strong and bright. Anna Davis was going to leave her mark on the world somehow.

Anna smiled as she read the text from Freddie and quickly replied. She thanked him again for taking her to the party and asked after his family. She'd had such a great time. And it had felt so good being around a real family again. She sighed. She was missing her mother greatly.

She had gone over a few scenarios in her head, trying to find a way to reach her without being traced, but it was virtually impossible. There had been one plan that she had mused on, dismissed and mused over again a few times. It would have to involve Tanya. And to involve Tanya would mean confiding in her about what had happened, even if just to make her understand the importance of secrecy. But Anna still wasn't sure she was prepared to do that yet. In a perfect world, no one would ever know.

'We have *so* much work to do, Tan,' she mused, looking thoughtfully out the window. 'Why don't we get away somewhere? You know, before we get the keys and the real work starts?'

'What, you mean like a little mini holiday?' Tanya's face lit up at the thought. 'Blimey, Anna, I can't remember the last time I got out of the city! That would be well nice. Where were you thinking?'

Anna bit her lip. 'I've got somewhere in mind. It's a lovely little town on the coast over in Norfolk. Very cute. I think you'd like it.'

'Ooh, that sounds lovely! I've never really been anywhere like that. Read about it and seen it on the telly and that...' She shrugged. 'Guess I never got round to it.'

Anna turned and frowned. 'Tan, have you ever been outside of London?'

'Nope.' Tanya shrugged again as if apologising for her lack of geographical experience.

'But what about when you were a kid? Did your parents ever take you away?' As soon as the words came out of her mouth she regretted them. Tanya's face reddened. Anna kicked herself.

'Sorry, Tan, it's none of my business. I shouldn't have asked that.' Anna jumped to a hurried apology, not wanting to upset her.

'Nah, 's'OK, mate.' Tanya smiled ruefully. 'My dad was away a lot, and me mum couldn't stand the sight of me.' Her eyes pierced Anna's. 'My upbringing wasn't quite as silver spoon as yours, babe.'

It was a barb, but just a little one and tempered with a smile. No serious damage was done.

As Tanya changed the subject to where to source their suppliers, Anna found her head wandering off in the direction of her mother again. She hadn't really meant to even suggest the trip out loud. It had just been a thought, and a potentially dangerous one at that. She hadn't fully believed that she could pull it off as an actual plan. But maybe she could after all. If everything went exactly as planned, if she was incredibly careful, and if Tanya was of course willing to help, then the idea that was forming in her mind might just work. But first she'd have to explain some things to Tanya.

CHAPTER TWENTY-FIVE

Freddie walked up to the large whitewashed mansion. It looked more like a villa really, out of place in North London. There were voices raised in bubbling laughter and general chitchat coming over the wall that cordoned off the extensive garden. CCTV cameras followed their movements. Paul glanced behind him as Freddie shifted the large bunch of flowers to his other arm and pushed the doorbell. The door opened and a slim, olive-skinned woman appeared. Her face broke into a smile as she saw who it was.

'Freddie! How lovely to see you!' Haroula reached forward and kissed him once on each cheek. She nodded to Paul.

'Haroula, you're looking as radiant as ever. These, of course, are for you.'

'Freddie Tyler, I'm far too old for you, and even if I weren't happily married, you're not my type – you're far too pale and skinny.'

He laughed and followed her through the house, their shoes clacking on the marble floor.

The patio was a hive of activity. Thirty or so people sat around tables and on benches, talking, laughing and enjoying their surroundings. A huge barbecue, with a grill two metres wide and three levels all working at different heats, was built into a large stone structure just to one side. Meats of all kinds were cooking away, big chunky cuts sizzling, smoke billowing up and travelling down the length of the garden. The smell was wonderful. Haroula led them towards the barbecue and the tall, overweight man proudly tending it. He had his back to them. The tight white linen trousers and floaty blue camisole she was wearing made Haroula look younger than her years. Her olive skin was smooth and unblemished, and the laughter lines around her big brown eyes only added to her attractiveness. Her arm extended forward now, towards her husband.

'Cos mou, Freddie's dropped in.' She reached up and kissed him briefly on the cheek. He turned around and smiled, putting the spatula down on the side of the grill. He motioned slightly with his head and one of the younger men nearby immediately took over with the food.

'You boys have fun,' said Haroula, walking away.

Paul had taken a seat near to the entrance of the house and was quietly watching a game of cards taking place on the table next to him. He had barely been acknowledged but took no offence. The Greeks only dealt with the people they ranked highest, the people of note. As Freddie's number two, he was treated politely but only included if he was to be of use.

Cos wiped his hands on his trousers and grabbed Freddie's outstretched hand with both of his own.

'Freddie, me old mate, how's things? What's 'appening?'

In his mid forties, Cos's thick head of hair was now a mixture of white and black. Like his wife, instead of subtracting from his swarthy handsomeness, it added an air of sophistication. His dark eyes twinkled with a mischievous grin.

'It's good to see you, Cos. Just sorry that I seem to have crashed your party.'

'Not at all.' Cos gestured wildly with his hand, trying to dispel Freddie's embarrassment. 'It's always good to catch up with an old friend.' He smiled warmly and Freddie relaxed.

'Can I get you a drink?'

'Whatever you're having, mate.'

Cos scanned the garden to make sure everything was as it should be. 'Shall we go through to the study? I take it this isn't purely a social call?'

'I wish it were, mate.' Freddie smiled ruefully. 'Sadly, though, there's no rest for the wicked.'

'Ain't that the truth?' Cos grinned back and the pair slipped off into the house.

They seated themselves in the comfortable back room Cos used as his study. Freddie scanned the room, looking at the impressive collection of books.

'So what can I do you for?' Cos asked as he poured two brandies into crystal tumblers. He passed one to Freddie, then sank into the comfortable leather chair opposite. Freddie swirled the amber liquid around in the glass.

'Got a couple of things I wanted to mull over with you, so to speak. Firstly…' He hesitated. 'You must have heard about Big Dom.' Cos nodded and waited for Freddie to continue. 'Obviously this has hurt us personally. It's not something we're prepared to allow to hurt us professionally.' He paused and breathed out loudly. 'To be honest with you, Cos, as embarrassing as it is at this point, we haven't heard a dicky bird. There's no gossip, no speculation, no leads whatsoever on our side of things.' He took a sip of brandy and placed the glass on the table. 'It can't be anyone over my way – we'd hear something. So it must be someone further afield. We're putting the feelers out where we don't usually meddle. I need to know if you've heard anything, friend to friend.' Freddie stopped there. He didn't want to offend a good mate and business contact.

Cos nodded, a serious expression on his face. 'I don't know anything more than you do at this point. If you're asking if there's been any involvement on my side, then no. But I'm pretty sure that's not what you are hinting at – you know me better than that.' He shifted his weight in the chair. 'If you are asking if I've heard anyone else in my neck of the woods having involvement, well…' He shrugged. 'I haven't as yet, but that's not to say I could give you my word that it wouldn't have happened. I keep on top of my business and my people. I work with a lot of people, mainly family, but like me most of them have their own agendas. I have thirty-four cousins, half of who, as you know, work in various underhand businesses. As closely as we work sometimes, I'm not up to date with their every movement…' He raised his hands up in a shrug of surrender. 'What can I say? It's plausible. You could be barking up just the right tree – I mean, it's green, it's made of wood, but let's face it, you're in a fucking forest, Freddie. It could be practically anyone. If someone wants to be king of your fucking castle, they have a lot to gain by taking out Big Dom. That's an attractive prospect for a lot of cunts.'

They both sat in silence for a moment, each lost in his own thoughts.

'I'm just surprised he didn't see it coming, you know,' Cos said quietly. 'I mean, he was one of the originals. Grew up in the old school. He never took his eye off the ball, never left himself open.'

'I know,' Freddie answered.

'Whoever did it, son, is looking for the biggest trouble he can get his hands on. And this geezer has currently got the upper hand.' He fiddled with the arm of the chair and gazed out the window. 'You know I can't get involved in this. But for the sake of my friendship with Big Dom and you, if I hear something I don't like, I'll drop you a visit.'

Freddie nodded. He didn't take offence to Cos not getting involved – it was part of the game. But he appreciated Cos's last comment. It meant that as long as it wasn't close enough to home to have any effect on him, then he would tip him the wink.

CHAPTER TWENTY-SIX

Leslie Davis walked downstairs slowly, unrested from yet another sleepless night. She paused as she caught herself in the hall mirror. She ran her fingers over her face, feeling the deep hollows under her eyes and the sharpness of her cheekbones. She sighed quietly to herself and continued to the kitchen, wrapping her soft, fluffy white dressing gown around her. She didn't bother turning the light on.

She made a coffee, moving around the kitchen silently, trying not to wake her husband. She loved him deeply. He had always been her rock, but right now even he couldn't help her. She knew he was going through the same as her; she could see the hurt and the helplessness underneath his solid exterior.

She got through her days as best she could, went through the motions, kept it all together, but her worry and heartache never went away. For some reason it seemed easier at this time of the morning, when the world was quiet. She sat alone at this time every day. Perhaps it was just that she was so tired she'd run out of feeling, but at this time in the morning she just felt calm.

She heard the soft thump of the post hitting the carpet. Tony thought she didn't know about the man posted outside the house each morning, rifling through the post before it was put through their door. Obviously she knew it was happening – she had seen the man in the car one morning by chance. Sometimes when she was particularly restless, she would watch them from behind the net curtains, rifling through their mail like pigs in a trough. They couldn't see her – it was too dark and she kept the lights off – but she saw them.

Leslie shuffled slowly to the post and took it through to the kitchen. She glanced at it uninterestedly. Bills and a postcard.

Her heart skipped a beat as she looked over the picture on the front. It was a silhouette of a woman holding a little girl's hand on the beach. She dropped the rest of the post and hurriedly turned it over.

Dear Leslie,

How are you? As usual it has been far too long since we last saw each other – fifteen years in this case! Do you remember, dear, the last time we had a good catch-up over a weekend away? We stayed at that little hotel right on the beachfront – you remember, that big old place in that sweet little seaside town in Norfolk? Well, it turns out I'll be going back there soon. I realise it's last minute and you're probably far too busy, but I wondered if you were free and fancied coming down this weekend to visit me and my niece, Tanya? You remember her, the one with all that red hair. You should bring your daughter too, if she's around. That would be fun.

Anyway, let me know. You have my number. If you do decide to come you'll find me along the promenade most days,

braving the weather as always. Do you remember that spot
where we used to sit to eat our fish and chips?
　All my love,
　Marge xx

Leslie's eyes filled up. There were too many emotions
running wild within her to cope with all at once. Relief,
happiness, excitement, terror, caution. She wiped her eyes
and read over the postcard again. It was definitely her. When
Anna was little, they had gone on a few girly weekends away.
They'd started when she was about two and carried on until
she hit her teens and was no longer interested in the small
town with its beach and shells and ice creams. The little town
she spoke of was popular with elderly holidaymakers and the
two of them had created a long-standing joke about a little
old lady called Marge who would holiday there come wind
or high weather, each in turn pretending to be their fictional
character, resulting in peals of laughter between them.

The man posted outside would probably be on the lookout
for anything coded, so could easily have photographed the
card before putting it back through the door. Tony would no
doubt let her walk right into it, create a trap. She pondered on
what best to do. Anna would probably realise this, hence why
it was sent in code in the first place. Perhaps she would find
another creative way of contacting her once she was there, so
as to not give anything away. Yes, that had to be it.

For the first time since Anna had gone, Leslie found some
energy inside herself. She ran upstairs to wake her sleeping

husband. She would go to Norfolk. The postcard said the weekend and it was Friday already.

'Arthur! Arthur, wake up! I have news – I have some real news.' Her voice went from loud excitement to conspiratorial whisper as she shook him awake. 'Get up! We need to pack.'

'What?' Arthur groaned as he dragged himself into an upright position, squinting his eyes painfully as his wife flicked on the light.

'Darling, it's Friday morning – we need to move now if we're going to get there tonight.' Leslie tutted excitedly, pulling out a suitcase from under the bed.

'Leslie… Les. Leslie!' Arthur raised his voice to get her attention. She stopped what she was doing, and he laid a hand on her arm.

'OK, calm down and tell me what's happened. From the beginning.'

*

Tony woke to the sound of the phone ringing next to his ear. He sat up groggily and stared down at the screen bleary-eyed, trying to make out who was calling him at such an ungodly hour. The phone rang off and he closed his eyes for a second before it started up with its annoying tinkle again.

'What?' he accused.

'It's Angelo. Sorry about the time, but you said to call you if I got any sniff of her. Well, I think I might have one. A sniff, I mean. It might be nothing, but better safe than sorry, right?'

Tony sat up and shook his head to clear it. 'Get over here and show me. And bring coffee.'

Half an hour later Tony was showered and dressed and in a thoroughly bad mood, having realised just how early he had been woken. It had been a long night the night before, with a lot of brandy and a lot of good-looking girls – the type that made themselves available to anyone with a large wallet.

Angelo passed him a large coffee and showed him the images of the postcard.

Minutes went past with only the sound of Tony sipping his coffee to fill the silence.

'It could be,' he said slowly, trying to rack his brains for anything she could have mentioned about Norfolk. To be honest, he knew very little of her life before him. When they'd first started dating, he had feigned interest to try to gain her trust. Once he had her where he wanted her, he put paid to her chatter whenever he grew bored by telling her to shut up. Now, though, he realised it would have been helpful if he could remember anything from her past.

'I don't know. She's never mentioned anything about her mum's mate down there. It could be her. On the other hand, it could genuinely be her mum's mate. Follow Leslie Davis. She ain't that clever. She won't even realise you're there.'

Angelo wasn't convinced. He had seen her once or twice looking at him with pure hatred blazing in her eyes, while he'd been tailing her on various trips out of the house.

'I don't know, boss. I think she's more savvy than you think.'

'Are you joking?' Tony snapped. 'She's an old bat who saw all the riches I gave her daughter and thinks I'm heartbroken.

She's just a woman, for Christ's sake.' Tony rubbed his face up and down roughly with his hands, a sign of agitation. 'I can't do this today. I have some meetings. Just go, take Dodge with you. Tail the old woman. You see any sign of Anna, you grab her and you bring her back here.' He slurped again at his coffee. 'If you do see her, use whatever you need. It don't matter what the mother thinks of me then. Keep me updated.'

Just at that moment Angelo's phone rang shrilly. He answered it quickly.

'Dodge?'

'Angel, I think you were right about that card. She's woken her old man up, all the lights are on and they're rushing from room to room like no one's business. Hang on! He's just driven a little two-door sportster out of the garage. Didn't know they had that.'

'I'm on my way.'

CHAPTER TWENTY-SEVEN

Leslie glanced in the wing mirror of the car and sighed inwardly. Arthur looked in the rear-view. They were still there. The black nondescript estate car that was keeping its distance but following them all the same.

'Did she say the name of the town on the postcard?' Arthur asked thoughtfully.

'No, she only put what she had to – gave us just enough to find her without saying too much.'

'Right, hold on to your hat then, Les, I'm going to open this baby up!' The little sportster roared to life as it jumped forward out of its leisurely stroll.

'Oh!' Leslie squealed. She turned round and watched the black car disappear as they turned a bend. 'You genius, Arthur!' she hissed, her face beaming in excitement.

He grinned. 'I've always wanted to do this. They won't know these country roads like we do,' he said.

But their excitement was short-lived as the other car shot round the bend and back into sight.

'Damn. Come on, Art, you can do better than that. Take them round the houses.'

Arthur glanced at her animated face out of the corner of his eye and smiled to himself. They hadn't had fun like this in ages.

An hour and a bloody good attempt later, the car was still managing to keep up. They had lost it once or twice, but not for long – it had always managed to catch them. Arthur slowed down and smiled sadly at his wife.

'Well, we tried,' Arthur said.

'Yes, we did.'

'I'm sure Anna's got a plan for when we get there.'

'Yes, she must do.'

They continued on in silence, praying that they were right.

*

Tanya sat motionless on one of the twin beds in their cosy little room at the bed and breakfast. Anna had insisted on this place rather than anything more plush. And now she understood why.

Anna bit her lip. It went against the grain of her whole new life to bring someone into her confidence. Tanya's silence was panicking her. Her eyes began to well up, and she tried to quell the tears before they spilled over.

Tanya just stared at her blankly as she lost the battle and a tear ran down her cheek. She wiped it angrily, hating to cry in front of anyone.

'No, oh no, mate, don't cry. Sorry, I'm just… I don't know, I'm shocked.' She handed Anna a tissue to wipe her face. 'I mean, I knew you was hiding from something – we all have our secrets – but I hadn't realised it was so, I don't know, serious.'

Anna hadn't gone into any further detail than she felt she needed to with Tanya. She had told her how Tony was now hunting her down and wanted to punish her. And she'd told her how he would be staking out her parents' house to find her. When she had explained her plan, she'd kept her fingers crossed that Tanya would agree.

'Of course I'll help. We're mates, roomies and business partners. We may as well be married!' She laughed. 'You just have to tell me where I need to be, what to say, what you want me to do and all that.'

'Are you sure?' She looked at her friend gingerly and Tanya gave a vehement nod. 'Well, let's start with wardrobe. You might be out there some time. I don't know when she'll get there. I had to be pretty vague.' Anna pulled out a woolly jumper from her bag and a pair of binoculars fell to the floor.

Tanya raised her eyebrows. 'Well, we are going very Tintin and Snowy, aren't we! Bags not Snowy.' She wiggled her face and they laughed together.

Less than an hour later, Tanya walked down to the promenade, having taken the long route shown to her by Anna. It wouldn't do to let anyone know where she was staying. She shoved her hands deeper into the pockets of the beige overcoat that Anna had given her. Tanya had gone pink when she'd opened it, all wrapped up neatly in silver tissue paper. It was the nicest present she'd ever received. In fact it was the *only* proper present she had ever been given.

She pulled her hat down over her ears, tucking stray strands of her hair up into it as she walked past all the little shops, lights twinkling in the windows and colourful displays reminding her that Christmas was not far off. This village was truly enchanting, each house and shop made of thick stone and the streets cobbled as if a hundred years old. She stopped off at a little coffee shop on her way down to the promenade, stooping to get through the low doorway, and grabbed a takeaway coffee to warm her hands with while she waited.

'Do you want cream with that, my love?' the plump, rosy-cheeked woman asked her in a soft lilting accent that Tanya quickly decided she adored. She smiled.

'Um, alright then, just a dash.'

'You're not from around here?'

The woman's interest was innocent but Tanya answered cautiously. 'No, I'm visiting an aunt of mine. She isn't from this neck of the woods either, just fancied getting away from the city.'

'That sounds nice, dear. Well, you be sure to come again now, and bring your auntie with you.'

'I will, thanks.'

Tanya smiled her goodbye as she stepped back out into the bracing cold and walked down to the bench Anna had described to commence her potentially long wait for Leslie.

CHAPTER TWENTY-EIGHT

In the end, Tanya didn't have to wait too long; she spotted Leslie's hesitant figure walking towards her about an hour later. She had spent a peaceful time, bracing herself against the bitter wind, just watching the waves roll in and back out again. She felt as though she was finally relaxing and letting out the breath that she had been holding in since childhood.

Leslie made her way up the beach, studying every figure she passed. As she began to scrutinise Tanya, Tanya got up and waved at her energetically, calling her over. Tanya's shrewd eyes had already spotted the two men following behind her at a distance and rightly placed them in her mind as Tony's men. Leslie glanced anxiously behind her and, as she did, one of the men melted out of sight while the other lifted a camera in front of his face, pointing it at the grey-blue sea. Tanya pursed her lips.

'Leslie! How lovely to see you after all this time! I bet you don't even recognise me now.' Tanya flashed a bright smile and drew the older woman into a full bear hug. Leslie hid her surprise and played along, realising at once that this must be part of Anna's plan. Tanya's grin was infectious, and she found that she was genuinely smiling back at the girl.

'I'm so sorry, but Aunt Marge can't make it now. She took ill all of a sudden but felt awful after inviting you up so I thought I'd come anyway.' Tanya let her forehead crease in concern as she talked, shaking her head solemnly.

'Oh, that's terrible, I do hope she gets better soon.' Leslie bit her lip and looked around, searching for a sign of her daughter. She lowered her voice. 'Tanya—'

'Not here,' she cut her off quietly. 'You've got two bleedin' followers, those bastards. Let's go shopping.'

She made a point of looking at the men curiously before taking Leslie's arm and steering her towards the quaint little shopping arcade across the road. They didn't talk about it further, just wandered slowly, looking through windows and commenting on the pretty things on view. Leslie kept the smile plastered to her face and a calm exterior, but inside she was bursting with impatience and longing. It had been so long, and she had come so far that this last leg of the race was impossibly hard. Twice more, Tanya turned and stared pointedly at the men, as if confused as to what they were doing there. Each time they quickly moved as if to look elsewhere. The last time she did this she adopted an air of annoyance, hand on hip, frowning at them.

This time Angelo backed off properly. All these birds had done so far was chitchat and shop – it was a waste of time. It could have been a ruse, so he would stick the weekend out, but they didn't need to be followed everywhere – that was just ridiculous. The whole thing was ridiculous; he was one of London's hard men, for Pete's sake, not some fucking babysitter. He blew out a long, slow breath and signalled

Dodge to follow him away. The last thing he needed was for the local police to be alerted by some little bird. They walked down the road to grab some food.

Tanya watched them leave in the reflection of the shop window opposite. When she was satisfied they were out of earshot, she breathed out a sigh of relief and looked around for a suitable place to talk. Her eye caught a tiny little shop window and door with an advertisement outside for afternoon tea. That would do. One way in and out, no surprises. As she opened the door she spotted a table at the back that was half tucked away and she headed straight for it, leading Leslie with her.

Anna would have loved this place, Leslie thought, taking in the little shop. She swallowed the lump in her throat and blinked rapidly before turning back to Tanya, who was ordering them both afternoon tea in her blunt East London accent.

'Please, where is she?' The hope and agony was clear in Leslie's soft voice, and Tanya felt a pang of envy course through her at the love this woman clearly had for her daughter. She was a real mother.

'She's here, Leslie, in Sheringham.'

'Where?' She made to rise, but Tanya stopped her.

'Leslie, you can't go to her.' She was firm, though her heart went out to the poor woman in front of her. 'It was dangerous enough for her to come here, and I have things Anna wants me to talk to you about.'

The tea arrived and she poured it, thanking the waitress, who tactfully ignored the distressed companion of the flame-haired beauty.

Leslie took a deep breath and shook off her disappointment. She reminded herself that the most important thing here was Anna's safety and that she was lucky to even have this meeting with Tanya. 'Tell me about my girl,' she said simply. 'I take it you're a friend of hers?'

Tanya smiled back at the older woman warmly. She wished again that she could have known the love of a mother like Anna's. She placed her longing aside and began to tell Leslie everything that had happened since Anna had left.

When Tanya had finished, she sat back and took a deep drink from her cup. Leslie's eyes were shining, her face full of hope and radiance again.

'I'm so glad she's OK. Thank you, Tanya.' Leslie squeezed Tanya's arm. 'Thank you so much for being such a good friend to her. She needs someone like you. She lost all of her friends, you know. When Tony got his claws into her.' Leslie's eyes clouded over again as she looked back in her mind's eye. 'He's an evil man. He tried to destroy her, to break her. We thought—' she faltered, 'we thought maybe we had lost her towards the end. That he'd won and finally broken her.' She stared through the wall, swallowing the hard lump in her throat. 'But then she disappeared. We don't know what happened to finally make her snap back; I doubt we ever will. She hid the worst from us. Or at least she thought she did.' The flicker of a sad smile played on Leslie's lips for a second. 'She lied to us about how bad things were, told us everything was fine whenever I asked. But I knew. A mother always does. Still, there was nothing either of us could do but wait until she came to us. It was heartbreaking, but what can you do when someone won't let you in? Whatever it was that finally made her go, I'm just glad she did it. She has such a strong spirit, you know, underneath her quietness.' Leslie's voice was full of pride for her daughter. Tanya nodded.

'Oh, I know. She has some serious determination, that's for sure. I'm glad to have her as my business partner. And my friend,' she added. She cleared her throat. 'There's something else I have to tell you.' She looked around, wary of anyone she might have missed. 'Don't touch it now, just in case. But I slipped a phone into your pocket earlier, on the pier.'

Leslie gasped, her eyes widening. Her hand automatically moved, but then she stopped it and placed it carefully back on the table.

'OK. It's a pay-as-you-go phone, totally untraceable,' Tanya continued as quietly as she could. 'It has a number programmed in the contacts, just under the word "Phone". That number is for another untraceable phone, which Anna has. Now this is important. You must *not* take it out of your pocket until you're in your house and then *only* in the en suite. Hide it under that sink. That is the only place in the house that Anna is absolutely sure no one can see or hear into.'

'OK, I will.' Leslie could barely contain her excitement. She was going to be able to talk to her little girl.

'The other thing is – Anna got this one specifically because she used to have the same model. There's a charger for it in the bottom drawer of the small chest of drawers in her old room.' Tanya recited the very specific information Anna had given her earlier that day. 'Don't go out and buy one or anything else to do with this phone.'

'No, no, I won't,' Leslie said hurriedly.

'If it gets discovered by Tony, then Anna will have to dispose of hers to avoid him being able to get to her. So please, be careful,' Tanya stressed. 'Oh, and whenever you speak on the phone, say the word "lemonade" first, to let Anna know that it's safe to talk. If you speak without using the word "lemonade", Anna will assume it's because Tony or one of his men is there listening, OK?'

'Got it.' Leslie nodded seriously.

'Anna will wait for you to call her when you're back. No hurry, she'll keep hers on her.' Tanya gathered her coat and stood up. 'I'll let you get on then. It was really nice meeting you, Leslie.'

'It was very nice to meet you too, Tanya. And thank you again. I really am so happy to see that Anna has such a good friend.' Leslie smiled. She meant what she said. It was obvious that Tanya came from a very different walk of life than she was used to, but Leslie could see that she cared greatly for Anna.

'Yeah, well…' Tanya shrugged and awkwardly pulled Leslie in for a swift, one-armed hug. 'See ya, mate. Get home safe, yeah?'

'And you both. Give her our love, Tanya.'

'Will do.'

Tanya stepped outside into the fresh, crisp air and breathed it in deeply. Pushing her hands deep into her pockets, she set off at a brisk pace. She kept an eye out for the two men but didn't see any sign of them. Satisfied after a few minutes that she truly was alone, she decided not to take the long route back to the hotel and headed straight for it. It was too cold to be out any longer than necessary.

CHAPTER TWENTY-NINE

Anna was pacing the room, wringing her hands when Tanya opened the door. She jumped forward and grasped Tanya, her eyes bright, the second she saw her.

'How did it go? Was she OK? Was it just Mum, or was Dad there too? Were you followed? Did you get the phone to her?'

'Jesus, gal, slow down, yeah?' Tanya laughed, holding her hands up in mock surrender.

'Sorry.' Anna stepped back and made an effort to compose herself. She waited for Tanya to take off her coat and hat quietly, but her impatience and fearful excitement sat bubbling away, just under the surface of her now calm exterior.

'OK, so it was just your mum. She's fine. Your dad's fine too. Slipped the phone into her pocket, told her everything you asked me to and parted ways happy. OK?' Tanya raised her eyebrows in question. Anna nodded, digesting. 'She's nice, your mum,' Tanya said wistfully. 'Must have been nice at yours.'

'Yes, it was.' Anna studied Tanya's face. She never opened up about her past and Anna had never pushed her. But she'd noticed how Tanya never discussed her family, and it was obvious that she wasn't in touch with any of them. In the few months that Anna had lived with her friend, she had never had any family over to visit or even had a phone call.

'So now you just need to wait for your call then, mate. Mission accomplished.'

'Yes, mission accomplished.' Anna nodded and looked out the window at the windy beachfront. 'Now for the wait.'

*

Dodge swallowed the lump in his throat as he waited under the furious stare of his boss. Tony didn't blink or break eye contact, just sat there, silently boiling with rage. When Tony was in one of these moods it didn't matter who you were or what you had done, there was every chance you would end up dead.

'You saw *nothing*?' he spat. 'There was nothing there *at all* that made you suspect she could've been there?'

'No, boss. Like I said, she just met that woman on the bench and went for a walk past all the shops. Anna wasn't there. We listened in to them but it was all just small talk, nothing about Anna. We tailed them as far as we could, but there was no one about, and the girl had eyes on us a few times. We had to disappear, she was one look away from calling the local plod.' Dodge fell silent and waited for Tony's response, his heart racing and his face smooth.

Tony said nothing as he processed everything. He'd been certain it must have been her. He couldn't believe that she'd managed to go all of this time without contacting her parents.

He eyeballed Dodge one last time. He enjoyed provoking fear in people. He watched Dodge's Adam's apple bob up and down as he swallowed again. Leaning back casually, Tony picked up his glass of whisky once more and fingered the large hunting knife he had out on the desk. Dodge's face immediately drained of colour, but still he didn't flinch or move. Tony felt a small flicker of respect for the man.

'Go!' Tony waved him away, and Dodge let out the breath he'd been holding in. 'Take the night off. See me back here tomorrow afternoon. I have plans to discuss with you.'

'Thank you, boss.' He nodded and swiftly retreated out of the room.

Tony stroked the hard, black handle of the knife and turned it slowly so that the light from the lamp glinted off the blade. This was the knife he was saving just for her.

CHAPTER THIRTY

Freddie and Sammy sat together in one of Freddie's offices, a Portakabin on a small junkyard near the docks. Freddie had acquired the junkyard early in his career, buying it from a tired old man who wanted to sell up and move to a quiet retirement in Spain. It had proved to be a shrewd move, working well as one of his legitimate businesses in which to hide a fair amount of his illegitimate money. It also provided a well-protected and very private office, due to the location and the large, none-too-friendly guard dogs watching out for any uninvited guests.

Sammy pursed his lips as he studied the plans in front of him for the umpteenth time.

'Is it really worth it, Fred?' he asked. 'How much went in there?'

'Just over half a mil.'

'Ah.' Sammy nodded and continued looking at the plans. He was a very logical man. He was working the process over in his mind and going through all the possibilities before he would give his answer. He didn't rush into anything without weighing up every single angle first. Freddie respected Sammy for that.

'It's ballsy, Fred. One wrong foot and that's it for all of us. There won't be no plan B here. It's risky. Even for half a mil.'

'I agree with you, Sam,' Freddie conceded, his face serious. 'But we have bent filth on the payroll working that night, running this from the inside. Once we're by that fire exit—' Freddie leaned forward and pointed it out on the blueprint '—then that's it. Five minutes while the stuff gets loaded and then we're gone. Done.'

The blueprints were the plans for the local police station. The station that was currently holding half a million pounds of Freddie's hard-earned money. Scottish George, one of Freddie's most trusted men, had kept his mouth shut when he had been collared with the money and was doing his time gracefully. He knew what was expected of him. In return, Freddie had put a large wedge aside to go to him upon release, as reward for his loyalty. He also made sure to keep sending George's wages to his family every month. Family were always looked after in situations like these.

Now, though, Freddie wanted his money back. He had several police officers on the payroll, and what Freddie gave them pretty much doubled their wages. Freddie couldn't stand them. A straight policeman he respected. They might be on different sides of the law, but he respected that they stood up for what they believed and worked hard doing what they said they were going to do. A bent copper, however, was scum in Freddie's eyes. A bent copper betrayed his own, and no matter what side of the coin you sit on, that just made you a scumbag.

But scumbag or not, they were worth having on the payroll at times like this. They had happily sat there raking money in all this time – now they could actually do some work for it.

They had to work it so that several of them were on shift at the same time. That was crucial. The security cameras would be taken offline for maintenance for a ten-minute window. Once they were down, the gate would be opened, and Freddie and his men would be able to drive into the back of the compound. They would drive around the back of the building to a small fire exit where one of the bent filth would be waiting to let them in. He would then lead them through another two locked doors, into the evidence cage. There were nine large, heavy bags full of money, which would have to be run back to the car quickly. They would have just ten minutes to get them loaded into the car, and they couldn't leave a single trace.

Sammy looked Freddie in the eye and nodded. 'OK. I'm in.'

CHAPTER THIRTY-ONE

It was dark outside as Anna left the comfort of the flat. A windy chill swept down her neck, and she nestled her head deeper into her thick scarf as she scanned the people around her. She was only going to the off licence, but she always had to be careful.

The road was lit up by street lamps and the light that spilled out from all the small businesses that ran late into the night. She passed an ice-cream parlour and an empty café. The road wasn't too busy at night here, but some cars still passed. One taxi, two, she noted. A small hatchback with neon strip lights underneath. She sidled to the left to avoid walking into a loved-up young couple.

Anna took a deep breath to calm her racing heart. This happened sometimes, the sudden anxiety. She didn't know what triggered it exactly, but sometimes she just suddenly felt anxious and alert. Tutting in annoyance, she pulled her phone out and tried to distract herself by texting Freddie. It had been several weeks since Freddie had taken her to the party at his mother's house and they had met up a few times since, for a quick drink here and there. They had formed a solid friendship, which Anna had begun to value immensely.

A woman burst into a fit of giggles behind her and she jumped slightly. Anna shook her head. This was ridiculous.

Finally reaching the off licence she stood up straighter and walked in, firmly leaving her issues at the door. The little bell above the door tinkled as she walked in. She picked up a couple of bottles of Pinot Grigio from the fridge. She and Tanya were having a girls' night in and had already run out of supplies.

She paid and left with the bottles tucked under her arm. Outside she noticed two men standing in front of the pub next to the alley, smoking. She could hear their voices. Northern. Not from around here. Two cars were driving past, one BMW, one Ford. One dark grey minivan with blacked-out windows. She carried on walking, focusing on the sound of her footsteps. The building wasn't far now. She could see it.

She paused. The minivan she had seen go past was coming back down the road towards her. Why had it turned around? Why was it going so slowly? She put her head down and picked up her pace. *Keep calm*, she told herself. Her heart pounded in her chest, and she felt the lump forming in her throat. The van cruised past her slowly and then suddenly pulled up on the side of the road. Two doors opened and then slammed closed. She could hear footsteps. This was it. He had finally found her.

She tried to run but her foot caught on something, and she stumbled. A bottle slipped from her grasp and hit the ground with a shattering crash. Glass and wine flew everywhere. Shaking, she turned around to face them.

*

Tony ignored his phone. He was enjoying the delights of his favourite whore house. The girl grinding up and down on his cock was doing a good job. He reached up and grabbed her tightly by the neck. The shock and sudden fear on her face urged him on. He pushed her down, reaching deeper inside her. She squeaked slightly, trying to breathe. Her face was turning red, and her eyes started to bulge. His excitement reached a high level and he flipped her over, ignoring the second call jangling away on the bedside table. Squeezing her neck harder he ignored her signalling for him to stop. He closed his eyes and imagined that it was Anna underneath him, Anna struggling for breath as he crushed her delicate neck with his hands. He finally climaxed and let go. She coughed and spluttered as she drew in oxygen.

Tony laughed and walked nonchalantly over to his clothes, his manhood still on show, shrivelled and spent, hanging down underneath his mountainous belly. He picked up his wallet and took out some extra notes.

'Here. To ease your discomfort,' he said mockingly as he threw them up at the girl he had nearly just suffocated. He knew she wouldn't say a word. She knew who he was and that it was better to not cause trouble. She nodded at him and tucked the money away quickly.

'I'll have you again next week. I think I'll become one of your regulars.' He grinned broadly as dread appeared in her eyes. *Oh yes*, he thought, *she'll do*.

His phone rang again shrilly for the third time. He tutted in annoyance. Could they not tell he was clearly busy by the first two unanswered calls? 'What is it?' he demanded, irritated.

'We've got her, boss. We found her.'

'What?' Tony's mouth widened in disbelief. 'Anna? You've got Anna?'

'Yeah, she's tied up in the back. We're nearly at your gaff. We weren't sure where to bring her, so thought we best head there.'

'I'll meet you there in twenty minutes.' He clicked off the call and stood still for a moment, taking it in. They had found her. She was his again.

CHAPTER THIRTY-TWO

With a screech he pulled away and sped home as fast as the traffic would allow him. The drive, usually a good twenty minutes, barely took him fifteen in his haste. He reached the electric gates at the front of his sprawling house and hit his steering wheel impatiently as they took too long to open.

'Come on, come on, come on, come on.' He felt like a kid at Christmas. Oh, what he was going to do to her tonight. This was the end of the road for that jumped-up bitch. She was going to pay for everything she had done, in full.

The gates finally opened and Tony sped up the drive.

There were two more cars parked up as he reached the front door and went into the house. Deano met him just inside.

'She's in the basement.'

'Good.' Tony smiled. 'So where did you find her?'

'Up the city. We were driving through and I spotted her. I knew it was her the moment I saw her.' He puffed his chest out, elated that he had been the one to catch her. 'She struggled a bit, tried to throw us off – making out she was someone else; calling for the police and that. I had to give her a bit of a cosh.' He searched his employer's face for approval, unsure how that news would go down. Tony smiled and nodded, and

Deano relaxed. 'Got her in the back and came straight here. No one saw; it was pretty quiet.'

'Cameras?'

'None that would have picked us up for nearly half a mile.'

'Good.'

Deano led the way through the house towards the basement. Tony had had the basement put in a few years back for times like this when he would have the need to cause pain to people in his home. He couldn't have the sound from the house travelling. The basement had been made soundproof though, so that wouldn't be a problem.

He reached the bottom of the stairs and marched over to where she was tied to an unused dining chair. Still out cold, her body was slumped forward. Her thick, dark hair had fallen like a curtain over her face, but he could see from the back of her head that they had gagged her. He smiled coldly. There would be no need for that gag. He wanted to hear every blood-curdling scream. He noticed that she had lost weight – she was far too skinny for his tastes now. Not that that really mattered anymore. She wouldn't be here much longer. Her hair was shorter too; she must have cut it. He couldn't see much of the rest of her, bent over as she was. He turned towards one of his men and clicked his fingers towards the opposite end of the room, where there was a large washbasin.

'Grab the bucket next to you and fill it up.'

'Yes, boss.' The young man's voice was low and quiet. If truth was told, he felt sorry for the girl. But he was part of the firm and this life, so his opinions would go with him to the grave. He filled the bucket quickly and carried it over to Tony.

Tony lifted the full, heavy bucket and with one swift movement chucked the contents up into the unconscious woman's face. With a gasp she woke up and jolted back. Her hair swept back off her face and she screamed out in terror.

About to throw the empty bucket at her, Tony's arm stopped in mid-air and his mouth dropped open in shock. He blinked and stepped forward, throwing the bucket to one side. Grabbing her face roughly with his hand, he moved it from side to side. 'This isn't Anna. What the fuck!'

Tony stared at the terrified woman in the chair. She did look incredibly similar to Anna. The same blue eyes, the same pale, heart-shaped face, the same full lips and neat nose, even the same hairstyle. It was uncanny. But it was not Anna.

Tony's men didn't make a sound, their faces all stricken with horror. Deano turned a sickly shade of green as everyone's eyes kept flickering towards him. He was the one who had seen her. He was the one who had stopped the car and grabbed her off the street. Not many of them had ever seen Anna up close; Tony was so possessive and secretive. They had only caught glimpses, always averted their eyes when she was around in case Tony kicked off. He had been known to scar men just for looking her way too long. Deano shook and looked down to the floor, swallowing hard.

Without warning Tony charged across the room and punched Deano hard in the face. He flew backward, his nose splitting and blood spurting out. He cried out, then stopped quickly by biting his lip. It would be worse if he made noise. Tony stood over him and he cowered, waiting for the next blow.

Tony breathed heavily, trying to control his temper. He was tempted to beat Deano half to death for this colossal mistake, but he needed him, and he was a good man to keep close.

'Get yourself cleaned up,' he spat. 'And I don't want to see you again tonight. Get out of my face.' Deano quickly left the room.

Tony began pacing again. It really was an uncanny resemblance. Even if Anna herself could see her, she would be shocked at how similar they looked. Tony stopped. If Anna could see her... He narrowed his eyes. Sitting down, he let a dark, twisted seed of an idea take root in his mind, and his mouth curled slowly into a smile.

*

Anna shut the front door and walked into the lounge where Tanya sat, arm outstretched with an empty wine glass.

'Jesus, gal, you took ages. I'm dying of thirst here.'

'Sorry, I got spooked by this van full of students on the hunt for an off licence and dropped the wine in the road.'

'What?' Tanya's face fell dramatically. 'Tell me you're 'aving a giraffe!'

'Nope. But luckily—' Anna brandished the remaining bottle '—I bought two! So we're OK!'

They both laughed and Tanya exaggerated her relief. Anna plonked back down on the sofa after removing her coat and began to pour the wine.

'Right. So where were we...'

CHAPTER THIRTY-THREE

The next day Anna woke up late, her head thick and fuzzy. She groaned as she made her way to the kitchen, where Tanya was pouring them both a cup of tea.

'What's up with you?'

'Too much wine,' Anna mumbled.

Tanya pulled a face. 'Shut up and have another; hair of the dog, that's what you need.'

'God, no, I couldn't think of anything I want less right now.'

Tanya sat down next to her and switched on the news.

'So what was it you said you wanted to do today?'

A woman's body was found in North London this morning by an elderly gentleman walking his dog…

'Nothing right now. I really did have too much last night.'

'We only had two bottles.'

'Exactly. That equates to an entire bottle each, Tanya.'

'Lightweight…'

'… was apparently tortured and mutilated before being sexually assaulted and murdered…'

'Christ, are you listening to this? That poor woman.'

'What?'

'This.' Anna pointed at the newsreader on screen and Tanya turned to listen.

'… to Jeremy, our reporter, who is currently at the scene.'

'Thank you, Carol. Yes, it is a terrible and sobering scene that greets us this morning here in Alexandra Park. I have here with me Alan Cambridge, who found the body this morning. Alan, can you describe to us what it is you saw?'

'It was awful. That woman, she… when I found her she was laid there with no clothes on; her body was totally covered in bruises and cuts. Looks like she'd been tortured. There was blood all over her, her hands were all bent and broken and someone had carved a big "A" on her breast. I've been here answering questions all morning with the police and I heard them say she'd been raped too. God… I can't stop thinking about it…'

'Of course. Thank you, Alan; we appreciate you reliving it for us. As I say, a very sobering scene here today, Carol. I think we are all now just hoping that this is the only body. Back to you at the station.'

'Very sobering indeed. We have just received news that the victim is twenty-four-year-old Karen Holmes, a newly qualified lawyer at a small firm in the city and daughter to Jessie and Adam Holmes…'

Anna gasped at the picture of Karen that flashed up on the screen.

Tanya's eyes widened as she caught sight of Karen too. She looked exactly like Anna. The mouth a little wider perhaps, her skin not quite so pale, but other than that it could be her twin.

Anna's face drained. It was Tony, she knew already in her gut. Her breath began to speed up and catch.

'Come on – breathe. It's OK.'

'It's not; it's not OK. It's him. It's him, Tanya.' She began to shake uncontrollably. 'He left her for me. He left her there in the open as a sign. He's showing me what he's going to do to me when he finds me.' The shock got the better of her and she burst into hysterical tears.

'You don't know that. That could have been anyone. I'm sad to say that there is unfortunately more than one total psycho in this city. I've met a few in my time,' she added wryly. 'Come on, it's just a coincidence.'

Anna sniffed and took a breath.

'A coincidence? What, with a huge "A" carved onto her? "A" for Anna, Tanya. It's him, I know it is.' Anna dropped her head into her hands and sighed heavily. The shock was wearing off. Now she just felt sick to her stomach. Tanya muted the TV and turned her body towards her friend.

'Look… if it is him, chances are he'll get his collar felt over this one. It's too public – the police will work it out. They'll find some DNA, something that leads them to him.'

'No,' Anna said quietly, shaking her head. 'They won't. He's too clever for that. Whatever else he is, he isn't stupid.'

They sat in silence for a while, both lost in thought. Eventually Tanya turned to Anna, biting her lip. 'Do you still want to do the club?'

'Yes, of course,' Anna answered straight away. 'Tony is a threat. He always will be. I'll always have to stay hidden, but I can't stop living my life. I have to keep moving forward. I have to build my life again.'

Anger at Tony set in. Her words grew stronger, loaded with emotion. 'I went through hell with that man, with that… creature. I found the courage to leave, to escape it all, despite the danger of even trying. If he had caught me, I would have died back then. But I still left, knowing that was a possibility. I can't have come all this way to start cowering now.' She stood up to her full height, walked over to the window and stared out over London. 'Yes, I still want to do the club. Our club is going to be the best club in London. I'm going to make damn sure of it.'

CHAPTER THIRTY-FOUR

Thea sat down at the desk in the small Portakabin and waited while Freddie poured coffee. She crossed her slim legs and looked around the sparse room with its faded grey carpet and scrunched up her nose.

'Why don't you spruce this place up a bit?' she suggested.

Freddie shook his head. 'No need. I've got nice offices – this is just for raw business.'

'Oh great, so you couldn't have asked me to one of your nice offices again then?' Thea quipped, rolling her eyes. 'This one stinks of the river.'

'That would be because it sits right beside the river, Thea,' Freddie replied drily without looking round. Thea pursed her lips and stared out the window. 'So. Talk to me – what's going on with the accounts?'

'Well.' Thea opened the large file she had brought in with her and pulled out two slim notebooks. 'You're going to have to think about buying somewhere new. These are the real accounts—' she pointed to one of the books '—and these are the legit accounts. I've put through everything I can, maxed every legal outlet's income, but there's still a huge discrepancy that's been building up for months. I physically can't launder anything more through these, and aside from your personal cash stashes, you still have nearly a hundred grand not accounted for.'

'Hundred grand… OK. I'll buy another house, use it as a rental.'

'That's not enough. I can only put standard rent through a house – you'll be backed up again in another few months. I need a high-flow, low-proof business.'

'I don't have time for another club.' Freddie lit a cigarette.

'OK, well something else then. What can you do that's low maintenance?'

Freddie leaned back in his chair and pondered this, not taking his eyes off his sister. He knew that business had been increasing more rapidly lately but hadn't given much thought to how to manage the extra money. Thea always just dealt with it. He could see the dilemma though. If his accounts were investigated now it would already look suspect, though they would still be passable. The front businesses definitely couldn't take anything more.

'What about a consultancy?' he wondered. 'A business-management consultancy. How much could you get away with there?'

Thea shook her head. 'It needs to be a cash-flow business. If you were audited it would be too transparent.'

'What about a café? Coffee, fry-ups, sandwiches…'

'That could work. Though you'd need at least two of them – one alone wouldn't take the difference.'

'OK. Done. Could you find some premises for me?'

'Sure.'

'And actually,' Freddie added, 'go knock on Lizzie Hayford's door, ask her to come see me when she's got a minute. I'll offer her the run of one of them. I heard her fella did a runner on her and the kids. Left her with nothing. She could do with the money.'

'OK.' Thea grinned. 'You're a soft git, ain't ya?'

Freddie gave her a level look. 'Not soft, Thea, smart. You look after those around you, you can count on them later. Always look after friends, family and neighbours. Loyalty is priceless.'

Thea nodded. 'Right, I'll get started. I'll call you later with some options. By the way, how's Anna? I liked her; she seems nice.'

'She's good,' Freddie answered shortly, with a tight smile.

'Just good? Any, er, plans to see her again soon?' Thea asked in an innocent tone, a gleam in her eye.

'Bye, Thea.' Freddie pointedly ignored her and waved her out of the Portakabin.

'Alright, was only asking! Jesus.' Thea rolled her eyes and left. Freddie watched her out the window as she made her way up the cobbled path to the main road. *Cheeky minx*, he thought.

His mind turned back towards business. He was going to need to think up something bigger in the long run to carry his extra income, but for now he had other things on his plate.

*

Anna put down the paintbrush and arched her aching back, looking around. They had been in here for five days now cleaning and painting the place. It wasn't good enough though, Anna thought. If this place was going to look as professional as it needed to, they would need to get proper decorators in. They couldn't half-arse anything. Not with everything they both had riding on this.

Anna's phone beeped in her pocket and wiping her paint-covered fingers on her top, she opened her phone to read the text. It was from Freddie, asking if she was free to grab some lunch. She smiled as she messaged back, telling him that she would meet him in an hour.

'Tan, do you mind if I skip off for a couple of hours?'

'Sure, where you off to?' Tanya asked.

'Oh, just for lunch.' Anna shifted her weight awkwardly from one foot to the other as Tanya gave a throaty giggle.

'I bet I know who that's with. Your mystery man, eh?'

'He isn't my "man", he's just a friend.'

'Mm-hm.' Tanya raised her eyebrow sceptically. 'Sure he is. Because you don't blush or nothing whenever we bring him up, no?'

'It's just lunch with a friend; there really isn't anything else to tell.' She shrugged and her smile faltered slightly.

Tanya studied her face and gave her a sympathetic smile. 'That bothers you, don't it?' she asked gently.

'What? No, not at all.' Anna frowned and moved about, agitated. 'I don't care. Why would I? I don't want a man in my life anyway, not after the last one. What I need are friends, and that is what I have.' She took a deep breath and gave Tanya a bright grin, then walked out the door purposefully, grabbing her purse on the way.

Tanya shook her head with a wry smile. Anna might be fooling herself, but she certainly wasn't fooling Tanya. She could see the way Anna lit up every time she spoke to this guy, the way she seemed to bounce through the day when she knew she was seeing him later. Sure, Anna had been knocked badly by her last relationship – Tanya knew that. But maybe it was time for her to begin opening herself up to new possibilities. Anna had become family. She loved the bones of the girl and wanted to help her find some well-deserved happiness again.

She turned her attention back to the task at hand and carried on painting.

'Sorry I'm late!' Anna sat down opposite Freddie and tried to catch her breath. He laughed at her, opening up his easy smile.

'That's alright – there was no need to rush. You look like you need a drink.' He caught the attention of the waiter, who rushed over immediately.

She grinned. 'I do, thank you.'

'What do you fancy?'

'I'll have a white wine, please. Pinot if you have it.'

'A bottle,' Freddie instructed. 'I'll join you,' he said, turning back to Anna. 'So how's things?'

'Good, thank you – very good.' She smiled and looked around the restaurant. Each time she met up with Freddie she felt herself relaxing a little bit more. Despite that though, she had still not told him the details of her venture with Tanya. He knew that she was starting up something new with her flatmate, but she hadn't elaborated. He hadn't pushed her on it

either, which was one of the things she liked about Freddie. She
didn't feel pressured to do or say anything she didn't want to.

She let her eyes roam subtly over Freddie as they ate. He
looked just as good as ever today, in a beautifully fitted black
suit and open-necked shirt. Not a hair out of place and his
aftershave romancing her senses just the right amount. The
girl who managed to settle down with Freddie would be a
very lucky woman indeed, she thought wistfully. Anna never
asked Freddie if he was dating anyone. It wasn't a question she
wanted to hear the answer to. He almost certainly was, she
thought. Why would he not be? He ticked every box.

'… so I took one home for Thea, and she loved it. Not
that it went down well there, of course.' Anna laughed with
Freddie and covered her glass as he tried to refill it.

'No, I mustn't. I have to get back to Tanya; we've got so
much to do still.' She studied him over the table as he just
nodded. 'Talking of Thea, she texted me the other day actually.
Invited me to go for a drink, which was kind of her. She's very
nice, your sister.'

'Yeah, yeah, she's a good sort.' Freddie made a mental
note to have a chat with Thea before she met up with Anna.
He didn't want her spilling any details about his way of life.
It wasn't time yet. He didn't know whether it ever would be
time to tell someone like Anna who he really was, but if and
when that time came, he wanted such information to come
from himself.

CHAPTER THIRTY-FIVE

The following morning Freddie sat upstairs in his bedroom, cleaning the gun he kept strapped under the mattress. It was a ritual of his to handle and clean all his various weapons once a month, whether or not they had been used. Always alert, Freddie wanted to be sure that if he needed to suddenly go for his nearest gun, it would be in perfect working order. When you sat in a position such as Freddie's, there was always the distant threat of some competitor or hungry kid further down the food chain. If one of them got too big for their boots and decided in their vast stupidity to try to take him out, he needed to be prepared. It had happened before; it would happen again. With Big Dom's demise still fresh and the culprit at large, Freddie was on even higher alert than usual. There was still no word on the street about it. No one seemed to be taking ownership of the crime, which in itself was odd. Why make such an outrageous statement, then walk away totally anonymous? It made no sense.

Finally happy with the gleam on the cold, hard metal of his gun, Freddie carefully restored it to its hiding place. He made his way downstairs to the kitchen, where he could hear his mother and brother talking. The kitchen was full of the aroma of roasting lamb, wafting from the Aga. Warm from the heat it was generating, it was a bright, cosy room and

Freddie felt a pang of regret that he had to soon leave it. Paul sat at one end of the table, his hands wrapped around a steaming mug of coffee. Mollie was sitting next to him with her own mug but jumped up and bustled over to the kettle when she saw Freddie come in.

'Ah, there you are. Here you go, love, made enough for you.' She poured another coffee and handed it to Freddie. He took it and smiled fondly at her.

'You're a diamond.' He drank from the cup deeply, savouring the warmth. It was a bitterly cold day.

'Fred, I heard something this morning on my way to the yard. Might be nothing, but it struck me as odd.'

'Oh yeah? What's that?' Freddie said, turning his attention to his brother.

'Thought I would pop in on Damien as I was passing, see what the latest shipment was looking like. Nice stuff, by the way. You wouldn't be able to tell the difference. Anyways, so he's telling me about his weekend and mentioned that there's been a couple of Greeks hanging round The Black Bear.'

'Oh?' Freddie raised an eyebrow. The Black Bear was one of their pubs, one that was fairly well hidden away from the general public. It was a hub of civilised criminal activity, all of which was under the management or watchful eye of Freddie. It was where his men spent a lot of their free time, and locals that weren't involved in his way of life avoided it. The only time that members of other London firms stepped foot inside that pub was if they had been invited for a meeting. It wasn't strictly off limits to anyone, but it was highly unusual for people in the know to ignore the unspoken boundaries.

'Did he say what they wanted?'

'That's the odd bit. They didn't speak to anyone. Apparently they sat there, had a couple of pints and left. Bill Hanlon told Damien that he'd seen them in there twice before. Did the same thing then too apparently, just had their drinks and pissed off.'

'That *is* odd,' Freddie agreed. 'Were they Cos's men?'

'No, apparently not. Bill said they were from one of the other Greek firms. They're all connected, of course, but these guys don't work under Cos.'

'Good.' He was glad. The last thing he needed was for an ally to start acting shadily. He liked Cos.

'Bit of a statement, ain't it?' Paul said, frowning.

'It is indeed,' Freddie mused. 'Find out whose crew they're on and get a tail on 'em. See if it's just that pair sniffing round, or if there are more. I want to know what they're doing.'

Freddie breathed out heavily. It could be nothing, but he doubted it. There was rarely smoke without fire. Downing his coffee, he grabbed his coat from the back of the chair and shrugged it on over his suit. Mollie handed him his scarf, which he put on and tucked into the front of his coat. Opening the back door, he shoved his hands deep into his pockets to protect them from the cold, then he turned back towards them.

'Sort that out this morning, then meet me at the docks for twelve thirty. I need to talk to Damien about upping the scale.'

'I don't know if he can, Fred. Apparently this lot was a scrape to get through.'

'Hmm. OK. Well let's go over the operation then, see what we can improve on.' He switched his attention to Mollie.

'Laters, Mum. Save me some of that, will you?' He motioned towards the Aga. Smiling, he gave her a wink and disappeared.

*

Sipping his own coffee, Paul went through the register of men he trusted in his mind. He needed the most discreet and efficient men for a tailing job. Heavy drinkers or gamblers were out of the question. Same with philanderers. Too easily distracted. He needed the straight guys. Bill Hanlon was the first man who came to mind. Yes, he nodded; he would definitely set Bill on it. Bill wouldn't so much as look at another bird with how loved up he was with his wife, nor would he be tempted to fuck up a job by drinking too much or hitting the cards. He knew Freddie was working on another job with him but was sure that Bill would be able to handle both. Archie Tucker was the second man he thought of for the job. Archie lived for 'the life'. Quiet and nondescript, he could blend into the background anywhere. Those two would do for now. If there turned out to be more of them nosing around, he would think of who else to set to the task.

Paul picked up his phone and scrolled down his contacts to Bill.

'Bill, it's Paul. I've got a job for ya...'

CHAPTER THIRTY-SIX

The wind ruthlessly hammered against Freddie and Paul's faces, the only part of them that was not covered up as they walked down the pathway to the dock. There was no protection against the weather down here by the river. It was swollen, brown with the muck and silt that was being churned up from the bottom. Freddie often wondered whether on days like this, the numerous bodies that lay at the bottom were at risk of dislodging and turning up on one of the banks. Not that he had ever disposed of anyone in the river, but he knew that Vince and Big Dom had used this option a few times back in the day.

Paul hunched his shoulders and blew into his hands, trying to warm them up.

'Fuck me, Fred. It's colder than a nun's snatch out here.'

Freddie pushed his hands deeper into his pockets. Their breath trailed away in white clouds as they walked briskly. They reached the small Portakabin at the end of the dock, past Freddie's own office, and Paul rapped on the door.

'Come in – it's open.'

Paul opened the door and shot inside, eager to get out of the biting wind. Freddie followed and quickly shut the door behind him. Damien was seated behind an old, chipped wooden desk, a man Freddie hadn't seen before sitting opposite him. He raised an eyebrow at Damien, who quickly got up and walked round to the two brothers.

'Freddie, Paul – good to see you. Let me get you a coffee; it's fucking 'orrible out there.' His eyes darted from the brothers to the newcomer and back again. 'This is Ted. He runs one of the factories we order the whisky from.' Damien poured two coffees from the ready-made pot on the side and handed them to Freddie and Paul. 'He was in town and I said about you coming in. Thought it might be good for you all to meet.'

Freddie nodded and sat down in one of the two empty chairs Damien had placed out ready for them. He didn't usually deal with suppliers once an operation was up and running. Damien had sourced this one, plus another couple, for the cheap spirits they smuggled into the country and sold through the clubs. It was a good earner, and the product itself was good. Joe Public couldn't taste the difference, and the profit through the clubs went up fivefold. It also made it easier for Freddie to launder some of his illegal money through the clubs.

Freddie steered clear of suppliers so that if they ever got a serious tug, they wouldn't know who to point a finger at. He trusted his own men implicitly, but he couldn't be sure of every single supplier on every single job. There were too many of them, and they had their own interests. Damien knew this though, and if he trusted this man enough to bring him in front of Freddie, then Freddie trusted that judgement. Damien was no fool. He wouldn't put Freddie at risk.

'You got some whisky to put in this, Damien?' Freddie motioned to his coffee. 'Could do with a bit of an Irish one on a day like this.'

''Course.' Damien smiled broadly and pulled a bottle out of a small filing cabinet next to the desk. 'Here you go.'

Freddie accepted the whisky and then turned to face Ted.

Ted smiled politely and held his hand out to Freddie. 'Nice to meet you, Freddie. It's good to put a face to the name.' Ted looked to be in his late twenties. He dressed smartly and subtly with neatly combed hair and a close shave. His tone was respectful and warm.

Freddie shook his hand and looked him square in the eye. 'Indeed. So long as this face and name stays in your head and nowhere else.'

Ted nodded. 'Of course. Goes without saying.'

'Good. Good. OK.' Freddie put his coffee down and got comfortable in his seat. 'Let's get down to business. Damien, Paul says the shipment is good quality. I trust his judgement. The demand is growing, so we need to up the order. I understand that you've had a bit of difficulty with this last lot. What happened?'

'Yeah.' Damien sighed heavily and his face turned grave. 'They've started doing spot checks on the ships. Luckily we always mask the product underneath legit stuff and in the middle containers just in case, but they got close, Fred. Real close. Apparently these spot checks are going to keep happening regularly. They went through random containers with a real fine-tooth comb. Didn't just take the contents on face value either, proper went through them. If they'd hit ours, they would have found the bottles underneath the other stuff in minutes. John kept an eye on things while it was happening, said they did the container right next to ours.' Damien paused to light a cigarette. 'It's become way more risky. I'm looking into ways to better hide the product. Might have to take up a bit more space, put more of the legit stuff in each crate and lower the secret bottoms. But we can't up the amount we're pulling through those shipments. If anything we may have to lower it. The more there is, the more chance we have of getting caught.'

'I see.' Freddie sat back and pressed his fingers to his head, rubbing at his temples. 'How long have these spot checks been happening?'

'Just this last shipment.'

Freddie nodded his acceptance of this and mulled the situation over in his head. There was silence for a few moments.

'I've got two supervisors at that customs' port on my payroll. These shipments are organised around their shifts so this doesn't happen. Where were they? What the fuck do I pay them for?' he asked Damien.

'Ben and Ralph,' Damien confirmed. 'They usually make sure there's no spotlight on our ships, but they weren't there. No one knows what happened to them; they just joined the missing list.' He shook his head. 'We already had the stuff on board, so they couldn't take it back off. They would've drawn too much attention to themselves. So I told them to continue and sit tight. That's when the check happened. After we got the all-clear, I got one of the guys to ask around. Apparently they were both fired last week. Their head office got a whiff of foul play and saw them off the premises. One of them was seen fighting with security to get back in, saying he needed his notebook. Made a right scene. My guess would be that the notebook held our details and that's why we didn't hear nothing.'

Freddie nodded slowly, mulling this over too. 'What number did they have?'

'A burner. It's at the bottom of the river. They didn't have nothing else. There's no trail. We delivered their pay in cash each time, no names.'

'Right.' Freddie was pissed off. They needed that port, and now it seemed they had lost it. He had another, but they had a good set-up at this one. It would take extra time and money to send it through the other available channels. 'What's waiting to be sent?'

'Ted has a shipment of vodka ready to move, but I've put it on hold until we have another route.'

'Can you get your crates down to Calais?' Freddie asked Ted.

'It'll take another day, but yeah, I can get it down there. If you can give me the contact details for that ship.'

'Damien will sort out the details with you.' He dismissed Ted with a flick of the hand and turned his attention to Damien. 'I need you to contact the Calais guys. Tell them there will be an extra load coming per month. Find out what ship you can get on and when. Find anyone that's going soon for this load, then arrange the regular shipment around their timetables. Tell them what's happened and remind them to be extra careful. As for Ben and Ralph…' He paused for a second. 'Let that go for now.'

There was a part of him that wanted to inflict punishment on them for allowing this to happen, when this was exactly what he had been paying them to avoid. But there was only so much that men like them could do.

'OK, I'll get on that today, Freddie.'

'And give the guys that were on that run a little extra in their pay this time. Paul will sort out the cash for you.' Paul nodded his agreement. 'Once we've done a couple of smooth runs on the new course, I want to discuss upping the amount we bring in each time.' Freddie put his coffee down and sat forward. 'Is there anything else before I leave?'

'Yes, actually there is.' Damien looked at Ted and then back to Freddie. 'Ted's cousin is another supplier on the market. He wondered if we could do an introduction. Maybe use him for the overflow orders.'

Freddie turned to Ted. 'And you don't want the extra business yourself?' he questioned.

'Your orders already have me running at full capacity.'

'And why should I use your cousin?' Freddie narrowed his eyes. 'I have other established suppliers that would take on the demand.'

Ted twisted his hands together in his lap. 'I'm guessing that you probably like to spread your business around so that if one of the factories go down, it isn't too much of a blow to you. So an extra supplier would be an asset. And on top of that, I'd like to bet that my vodka and whisky are some of the best you've had. My cousin uses the same methods. I can guarantee the quality.' Ted finished his sales pitch and swallowed down the anxiety he was feeling under Freddie's steely, unwavering gaze.

Freddie turned his attention to Damien and raised an eyebrow in question.

'I don't know him personally, Fred.' Damien put his hands up. 'I only take on suppliers I know, so you'd have to make the call on this one.'

'Yes,' Freddie agreed. Damien only trusted people that had already proved their worth to him. He wouldn't take on anyone that he wasn't a hundred per cent sure of personally. He stared at the hopeful, worried young man in front of him. He was bricking it – that much was obvious. He didn't break eye contact though.

A faint smile almost crept onto Freddie's face. He remembered what it was like, being a nobody, sitting in front of someone as respected and feared as he was.

'OK. I'll give your cousin a meeting.'

'Thank you. Thanks so much, Mr Tyler. I really appreciate it.' The gratefulness spilled out as he reached forward to shake Freddie's hand. Freddie gave him a tight smile, shook his hand and stood up.

'Let me know when you've sorted everything, Damien. Later.'

'Will do. Thanks, Freddie.'

Freddie sat in Sammy's office without removing his coat. For once he felt like he was actually dressed appropriately for the Arctic setting Sammy kept his air conditioning on.

'How you been?' He smiled warmly, a genuine smile he reserved for friends.

'Good, mate, good.' Sammy looked excited and animated. This was a good sign, Freddie thought. It meant he thought it would work. Given how carefully Sammy made these decisions, Freddie trusted his instincts above almost anything else. 'I've put together a list of people I think we would be best with. Let's go over them, see what you think.'

'That sounds perfect, Sammy,' Freddie said with a wide grin. 'Absolutely perfect.'

CHAPTER THIRTY-SEVEN

Tanya shook her head and Anna held her hand up to the woman shaking herself around the small stage in front of her.

'Thank you, that's all we need for now.'

'But I ain't even got my top off yet. Don't you want to see the goods?' The greasy young woman chewed loudly on her piece of gum as she waited expectantly, one eyebrow raised and a hand on her hip.

'No,' Anna replied in a clipped voice. 'That will be all.'

'Fuckin' time-wasters.' The woman scowled and stomped off.

Anna pulled an amused face at Tanya. 'Where did that one come from?'

Tanya looked down at her list. 'Gumtree.'

'Oh. Well, that explains it. I think we should take that ad down.'

'Yeah, probably,' Tanya agreed, looking glum. She dropped her notebook onto the small round table between her and Anna and rubbed her face with her hands, frustrated.

They had been working flat out to get the club ready, but they had already flown past the date they had wanted to launch. No matter how well they planned, there were still all the unexpected snags and the small matter of finding just the right acts.

'I wonder if we should consider trying an agency, Tanya,' Anna suggested again.

'No, we talked about this. They are way too expensive. Paying their rates would leave us brassic. And the girls don't get paid that well either – both parties are better off going direct.'

Anna sighed. 'Well, we need to do something. This place is costing money every day it sits empty, and we can't expect the staff to wait for their start date much longer.'

'I know. Look, we're getting there; we have two – possibly three – already. This next one looks promising; she worked over in Circus for a bit.'

'Is that good?'

'Yeah, really good. They have blindin' acts, real talent.'

'OK, call her in.'

Tanya stood up and disappeared. A moment later she was back and a tall, slim, pretty young woman walked onto the stage. Her long, pale blonde hair curled almost to her waist, and her sparkling smile was infectious. Anna sat up. This one was beautiful. She prayed that she was blessed with talent too.

'Hello, Sophie, is it?'

'Yes, that's me,' she said sunnily.

'Go ahead.' Anna sat back.

'OK, well just to let you know, I've prepared a belly dance for you to see, but I'm also a qualified aerialist. If you're able to get rings fitted, I can put on a lot of different shows with them and with sashes or fire if you want. I'm very flexible; I can tailor my shows around whatever style you want,' Sophie said eagerly.

Anna's eyebrows shot up and Tanya gave her a wide grin.

'That sounds awesome,' Tanya said. 'This is the sort of thing we've been looking for. Go on, show us your dance then.'

Sophie placed her phone on the floor and pressed play on the music she had prepared. The upbeat tones hit their ears and she stepped back and began moving to the music. Anna and Tanya watched her dance gracefully around the stage, entranced. The Arabian-style outfit she was wearing showed off her lithe body and her elegant, artistic style perfectly. Tanya grabbed Anna's arm and squeezed it.

'Definitely,' Anna murmured under her breath.

The music slowed and the dance came to an end. Sophie finished off in a bow. Anna cleared her throat and gave her a winning smile.

'Thank you, Sophie, we will—'

'When can you start?' Tanya burst in. 'Sorry,' she said quickly to Anna. She turned back to Sophie with shining eyes. 'You really are the best we've seen and although my partner and I need to discuss the details, we definitely want you on a permanent rotation. If you want.'

'That sounds great, thank you,' Sophie said. 'How many shows are you looking for me to do a week?'

Anna sat forward and placed her hand on Tanya's arm. She didn't want her getting too carried away just yet. 'We'll have to talk that over tonight. Would you be able to come back for a chat tomorrow afternoon, to go over the details?'

'Yes, that's no problem.'

'Great, come over at two. And if you have any video footage of your aerial work, I'd really like to see it.'

'Sure! I'll email something over to you,' she said.

'Here are my details. Number there too, in case you need to contact us before tomorrow,' Anna said, handing over the piece of paper.

'See you tomorrow then.'

'Bye.' Sophie waved at them over her shoulder as she left.

'Well,' said Tanya, bubbling with energy all of a sudden. 'She's a blinder. We should make her one of the central acts, prime time, then build the others around her.'

'Well, yes,' Anna replied drily, 'except we actually need other acts to put around her before we get to that point.'

'Oh yeah.' Tanya remembered how many they needed to get still and groaned. She slumped back in her seat and pulled a face at Anna. 'This is so tedious. It's like when you're a kid and you have to sit through eating endless bowls of cereal while you try to get down to the little toy prize. And I'll tell you what, it was never Lucky Charms in our house either, it was always the boring shit that tasted like cardboard. This is definitely the same feeling.'

'OK, well, let's call forward the next bowl of cardboard then,' Anna replied. 'Onwards and upwards!'

CHAPTER THIRTY-EIGHT

Tony locked the door of the large warehouse full of dusty antiques and turned the sign to 'Closed'. He switched the light off and put the chain on. It was closing time as far as Joe Public was concerned. His day manager had gone off home for the night and now the real work would begin. He squinted out of one of the many small panes of glass that made up the large area of window on one side of the door. Each pane was grimy with years-old soot and grime, right up to the lead. They were old windows. Probably antiques in themselves, he thought. He made no move to clean them though. It made it difficult for anyone outside to peer in. Though if that wasn't enough to deter them, the back-to-back shelves full of dusty paintings and vases and lamps cluttered up the view to the back.

Following the light on his phone, Tony made his way to the back wall. Pulling aside one of the many paintings, he entered a code on the keypad behind and a panel of wall popped open with a small click. He walked through the door into the light of the operation behind and closed it again.

The heroin lab had been up and running for some time now and had quickly filled the gap the other operation had created when it had been closed down, just as Tony had predicted. If anything, it had actually made things smoother, as there was no longer the hassle of having to transport it to the different clients in London from Stevenage. Instead, they now came to the shop and picked it up from Tony's man at the front. The delivery process was much more streamlined all round.

Now, Tony sought out the man he referred to as his 'night manager'. The man who oversaw the process of creating the product. Wrinkling his nose at the smell of the chemicals as he passed each room, he walked down to the office at the end. He opened the door without knocking and found who he was looking for.

'Tom,' he said, nodding in greeting.

'Tony, how ya doing?' Tom hid his initial surprise at seeing his boss quickly. Tony was known for turning up at odd times. It kept them all on their toes.

'Good, good…' Tony muttered. He hated small talk with small people. 'I need you to change some quantities. We don't need as much grade 4. Just make about half of what we had last month. What I need is more black tar.'

Tom frowned. 'Black tar?'

'Yeah, that shit's selling out faster than we can make it. Higher profit margin on it too, so triple the output on that.'

'OK.' Tom grabbed his calculator and started jotting down some numbers on the scrap pad in front of him. 'It takes much less time to make the tar so in that quantity, if we're dropping half the grade 4… yep. Yep, that should be fine. Staff can stay as they are, we can meet that.'

'Good.'

'That stuff is much, much more impure though,' Tom said with a slight frown. 'Users are much better off with the powder.

I've raised the proof levels to around ninety per cent last month. It was the best stuff on the market. Tar is twenty-five, maybe thirty at best…' He looked highly put out.

Tom was a highly skilled chemist by trade, struck off after he was caught stealing a number of opioid-based painkillers to sell on the side. He had put his knowledge to good use and now prided himself on being one of the best in the business when it came to producing class A drugs. To him, being asked to produce mediocre product felt like being asked to clean toilets for a living. His professional pride was being mortally wounded. Tony, of course, did not pick up on any of this. His only priority was the business.

'Do I look like I care what's good for the punters?' he asked, his tone incredulous. 'I couldn't give a fuck what they put in their bodies. I don't care if they want cream fucking cheese pumped into their veins; all I care about is that I am the one providing it and getting their cold, hard, wasted cash.'

Tom nodded, looking down. He wasn't about to disagree with Tony Christou.

'If they're stupid enough to pump themselves full of shit, let them.' Tony turned to leave, eager to get away from the cloying, sickly sweet odour of the drug being made around him. 'Fill the order, and send someone to let me know when it's ready.'

'Of course. Good to see you, Tony. Best wishes to Anna,' Tom called out politely to his boss's retreating back.

Charging down the corridor, Tony scowled. Why the fuck did people have to keep mentioning her name? The memory of her made him more and more angry these days.

The calm and satisfaction that had enveloped him after he had slowly tortured that girl in his basement was beginning to ebb away, like it was a distant dream. He had loved every second of it. The terror in her eyes. Knowing that he could go as far as he wanted and no one would stop him. He had taken pleasure in hurting her deeply and slowly. The ending was the best bit. The helplessness in her eyes – Anna's eyes – as he'd squeezed her neck and watched the life drain out of her. As he'd watched her slip away, her expression still full of the horror he had put her through, he'd suddenly felt calm – clear and light, as though the dark fog he constantly wandered through had lifted.

Now though, the effects of that short-term fix were wearing off, like the effects of a weak painkiller on a headache. Tony took a few deep breaths and unlocked his car. He jumped in and turned on the engine. He knew that this bloodlust would never stop until he did all of those things and more to Anna herself. It was all because of her that he felt this way, and it was only her demise at his hand that could fix it. He still couldn't believe she'd had the audacity to walk out on him and take some of his cold, hard cash to boot. It was an outrage. No one mugged Tony Christou off like that. Especially not a woman. He needed to satiate his need for revenge and soon. It was time to step up the game.

He scrolled through his contacts until he found Angelo's number.

'Boss.'

'Angelo. I need you to get hold of Trevor Young.'

'The tech guy?'

'That's the one. Get hold of him and tell him we need bugs – small ones, high power. I don't care how much they are. Get three, then next time the Davises are out I want you to go in the house and plant them somewhere they won't be found. One in the lounge, one in the bedroom and one in the kitchen. Got it?'

'Yes, boss.'

'I want someone recording details at all times. She'll trip up eventually. And when she does, we'll be listening.'

'OK. I'll get a team together.'

'Only from the inner circle, remember that,' Tony warned.

'No problem.'

'Good.' Tony put the phone down and drove away.

Anna was close to her parents. There was no way she would just abandon them. Either she had already got in contact with them, or she would soon. Whichever it was, her parents wouldn't think not to talk about her openly in their own home. This would be the move that finally smoked her out. All he had to do was be patient.

CHAPTER THIRTY-NINE

'It's here, Anna. It's really, actually here! This is actually happening!' Tanya was darting around the office at a hundred miles an hour, wringing her hands and biting her lip, looking like she might pass out from excitement and fright. Anna raised her eyebrows, her eyes wide. She had never seen her friend like this.

They had worked their fingers to the bone scrubbing and clearing the place out. They had organised redecoration, furniture and floor plans. They had advertised for, interviewed and hired a small army of people to work the club, the door, the kitchens and, of course, to perform in the shows. They had researched and even helped choreograph, to ensure that their acts would be the best. They had sweated and bled, shouted in frustration and cried with laughter to get this place perfect, shining and ready to go. And now here they were. Here they were, hiding in the back room like absolute wimps. Anna took a deep breath and twirled the office chair she was sitting in to the side. Standing up, she straightened the simple, tailored black dress she was wearing and walked over to Tanya. She grasped her shoulders tightly to stop her.

'We've got this,' she said firmly. 'You and me, we have got this. We did this!' She motioned around her with one sweeping arm. Tanya's eyes scanned the small, cosy office. 'We made this club from nothing. Just us. And you know what? It's absolutely amazing.' Anna smiled broadly, excitement beginning to flow through her veins. 'Tonight is going to be so much fun, and everything's going to go just fine. More than fine.'

Once they had overcome all the snags and setbacks and earmarked a realistic date for opening night, Anna had focused her energies into marketing it. They needed to have a successful first night in order for word to spread. A dead first night could kill them, and that just couldn't happen. They had sunk everything they both had into this – failure was *not* an option.

Hitting the pavement, Tanya and the new waiting staff spent days handing out fliers to passers-by and through local offices, offering a free drink and free entry to anyone who registered their attendance on the website. Sure enough, the guest list began slowly filling up and now they were expecting over a hundred people. If they could get a good buzz going outside and get the local traffic in, they would soon fill the place to capacity and might even have to turn people away. It would do them the world of good if that happened, Anna thought with excitement.

'Come on. Get yourself together,' she said with a laugh, nudging Tanya.

'Yes.' Tanya shook herself slightly and stood up straight. 'Yes, it'll be fine. It'll be brilliant. *We* are brilliant.'

'Exactly! Now, can you go and check that the girls out the back are ready and warming up?'

''Course.' Tanya ran her hands through her thick, loosely curled hair one last time and rechecked her flawless make-up in the mirror.

Rubbing her red, shiny lips together, she turned to give a dazzling smile to Anna and then walked out of the office with purpose. The chilled club music that was playing in the main bar came through loud and clear for a few seconds until the thick door clicked softly shut, leaving Anna in the quiet. She leaned back onto the front of her desk for a minute, her eyes glazing over. She had wanted to do something for herself for a long time. But before she ran away, it had been nothing but an impossible dream. Tony's cruel laughter bounced around in her head. She had asked him once if she could work again. She had been so naïve back then.

*

'You what?' Tony sneered down at her. Anna lowered her eyes immediately, her cheeks burning, but still she persevered.

'I – I have some ideas. I'm actually pretty good with websites and brand developing. I – well I did do this before, you know. I think I could make it successful—'

'Did this before what?' Tony demanded, pushing his face down into hers. She flinched but forced herself not to move away. That would be a mistake. *'Before you met me? Before I took your fucking ungrateful arse in? Before I gave you a fucking palace and everything you could ever need? You ungrateful bitch.'*

'No, no I didn't mean it like that.' She kicked herself. *'I'm grateful for everything. I just thought I could contribute? I made good money…'*

Tony snorted and paced around as if she had said something highly offensive.

'Your "good money" is nothing but pennies next to what I make. And you think I'm going to sit by while you fuck off, pissing away your time playing around like lady muck at pathetic shit like "brand building"? You think I'm going to allow you time away from running the home I fucking gave you, which is your actual fucking job, to take the fucking piss out of me?' His voice rose with every sentence until he was screaming in her face, spittle flying out of his mouth and onto her fair skin. 'You don't deserve the shit on my shoe, you fucking bitch. Yet I give it to you. I give you fucking everything and this crap is what you come to me with?' He shook with rage, his black eyes glinting dangerously.

Anna felt the tears begin to sting the back of her eyes. Her hands trembled as she tried not to move. He was going to punish her anyway – she could already see that. She might as well have one more try.

'I know that you do a lot for us. I just wanted something to use my brain on, that's all. It wouldn't even have to be full-time.'

The punch to the face sent her flying across the room. It happened so swiftly that as she was heading backward, she wondered for a moment how she was moving. The crack to the back of her head as it connected with the wall soon enlightened her. She slumped to the floor, the blinding pain resonating through her head so badly that she nearly passed out. Black spots danced in front of her eyes as she tried to hear through the ringing in her ears.

A hand gripped her face, squeezing her cheeks tightly and jerking her head to the side. Tony's face came up to hers, shining clearly with the ugly, pure evil he usually kept hidden inside. She cried out in pain.

'You,' he said in a shaking, deadly voice, 'are a nobody. You are worth nothing outside of these four walls and never will be worth anything. You're too stupid, too weak and pathetically average.' Pressing his nose against hers he looked into her pained eyes for a moment before shoving her face away. 'Go and sort yourself out – you look a mess.' He curled his lip in disgust and walked out.

Anna waited until she heard his office door shut at the other end of the house and then relaxed forward away from the wall. She touched her face, checking it for damage, then tentatively reached her shaking fingers around to the back of her head. Pressing where the pain seemed to be coming from, she immediately retched. There was a huge lump, and she could feel the sticky wetness of blood. She pulled her hand back to the floor in front of her, steadying her swaying body, trying to calm her stomach down.

Ignoring the blood on her fingers, she pulled herself slowly into a kneeling position and waited for the world to stop spinning before she gingerly stood up.

She closed her mind to what had just happened and focused on trying to fix the damage. There was no point thinking about it. If she thought about it too deeply she would begin to panic. Because there was no way out. There was no exit from this hell. And the more she allowed herself to think about it, the worse she felt. She closed her mind and curled up into a ball. She just had to survive right now.

CHAPTER FORTY

Pulling herself back to the present, she shook off the memory. Her lips hardened into a thin line. She had come a long way since then. He had damaged her, yes. But he hadn't defeated her, and she grew stronger with every single day of her new life. She would always be looking over her shoulder, always hiding from her past, but she wouldn't wither away like some little lost soul. She would adapt and flourish. Her panic attacks had become less frequent. The flashbacks and nightmares still haunted her, but they were weaker. These days she felt strong.

Walking to the mirror, Anna stared hard at the woman in front of her. This woman was so much more than that psycho had tried to make her believe. These days she was Anna Davis, independent woman, best friend, business partner. She was so much more than Tony's punchbag. And he couldn't take anything away from her anymore. She wouldn't let him. And she certainly wasn't about to let the shadow of him take tonight away from her. Not this night, nor any other. He couldn't hurt her anymore.

Tanya turned towards the group of people standing by the bar and grinned widely, her green eyes twinkling.

'This is it, guys. Let's give these bastards the best night of their lives!' There was a cheer and laughter as the staff became infected by Tanya's excitement. 'When I open those doors, Club Anya will officially be open and within the following ten minutes, this club will be crowned the best gentlemen's club in all of London!' She fist-pumped the air and more cheering ensued. She saw Anna enter the room from the back, out of the corner of her eye.

Anna smiled, shaking her head. Wherever they went no one could help but be totally entranced by Tanya. She had the staff hanging on her every word. She didn't join Tanya. The front of house and all the staff were totally under Tanya's rule. It was the back office that Anna ran. It suited them both and made the most of their talents.

'So,' Tanya continued, quieting down but still wearing a warm smile, 'go to your posts and give it your all. Bar staff, I want speed, attention to detail and most of all I want big smiles for the punters. They need best friends – that's you. Doormen, keep it friendly but stick to the rules and I trust your judgements.' The two burly men to the side nodded their agreement.

'Anything for you, Tan.' One of them winked fondly at her.

'Girls.' Tanya stopped and put her arms out wide. 'You gorgeous, beautiful creatures. You know that I know what it's like. You are the frontline troupers, the diamonds that they're here to see. Just you remember that's what you are. *Diamonds*,' she stressed. 'This ain't like those shit-arse clubs back East, with back rooms. You're here to dance and put on a good show. Make them work for it, make them part with all of their money – you know the tricks. But anyone getting handsy, signal the boys to show them out. OK?'

'Yes, Tanya. Thanks, Tan,' the girls chorused. Most of them had worked in clubs such as the one Tanya had worked in. All of them were excited to be working here. Anna had been unmovable on the fact that this was to be totally above board and not just that, but that the girls were to put on shows that outshone all of the other clubs of this type in the city. Between the two of them and a freelance choreographer, the girls were ready to perform a new mix of stripping and theatre. This way, the men got their fix of flesh, but there was something extra that made the experience a whole lot more interesting.

'Boys.' Tanya turned to face the small cluster of kitchen staff. 'Your food is pukka. Let's make sure we stay up to standard and get as much out there as they can eat, yeah?'

They grinned. 'Yes, boss.'

'OK!' Tanya clapped her hands together. 'Come on, Anna. Let's go and open this club.'

Anna walked with Tanya, skipping along to the double front doors. She unlocked them and stepped aside for the two bouncers to take their places. Tanya walked out into the cold night air to greet her public.

Click. Click, click. Flashes accompanied the sounds and Anna froze, just inside the door. Her heart jumped wildly and she quickly stepped back into the shadows. It was the local press. She had called them herself, offering them free drinks all night to promote the club. She kicked herself for almost forgetting. Tanya, smiling for the cameras, turned to the side. Not finding her there, she looked back and gave Anna a quizzical look. Anna shook her head and motioned towards the cameras. Confusion filled Tanya's face for a second and then understanding dawned. She signalled her comprehension and turned back to face the press.

The night carried on as positively as it had begun and turned out to be a roaring success. To Anna's glee, they did indeed end up having to turn guests away and even ended the night with a few future table reservations.

As they said goodbye to the last merry, drunken guest, Tanya closed the front door and leaned her weight against it while she turned the lock. She was exhausted but exhilarated at the same time. She still felt like she needed to pinch herself, just to check that all of this was real. Looking around at the end-of-night mess, a slow smile spread across her face and she hugged herself. It really was real. No more stripping for lecherous perverts, no more extra services in the back room in order to scrimp together the money for her dream. Her dream had finally become a reality. Thanks to Anna. Her eyes wandered to the closed door of the back room.

Her life had been transformed since Anna had arrived. Until then it had felt like she was wading through thick mud, in the dark. She had waded and waded, trying to find the exit. She could even see the door sometimes, but without the money she needed, it was as if the door was locked and bolted to her. Then Anna had come along and handed her the key. For this, more than anything else, she would always be more grateful than Anna would ever know.

Tanya looked around at the goings-on with a critical eye. The tables were being wiped down, the floors were being swept and the glasses were being polished. She nodded to herself and stepped behind the bar. Picking out a bottle of champagne from the fridge, Tanya collected two clean flutes. She flicked her hair back over her shoulder and, awarding one of her barmen with a wink and a smile, walked through to the back office.

The door opened and Anna looked up from the receipts she had been going through. Tanya appeared with the bottle and she smiled, ready for a drink after the long night.

'Oh yes, I think we have definitely earned this one.' She cleared space for Tanya to put the bottle and glasses down and waited while she popped the cork.

'Whoop! Congratulations to us! Our first night as successful club owners. And we were a success, right?' Tanya paused and cocked her head to one side.

'Yes, we really were,' Anna said excitedly and turned her laptop towards Tanya to show her the night's takings.

'Well, aside from the fact our choice of talent is obviously great, I think we have our location to thank for that. We couldn't have been more lucky with this place,' Tanya commented, as she poured the champagne. She looked over the columns in the outgoings section of Anna's neat spreadsheet. 'There is one more expense that needs to be accounted for though.'

'Oh?' Anna leaned over and studied her list, frowning. She couldn't think of anything that she'd missed. She'd gone over it a hundred times; her paperwork was airtight.

'It's not exactly something we can put through the books. We will need to pay out for protection. This sort of club…'

She gestured around her. 'Well, it's part of a different sort of world than a normal business. We're running a gentlemen's entertainment club on turf that belongs to a particular firm. That's how it has always been,' Tanya explained. 'We'll need to pay something out to a guy called Vince. In return, he'll make it known to all of the other criminal firms around, and the little fuckers looking for places to scam, that this place is off limits. Anyone causes real trouble, they sort it out; anyone causes us financial damage, he pays out, that sort of thing.'

Anna raised her eyebrows, not impressed by this bombshell. 'Why didn't you tell me this before? And why can't we just run independently?'

'Honestly, I just forgot that you weren't from this sort of life.' She shrugged. 'In our world, it goes without saying. And yes, technically we could run independently. We could say "no thanks", politely, and Vince would let us be. He's actually a good guy, very fair. But within a week we would have three other firms in here trying to take over, trying to bully us into running scams and schemes. Because this would be known as the only club without a firm. Not only that, but a neutral club smack bang in the middle of the West End, which is a pie *everyone* wishes they had a finger in. We'd be a target for anyone trying to gain some ground here.'

Anna turned this over in her head. It annoyed the hell out of her, but she could see the truth and sense in Tanya's words. After years of living around Tony's firm and various criminal businesses, she had been elated to have escaped that world and thought she had washed it off completely. Now it seemed she would have no choice but to accept that it would remain a part of her life. She would have to be careful. People talked, and the criminal underworld wasn't that big.

'I see,' she said heavily. 'OK. I guess we have no choice then.'

Tanya studied her friend's weary, worried expression. 'Don't worry about it, mate. I'll deal with it, alright? I'll arrange a meeting and sort it out myself. You don't need to be involved. I'll just let you know how much, and you can work your magic with the figures.'

Great, Anna thought sarcastically. *Financial fraud, here we come.*

'They'll want to see the accounts for the first week before they decide what to charge us. They only charge what they know is affordable with a club's earnings.'

'OK, I'll leave it with you then. Please don't tell them my name, will you? Tell them it's just your club, with a silent partner.'

'Of course.' Tanya leaned forward and squeezed Anna's cold hand. She bit her lip but said no more. She knew Tony still had men out searching for Anna. She knew Anna would have to live in the shadows forever, if she was to stay safe.

'Right. Well, let's celebrate, shall we?' Anna grasped the full glasses and handed one to Tanya. 'Cheers! Here's to our new club, our ongoing friendship and many more happy years together.'

CHAPTER FORTY-ONE

Christmas passed quickly for everyone. Freddie invited Anna to his home for the day itself, on strict instruction from Mollie, but she had politely refused. Much as she'd been tempted, she and Tanya had already decided to spend the holidays together. They were as close as any two sisters could ever be and were now family to each other. Anna spoke to her parents and shared holiday laughs with them over the phone while Leslie and Arthur huddled together by the secret mobile in the en suite, the door locked behind them. In the end they were on the phone for so long that Arthur went downstairs, dished up their Christmas dinner and brought their plates up on trays. They sat cross-legged on the bathroom floor with their meals, keeping Anna on speakerphone, listening happily while she told them stories of her new life.

When Anna finally ended the call, Leslie wept in Arthur's arms for a few minutes.

'It's OK,' he said gently. 'I miss her too. But I'm just glad that she's safe.' He looked around at the bathroom. 'Might start thinking about redecorating in here though. Maybe add a couple of armchairs!'

Leslie laughed and wiped away her tears, then she sniffed and hoisted herself up from the unforgiving tiled floor.

'Well, maybe at least a thick rug,' she said. She sighed and hid the phone back under the sink where they kept it. Arthur stood up and stretched. 'I'm fine, Art. I just miss her. It's Christmas – she should be here, lounging downstairs in her pyjamas, playing with her presents and picking at the stuffing.'

'She hasn't done that for years, Leslie,' Arthur said sadly, 'but I know what you mean.' He patted her on the back and followed her back out into the main house.

*

Over in East London, Anna put the turkey on the table and offered Tanya a cracker. Tanya pulled it with her and then handed Anna a sickly looking pink drink.

'What on earth is that?' Anna asked with a laugh, already fairly tiddly from Tanya's other adventurous creations.

'Alright, don't judge it just yet, yeah?' Tanya said, giggling. 'That, my friend, is a "Double Bubble" and it's going to be our New Year signature drink for all the ladies that frequent our fine establishment.' She hiccupped. Anna burst into peals of laughter.

'I do think you're a bit pissed, Miss Tanya! Which is entirely your own fault, you redheaded, alcoholic drink-forcer person. Oh God, I think I am a bit too. Anyway, what the hell is a "Double Bubble"?'

'It's champagne with bubblegum syrup. It's fucking immense. I've had two already in my little, you know—' she waved her hand over to the sideboard where she had been messily mixing up drinks '—experiment area.'

'Oh God. OK, go on then.' Anna took a big gulp of the new drink and grimaced. It was sickly sweet but also, as she swallowed it, very refreshing. 'Wow. That is super sugary.'

'I know, right?'

'Not quite my thing, but it's a great one for the New Year ladies. Good shout.'

Since their recent grand opening, the club had become popular with not only the men but a lot of women too. As the girls weren't just stripping but performing acts with storylines and backdrops and dancing, it had become a novelty for everyone. These days, seeing naked women perform was not such a taboo. Not that Anna had mentioned this to her parents. As far as they were aware, her club was the kind you went to for a bit of a boogie and a couple of drinks, nothing more.

Tanya was having the best Christmas Day of her life. Christmas for her had always been a lonely affair, filled with microwave meals and a shedload of booze. It was still filled with a fair amount of booze, but this year, for the first time she could ever remember, it was actually a real Christmas. It was being spent with someone she loved, there were actual presents and a real Christmas dinner with a whole roast turkey. Anna had gone the whole hog, making little stuffing balls and a mountain of vegetables and roast potatoes, and there was even a homemade Christmas pudding. The flat was full of festive decorations and the tree was the most beautiful thing Tanya had ever seen. They had put it up and decorated it together. It filled Tanya with a warm happiness that she had never felt before every time she looked at it. *This must be what other people feel like every Christmas*, she thought.

She thought back to her miserable Christmases as a child. If her father had been there he would sometimes fish out a toy or a treat for her. But those Christmases would be all about her mother trying to shove Tanya out of the way. Tanya would always end up in her room while they spent the day either laughing drunk together, or fighting drunk together. If her father wasn't there, it would be much worse. Tanya would be punished for tying her mother down and being such a burden. There would be no dinner of any kind, let alone a proper Christmas one, and there had never been a tree.

Anna watched Tanya's face soften as she stared at the lights twinkling on the tree. It had broken her heart when Tanya admitted that she'd never had a tree before. It was obvious that all of this was new, and a hard lump formed in Anna's throat. What sort of childhood had her friend had? Tanya had actually cried when Anna had given her the silver locket she'd bought her. Inside was a picture of Tanya and her hugging on a rare night out. She had put it straight on and cried into her hands for a good five minutes.

'I'm sorry! I didn't realise my face was so upsetting!' she said with a laugh, running over and hugging her friend tightly.

'No, it's just— I'm sorry, it's just… this is the nicest thing anyone's ever done for me. This is the nicest thing I have ever had,' Tanya said, between heavy, heartfelt sobs. Anna had rocked her and jollied her out of it.

Tanya had bought Anna a beautifully soft pair of leather gloves that she had admired on a shopping trip. Anna was thrilled.

As they sat down to dinner, with an array of cocktails surrounding the mountain of food, the two young women smiled at each other.

'Come on then, dig in!'

*

Over at Freddie's house the festivities were in full swing and the volume was deafening. Christmas songs were pumping out of the sound system Freddie had set up in the lounge, and the air was filled with wonderful smells from Mollie's kitchen.

'*Siiiimply, haaaaving, a wonderful Christmas tiiiime!*' Thea sang along as she danced around the living room with Paul, each a little rosy-cheeked from the rather potent eggnog Thea had made. Paul loved Christmas. Freddie looked on at him in bemusement as his brother twirled Thea round and round, a huge smile on his face. If their men could see Freddie's hard second-in-command now, they wouldn't believe their eyes. He rolled his eyes and turned his gaze subtly over to Michael. He was sitting in one of the other armchairs, watching Thea and Paul with a glazed expression on his face as though lost in thought. He wasn't smiling. He rarely did these days. It was worrying Freddie deeply. He refused to open up and got angry when people tried to push him, so they had no choice but to back off. He wasn't happy though, that was a certainty. Freddie just wished he knew why.

'Hey, Mickey,' Freddie called. 'Michael?'

Michael turned his head towards Freddie and blinked, coming back to the present. 'What?'

Freddie contained his annoyance at the rude tone his brother kept using towards him. He saw Thea's eyes widen for a second though, before she pretended she wasn't listening, obviously shocked that he would talk like that to Freddie.

'Your seventeenth birthday is coming up. What would you like us to get you? Anything you particularly want?'

'Driving lessons. I'm going to need those,' he replied curtly, looking away.

'Right. OK then, driving lessons it is. Then if you pass in time, I'll get you a motor for your eighteenth. You can come and pick one with me. That sound good?'

'Sure,' he answered flatly.

Sure. Freddie let it echo in his head. No 'thank you', no smile, nothing. As if he were somehow just entitled to it, like it was owed to him. Had he spoilt him? Was it his fault? He didn't think so. He made sure Michael had what he needed and had sent him to a good school to help build a better future for him, but he didn't think he'd spoilt him.

Michael stood up and left the room, heading upstairs. Thea frowned and looked to Freddie.

'What was that about?' she asked, confused.

'I don't know,' Freddie answered quietly.

Mollie bustled through, her face as red as the festive Christmas dress she wore underneath her snowman pinny. Oblivious to the undercurrent of Michael's mood flowing through the room, she was excited and happy. She had all her children under one roof and they would stay with her, eating and laughing and celebrating with her, all day.

'Come through, come through – dinner is ready! Go and clean up and come through, all of you. Be a dear, Thea, and get Michael. I've made all his favourites! Come on now!' She disappeared back to the heavily laden and decorated table to make sure it was still as perfect as she'd left it thirty seconds before.

'I'll go get him,' Thea said after a nod from Freddie. Freddie and Paul shared a look. Somehow they needed to get to the bottom of this, before it hurt Mollie.

CHAPTER FORTY-TWO

Tony's men walked into his house and headed for the large office he kept for secret meetings like this one. Nobody knew why they were there. Angelo sat to one side of Tony, who was positioned at the head of a long, dark table. He was whispering urgently into Tony's ear about something, while the rest of the men chatted between themselves. Tony nodded and then sat back, looking at the faces around him. Immediately everyone fell silent and directed their attention to their boss.

'Gentlemen.' Tony spread his arms out wide and smiled. 'Welcome. Have you all got a drink? Yeah? Dev, you got one?' Dev nodded and lifted his glass to show Tony. 'Good. You lot are here because although I have a small army working for me, you few are the ones I actually trust. You are the few I know that no matter what, you are loyal to me. And I value that loyalty.' He nodded to himself gravely. 'I value that a lot. And I want to reward it. So I have a job for you. It's a fucking big 'un. And it's dirty. Some of you've already been doing a bit of work on it, most of you are still in the dark, but today I will enlighten you all.' Tony reached into his pocket and brought out his cigarettes. He lit one and took a deep drag before continuing.

'Tomorrow is the start of a brand new year. *Our* year. As you know, our businesses are limited to the north of London.

They're lucrative, of course, but they *are* limited. And why is that? Why are we so limited, when we're the best at what we do? We run bookies, dens, sharks, laundering—' he ticked them off his hand, one by one '—and we run them well. We have the corner on the crack heroin market. So why,' he asked, narrowing his eyes, 'are we being kept in our fucking box, up here on the sidelines?' He eyed each of the men in the room, seeing who had worked out where he was going with this yet.

'We're being kept up here, in our little patch, because the boys running around creaming all the money in Central say so. Because they don't want anyone else coming over to their little goldmine and taking any of it. Now—' he shrugged '—I can understand that. I would want to keep other people off my honey pot too, if it were mine. But that's the thing, ain't it?' He leaned forward. 'It ain't mine.' He flicked his cigarette ash carefully into the ashtray in front of him and took another large drag.

'The problem here is that the more I think about it, the more unfair that seems. Why shouldn't it be mine – ours? Who decided that it belonged to those fuckers and not us? Now my cousin, Cos, he's in with them. They throw him a few bones and a friendly smile and he rolls over. He doesn't step on their toes, and they won't step on his. But of course they won't!' His voice rose. 'Why would they bother with the North when they have everything else? They're laughing at us.' He banged his fist on the table. 'Now Cos might be happy never striving for more, but I'm not. And I don't think any of you are either. I think, like me, you would like to taste a real piece of the pie for once. So this, boys, is what we're going to do.' He stood up and leaned his weight forward over the table. 'We're going to take Central London. West End, East End, all ours. We'll leave the South; those bastards can keep their shitty side of the river, but we're taking the rest.' He stared around at the men in the room, a mixture of shock and excitement in their faces.

'You will all have heard about Big Dom's sudden demise a few months back. That was me. Angelo here took him out on my orders.' He patted Angelo on the back and the baby-faced young man nodded confirmation to the rest of the men, smiling. 'Big Dom was the first domino to fall.' He smiled at his own wit. 'We toppled their old king. We haven't been able to get near Vince, but that's OK for now. We made our statement with Big Dom. Their people are uneasy and are losing faith in their boss's ability to keep them safe and deliver retribution. We've scouted their businesses and found a way into several of them for a sudden overtake. The plan is to strike when certain players of theirs are out of the way. At the same time we create a diversion to pull away any remaining men in our way. At this point, there will be several of you with small teams in place to play out a takeover – all at once. Overthrow one place, they can oust us. Overthrow a number of places and they have a problem on their hands.' He looked pleased with his plan.

One of his men put his hand up to get Tony's attention. 'What happens then? They'll still make an attempt to get control back. Even if they go for one at a time, we'll be too thinly stretched.'

'By this point there will be a secondary, much larger team in place, armed and ready to come in and secure each location. When they come – and they will come – we'll extend them an offer to join our firm, the winning firm. These days, the man they all follow is Freddie Tyler. Vince has retired. Freddie is who we're really up against. He's the one we need to take out.' Tony filled his tumbler up with more of the whisky placed within his reach. 'Freddie has no clue that we had anything to do with Big Dom's death. He thinks he has a good relationship with the Greeks. So before he hears that anything has even happened, I'll be having a friendly lunch with him. Introducing myself, offering a business-related hand of friendship. And before he even gets through his main course—' a manic, excited glint shone brightly in Tony's eyes '—I'll walk up behind him and I'll slit his pathetic, weakling throat. That,' he spat, 'is the point at which *we* will win. That's the point at which London will be ours.'

CHAPTER FORTY-THREE

The two nondescript black SUVs pulled up down the abandoned side street. There were no CCTV cameras down here, or in fact on any of the last mile of road they had been driving down. They'd had to travel the long way round in order to avoid cameras.

Freddie looked at his watch. He was dressed head to toe in black, as was Sammy, who sat next to him in the driver's seat. They each wore black leather gloves, and their balaclavas sat on the dashboard ready for later. In the second car, Paul waited alongside Bill Hanlon and John Daley, another of Freddie's men. They had all been briefed on their roles, down to the last tiny detail so that the entire operation would be completed in eight minutes.

Freddie was on edge. This was good, he reasoned. It would keep him alert. Sammy sat beside him, decidedly more relaxed.

'You OK? You seem tense.'

'I *am* tense,' Freddie admitted. 'It's a risky one – you said that yourself.' He glanced back at Sammy. 'You look like we're just popping for a quick pint.'

Sammy laughed. 'It's a solid plan, and I have every faith in it. If something happens we can't control…' He shrugged. 'There's no point worrying over it yet, eh?'

Freddie nodded. He couldn't argue with that, but he was still too wired to relax. His watch beeped and Sammy started the car. It was show time.

The CCTV was now down throughout the police station for the next ten minutes. As they pulled out of the narrow side street, Freddie watched Paul through his wing mirror, following in the second car. They turned the corner and came to a stop outside a pair of wire gates. Barbed wire curled across the top in aggressive loops all the way along to the tall walls either side, topped with cemented-in spikes of broken glass. They were at the back entrance. Freddie and Sammy reached for their balaclavas and put them on.

As they approached, the gates began to open. The guard in the small Portakabin inside the gate lifted his hand in greeting and then disappeared for his tea break, as planned. John jumped out of the car behind, gun in hand, and took his place inside the gate. Checking around, he waved them through the second the gate was wide enough. The two cars slipped through and headed straight for the small door to the right of the large, brick building in front of them. It was eerily devoid of movement. Police cars and vans littered the space around them. A sliver of light appeared from the door they were aiming for as they backed the vehicles up as close against it as possible. The light grew stronger as it was opened fully by one of their paid plods waiting on the other side.

Freddie and Sammy jumped out and were joined by Paul. Bill swung the boot open on both vehicles as the three of them walked in with purpose.

The outer door was closed, the plod standing by ready to open it again when they came back through. It had to be opened using a code, and it would trigger an alarm if left open for more than a minute. Freddie nodded a greeting to the man. They quickly made their way through the next sealed door where another of their payrollers, Gavin, was awaiting them. He smiled as they entered and began walking with them through the hallway to the room they needed to get to. They reached the door and he slid a card through the reader to unlock it. Freddie looked at the card.

'It's the visitor card. Can't be traced to me. Don't worry.'

'If it was traceable, it wouldn't be me that has to worry, mate,' Freddie replied.

The door opened and Freddie whistled as he took it all in. There was a small armoury in there of confiscated weapons, alongside enough drugs to satisfy the whole country for a month. It was a criminal goldmine.

'Where is it?'

'Here.' Gavin skipped forward and dragged out a large evidence box from a wall of boxes. 'It starts here and goes about six boxes that way.' He pointed along the wall.

'Paul, start that end, Sammy go for the middle. We have five minutes to get this done. Go!' he ordered.

The three of them began hoisting the sealed bags of money over their shoulders. Laden with as many of the heavy bags as they could carry, they jogged through the doorway and down the hall. They burst through the next door, breathing heavily, and Freddie looked up to check that the outer door was being opened so that they didn't have to stop. It was opened and swiftly held back as the three shot through with their first load. Lurching forward, they all dumped their bags on the ground outside the building. Bill jumped forward and started loading them into the boot spaces.

Freddie caught his breath on the run back through to the evidence room. They loaded up again and started the journey back to the car. Freddie's back muscles strained under the weight of the heavy bags. His breathing became more ragged and beads of sweat began forming on his brow. *Christ*, he thought, *I need to make it to the gym more.*

Bill was ready to grab for the bags again but his face was tight.

'You need to make this run quicker, boys – we're pushing it,' he said with urgency.

They redoubled their efforts and flew down the corridor to get the last few bags. Freddie had been right: three runs with three people would just about do it.

The static sounded on the walkie-talkie attached to Freddie's belt as someone got ready to talk. He froze for a millisecond, then carried on, keeping his ears trained on the voice coming through.

'Gate to runner, there's a car approaching. It's stopped up the road, lights on facing the gate.'

Freddie swore loudly. He wound another bag over his back. Paul stared at him, eyes wide.

'Can't see if it's wrapped in bacon. The lights are too bright, and it ain't moving.'

Freddie squeezed his eyes shut for a second. He went to grab his last bag, but Sammy took it off him, gesturing to the walkie-talkie.

'I'll take this, you do that,' he said. He began the third run back, and Freddie and Paul joined him. As they ran, Freddie opened up the line and began to speak into the small device.

'Runner to gate, has it moved yet?' They ran quicker than ever back through to the outer door. Worst-case scenario, he reasoned, it would be a copper who smelled a rat, calling in to check things out. They should still be able to get out, but it would still have to be dealt with.

'Wait,' John's voice came through the radio. 'Oh for Pete's sake, false alarm. It's just some couple having a barney. She's stropped off and he's driving away,' he added.

Freddie let go of the huge breath he had been holding in as Bill carried on shovelling the bags in, his face betraying nothing. Freddie threw the last of his load in the back and checked nothing was missing.

He glanced at his watch. 'We have to go now. Right now.'

They jumped in and both engines roared to life.

'Runner to gate, open up and get ready.'

'Gotcha.'

Ahead of them, the slow gates began to open up. As they neared them, they were just wide enough to head straight through. Freddie opened the back door of the car from the inside and, running alongside the vehicle, John leaped in and slammed it shut behind him. The car didn't stop. John pulled his balaclava off and straightened up in his seat. He peered his head through the middle.

'We fucking did it,' he said, grinning.

'Not yet,' Freddie said curtly.

They made it through the gates and Freddie watched in the mirror as the second car did the same. He breathed an audible sigh of relief.

'*Now* we've done it.' Opening the radio line to the other car, he continued. 'Let's get this to the yard, burn these clothes and get down to Ruby Ten to celebrate. Get your wives and girlfriends out. But just tell them it's a jolly. Our work here tonight is between us.'

A cheer came down the line from Paul, and Bill murmured his acceptance. Freddie sent a text to Anna. She wasn't his girlfriend, of course; he didn't know what she was. But whatever she was, he wanted her here with him tonight. He wanted to celebrate with her. Even if she didn't have a clue what it was about.

CHAPTER FORTY-FOUR

Anna looked at the long queue in front of the club where she was meeting Freddie. She ignored it and walked past it, straight to the bouncers at the front. Freddie had instructed her to come straight in.

She had been excited to receive the message from Freddie. No matter how hard she tried not to think of him, he still filled her thoughts whenever she wasn't busy. It was dangerous, because she knew without doubt that he only cared for her as a friend, but she couldn't seem to help her excitement whenever she had a chance to see him.

She should have been working tonight, but Tanya insisted on her meeting with her mystery man instead. Now here she was. She wished Tanya had been able to come with her, but this was how it was these days. One of them had to be at the club.

She walked through the throng of people enjoying themselves on the dance floor. Freddie had told her that it was a get-together with a bunch of friends. *What had he told them about her?* she wondered. Maybe he would even have another girl there with him, one he was seeing. She paused in her step, ice grasping her heart with its cold fingers.

Would he do that? Would he parade another woman in front of her? Would this be a perfect opportunity to introduce some casual fling to his friends, making it less casual and more like a full-on relationship? It wasn't like he would have any clue as to her feelings for him, so he wouldn't have any cause to act delicately in front of her. She breathed deeply and reined in her dramatic train of thought. This was ridiculous. Freddie was a great friend and someone she cared for – that was all. She was just lonely and worried that a girlfriend would get in the way of their friendship. That was all this was.

Holding her head up and straightening her shoulders, Anna walked into the VIP area. There was a group of about twenty people milling around the two large tables. The chairs looked luxuriously comfortable, and a number of women sat chatting together, cocktails in hand. Was one of them with Freddie?

'You made it!' Freddie's voice was warm and jovial, and he wore a relaxed smile on his face. She couldn't help but smile back. His was so infectious.

'I did. Well, Tanya insisted. She took my shift tonight so that I could come.'

'Good of her to do so,' Freddie commented, handing her a glass of champagne. 'Cheers to her then.'

'Cheers to her,' Anna agreed and chinked her glass to his.

Bill Hanlon stepped over and nodded hello to Anna. 'Nice to see you again,' he said. 'This is my wife Amy. Amy, this is Anna.' Assuming that she was Freddie's latest bit of stuff, Amy smiled at the younger woman.

'Nice to meet you, love. Not often Freddie brings a girl along these days. He's always too busy running things. Good to see he's met someone though. How'd you two meet?' She waited expectantly.

'Well, er…' Anna laughed awkwardly. 'We're just friends. I met Freddie when I moved to the area a few months back.' She glanced up at him, but he was totally engrossed in a conversation with Bill.

'Oh!' Amy said, her eyebrows shooting upwards. 'Well. That's a new one!'

'Sorry?' Anna asked, confused.

'Well, um… anyway, how you doing with that drink? Fancy a cocktail? We've got some jugs over here.'

Amy led her over to the table full of women. Some smiled at her as they approached, others looked her up and down critically. One woman in particular gave her a hard stare. Anna blinked. What was her problem? The woman in question sat with her long, bronzed legs crossed to one side, showing off a pair of very high stilettos. Her flimsy, gauzy dress hung off her shoulders, showing her plump cleavage off to perfection. Immaculate make-up enhanced her features, and her blonde locks were styled as though she had just come from a photo shoot. Anna took this all in and immediately felt incredibly average. She had come in a simple black wrap dress and not-too-high heels, and although she had taken some time with her make-up, she had done little more than run her fingers through the ends of her hair.

'Darcy, Lola, this is Anna. She's here with Freddie.'

Anna sat down on the seat offered to her and smiled at the two women. Amy sat next to her and handed her a shot of something.

'Oooh, you dark horse, how did you snag him?' Darcy shrieked. 'Well done, gal. Good to meet you.'

'Oh, it's not like that,' Anna protested. 'Really, it's not.'

'Of course it isn't like that,' a voice behind Anna said, laughing venomously. 'Look at her. She's hardly his type, is she? Looks like she's just stepped out of a library.' Anna turned to find it was the woman with the hard stare. 'He's got some business-related use for you, hasn't he? He must do. It certainly ain't "like that",' she mocked, snorting. 'This is Freddie Tyler we're talking about. He can have the cream of the crop; he don't have to put up with sad rags like 'er.'

'Cream like you, you mean?' Amy quipped. 'You already tried that, didn't you? He didn't want ya, did he? Off you trot, you old scat bag. You're only here because you got in with John, ain't ya? Go shower him with your cream, then, and fuck off.'

Anna was surprised at how loud a person as petite as Amy could be. The other girls all jeered at the bronzed woman, backing Amy up. Scowling, she tottered off without a further word. Amy turned to Anna, who was red-faced and feeling more inadequate than ever.

'Don't pay no mind to that strumpet, love, honestly,' she said kindly. 'No one likes her. She's a nobody – just some 'orrible little creature, trying to sleep herself up the ladder. She's a right piece of work. Got two kids at home by different dads, treats them like shit. I've seen the poor little mites. Always look cold and dirty, they do.' She shook her head. 'Skinny little things too. She don't feed them. Leaves them to it. Minute she gets a bit of attention, she can leave them for days. It's a miracle social services haven't taken them off her,' she huffed.

'Smacks them about something rotten too,' added Lola. 'My aunt lives near her, says she's seen her going for them loads of times.'

'Well, anyway,' Darcy changed the subject, 'fuck her. Let's get drinking, eh, girls? Here's to Anna and Freddie.'

'Anna and Freddie,' the others chorused.

'No, I—' Anna started but then gave up and laughed, downing the shot along with them. She looked over to where Freddie was still talking to Bill. The top two buttons of his impeccably white shirt were open, showing off the taut lines of the top of his chest. Her breath caught in her throat as she imagined touching it. He laughed at something and his face lit up. He was beautiful. He looked hard and masculine, but somehow beautiful at the same time, she thought.

She was going to have to admit it to herself at some point, she realised. She was going to have to accept that somehow, despite everything she had been warning herself against, she really was falling for Freddie.

*

Across the room, Freddie welcomed Vince to the celebrations. 'Hello, mate. I'm glad you could come. Here, have a whisky.'

'Thanks.' He took the drink. 'How'd it go today? Well, I take it, by the looks of things.'

'Everything went to plan. The money is back at the yard, so once I've paid the men I'll run it through the laundry and get your half over to you, soon as I can.'

'Good man.' Vince looked around. 'Which one is this bird of yours then? I'd like to meet the woman that caught Freddie Tyler's attention.'

Freddie tensed. 'Actually, Vince, I'm still flying solo,' he said before switching the conversation back to business. It was too hard to explain Anna to Vince. It was a sore subject. Every time he saw Anna, he felt more and more drawn to her. He couldn't pull himself away, even though he knew that she didn't feel the same. And even if she did, once she discovered the sort of person he really was, she would soon turn away.

She was gentle and good. She clearly wasn't bought up in this world. He could never let her know who he really was. He wouldn't be able to bear seeing the disappointment in her eyes when she found out.

CHAPTER FORTY-FIVE

A few days later Tanya sat down opposite Anna in the back office and took off her hat, shaking out her long hair. It had been snowing all day, and she was glad to be in from the harsh conditions.

'How did it go?' Anna asked, wiping the droplets of water that had fallen from Tanya's coat off her desk.

'Well, I think. He started off high, but I managed to negotiate down a bit to what I think is pretty reasonable from my experience.'

'What sort of figure are we looking at?' Anna asked nervously.

'Two hundred and fifty a week.'

'What? That's a lot of money to basically just not be done over, Tan. Especially when that's the job of the police anyway.'

'The police?' Tanya raised one eyebrow. 'They don't touch these clubs; they steer well clear. I think it's pretty fair. Our profits are high; this won't hurt us. Other people will though. And at least it's only that much. He started out wanting five hundred a week.'

'Jesus.' Anna sighed. 'OK then. Two fifty it is. I'll have to put it through as an extra member of staff and pay it out that way. Let me know what I have to do with the money.'

'Don't put it through that way. Have it down as petty cash. With the amount of traffic coming through here we can claim needing all sorts of extras for the kitchen and cleaning products, things like that. I'll get the cash over to them. If you could create a petty-cash list to use against it each week, that would be perfect.'

'OK. I'll get you the cash out each month, just tell me when.'

'Perfect. So, on another matter, when are you bringing this Prince Charming of yours over to see the club? And by club, I mean me.' She smirked at Anna. Anna laughed.

'He's not my Prince Charming, OK? He's just a friend. He's made it super clear that he doesn't think of me that way.' Anna leaned back as she finally admitted it out loud. 'Maybe if he was interested then that would be nice, but he isn't.'

'I knew it!' Tanya said, pointing a finger at Anna. 'You can fool yourself, lady, but not your best friend.'

'Yes, well, it doesn't matter anyway, so there's no point talking about it.' Anna gave her a tight smile and straightened her jacket.

'Oh, come on. Do you really think that he would do all these things with you if he didn't have feelings for you? Do you really think you would have met his family, gone off to the beach, shared nights out with him and his friends, if you were just some mate? Nah.' She shook her head. 'No way.' She walked back towards the door. There was a lot to do before the club was ready to open tonight. 'Who is he anyway, this little heart-throb of yours? What's he do?'

'Nice try,' Anna said and raised her eyebrow at her. Tanya scowled, annoyed. She had never given Tanya any details about

Freddie. It wasn't that she didn't trust her; it was for the same reason that she hadn't told Freddie about the club. It was just another way of keeping safe, compartmentalising her life. It was a habit she had formed out of fear. Perhaps it was time that she stopped living like this to such an extreme. She would always be hiding, always looking over her shoulder, but surely she should open up to close friends?

'OK. I'll bring him to the club one night. I'll introduce you.' Tanya's face lit up, excited to have finally been let in. 'But,' Anna warned, 'just remember that we are nothing more than friends. Don't go running away trying to orchestrate anything.'

'I won't, I promise. Just let me know when,' Tanya said, leaving the room to start her shift.

Anna watched the door slowly close and stared at the dark wood. Her stomach turned in knots. This was the right thing to do, she told herself. She had to stop living in fear and start enjoying life.

*

Arthur looked over his newspaper and called out to his wife. 'Leslie? Are you getting that?'

The doorbell went again, twice this time. Whoever it was, they were impatient. Arthur sighed and stood up with a glum expression as his knees ached. He wasn't as young as he used to be. He made his way through the hallway and pulled the door open, ready to take in a delivery or say no to new windows.

Bam!

The door slammed back and knocked him flying across the hallway into the opposite wall. He cried out in shock and put his arms out in front of him to shield himself from the swarm of men who were now entering his home. What was going on? Were they being robbed? The two men closest to him held large knives up and pointed right at him. A silent warning to stay still and do as he was told.

Tony walked in last, his men having cleared the way for him. Arthur's eyes widened and his brow furrowed as he realised who it was.

'How dare you.' His voice shook with anger.

'Don't even start with me,' Tony snarled back. 'I tried asking you nicely. I gave you every opportunity to cooperate.' Tony shut the door and looked around. 'Where is she then?'

'Who?'

'Your wife, of course.'

'I don't know,' Arthur replied truthfully. Tony narrowed his eyes but Arthur held his stare defiantly.

'Go get her.' He clicked his fingers at two of the men near the stairs. One began his search in the lounge and the other upstairs. Within a minute they heard Leslie's screams.

'Get your hands off me immediately!' Her indignant tones wafted down the stairs before her feet, body and finally her furious face came into view. She strode over to Tony, ignoring the men around her. Standing to her full height she gave him a scathing look. 'How dare you enter our home like this, Tony Christou? This is absolutely unacceptable.'

'What is unacceptable,' he said in a deadly tone, 'is that you've lied to me, Leslie. You've purposely kept information from me. Haven't you?'

'Not at all.' Leslie stepped back and tried to regain some composure. She glanced around, assessing the situation. Six men, at least two with knives. Most likely all of them were armed. Tony was practically frothing at the mouth. They would have to tread very carefully.

She forced what she hoped was a friendly smile onto her face. 'Why don't we stop all this nonsense,' she said, trying to sound calm and authoritative, 'and go through to the kitchen where we can talk like civilised people. And I think it would be best if you asked your friends here to wait outside. There is no need for them to be here.'

Tony shook his head and grasped the top of her arm. She shrieked and tried to pull away, to no avail. Tony was much stronger than she was. Arthur jumped forward but was stopped, the knives pushed closer into his face.

'We've gone way beyond niceties, Leslie,' he answered. Dragging her through to the lounge he shoved her onto the sofa. Arthur was deposited next to her, and he immediately put a protective arm around her.

'What is this about?' he asked. 'We have nothing to tell you.'

'But that's not true, is it, Arthur?' Tony paced up and down the lounge slowly, touching all the little knick-knacks on the shelves and sideboard as he went. He paused as his hand reached a figurine of a family hugging. Two parents, one child. He picked it up.

'The thing is, Arthur… I didn't really trust that you would tell me if Anna got in touch with you. I felt like you were both just lying to me. In fact, I was beginning to feel… like you actually wanted Anna to stay away.' Tony pulled an exaggerated look of confusion. 'I couldn't understand it. What sort of parents wouldn't want their daughter back home where she belongs? So—' he stroked the figurine '—I've been listening in on you.' Tony pulled the tiny bug from the bottom of the figurine and held it up as he watched the colour drain from their faces.

'It's a funny thing, really, but my men overheard you talking about things Anna had told you on the phone. Now I checked your phone records and there ain't nothing there, and I've had my men follow you and you haven't used any phone boxes either, so you must have a phone I don't know about.' He watched them exchange fearful glances. Bingo. He was right. He turned to the three men closest to the door of the lounge. 'Search the house.'

CHAPTER FORTY-SIX

Leslie groaned at the smashing sound coming from every room in their house. Tony smiled.

'They don't care much about breaking things. You can save us all some time and possibly some of your more fragile possessions by just telling me where it is.'

Leslie narrowed her eyes and said nothing. Arthur pressed his lips in a firm line and held his wife closer. Tony just shrugged and sat down in one of the comfortable armchairs to wait.

The group sat in silence as everyone waited for the phone to be found. Leslie squeezed her eyes shut, trying not to cry. She tried to hold on to the hope that they wouldn't find it.

Fifteen minutes passed and the little seed of hope she had been holding on to began to grow. Maybe it would be OK. There was nothing he could do to her or Arthur that would make them give it up.

Another five minutes passed and suddenly her hopes were dashed. There was a triumphant call through the house.

'I've got it! Twats hid it behind the bathroom sink.' He entered the room and handed it to Tony. 'It was off, but I've turned it on. It's fully charged.'

Tony grinned evilly at the devastated pair on the sofa. 'Ahh, here we are,' he said jovially. 'The phone you use to call your beloved daughter.' His face darkened and he threw the handset over to them. 'Now, here's what's going to happen. You're going to call her now, in front of me. You're going to act normal. You will arrange a time and a place to meet her, soon. Then you will end the call.' He paused to let them take it in. 'You will not tell her I'm here. You will not warn her off. You will not do anything to get in the way of her coming to that meeting spot. Because if you do—' he leaned forward '—I will slowly and carefully slice off both of your faces, here in this very lounge.' He looked down. 'And I'm sure you don't want this nice carpet ruined. Looks expensive. Now make the call.' He sat back and waited, not taking his eyes off them.

Leslie slowly took the handset from her husband with trembling hands, clicked through to the only contact in the phone book and pressed the call button. It connected quickly.

Please don't answer, she begged in her head. But the ringing ended and the call connected. She heard the silence as Anna waited for her to say the code word, to say 'lemonade', indicating all was still OK. Leslie swallowed the lump of fear in her throat.

'Anna, darling.' She brightened her tone, trying to sound normal to Tony, withholding the code word so that Anna would know things weren't right. She heard Anna catch her breath. 'Just wanted to call to see how you were,' she continued, then swallowed again, trying to keep her composure. She squeezed Arthur's hand. 'And I wanted to remind you that I still have things set up all nicely with Jackie.'

'What?' Tony snarled. Something didn't sound right. What was she talking about? 'Make the fucking date,' he hissed.

She turned her head and looked into his eyes, a calm steeliness appearing in her face.

'Destroy this phone, Anna,' she said, her voice strong and flat. 'Destroy it right this second.' Tony jumped up with an angry snarl and launched himself across the room. 'We love you. Go, right now!' she shouted quickly.

He ripped the handset from her grasp and backhanded her hard, to the floor. He put the phone to his ear, but Anna was gone.

'Nooooooo!' he roared. 'You fucking bitch! You stupid, thoughtless fucking bitch!' He went to strike her again but she moved back and held her finger out to him in warning.

'I wouldn't do that if I were you,' she said quickly, backing up to get as much distance from Tony as she could. Leslie's face was red, half from where Tony had struck her and half from the adrenaline coursing through her veins. 'I've made provisions for this. You lay one hand on me or Arthur and that's the end for you.'

'What the fuck are you talking about?' he spat.

'I have a friend whose husband is in command of the anti-terrorist squad in the police. After Anna got in touch, I wrote a letter. It has everything in it, all the business dealings Anna has told us about, all the things you did to her – times, dates, even several places you use to do business.' She stood up slowly, holding the wall behind her. 'It has other things too. Names of the people you work with, details of the connections between you. There's enough in there to bury you if it ever sees the light of day. The letter also describes the threats you have used against us and states that if something should happen to us, it's you who should be investigated.' Leslie's voice shook. 'The letter is still sealed and sits in their safe. If I don't call her every Sunday morning, or if I suddenly disappear, she is to immediately give the letter to her husband.'

Tony's face turned purple and he began to shake in fury. He was torn. He wanted nothing more than to hurt the pair of them and scar that meddling cunt of a woman for life. But on the other hand, this letter could have serious consequences, and he had a big job going through. The last thing he needed was a tug by the Old Bill.

He grabbed her by the throat. One of his men held down Arthur, who was fighting to get to Leslie and yelling at Tony to stop. Leslie's eyes began to bulge yet still held that confident, steely expression, despite his hand halting her breath. She looked triumphant, like she was still winning. That was what finally stopped him. He threw her back across the room with a roar and punched the big mirror above the fireplace in frustration, with all his strength. Glass flew everywhere, littering the cream carpet with small, sparkling shards.

He had been so close. Without another word, Tony strode out of the house and left. His men followed.

Leslie and Arthur listened as the car doors shut and two vehicles screeched away down the road, then… silence.

Arthur stood up and checked to see that they were all definitely gone. He double-locked the door, then returned to his wife. 'They didn't win, Arthur,' she told him. 'We kept her safe.'

'Yes, we did. You did,' he corrected himself. He held her close and kissed the top of her head.

'We need to get away from here for a while. I think we should go right now. He's forgotten to leave anyone to watch. Let's pack and get out of here before he remembers. We can call Jackie from wherever we are tomorrow to warn her. Anna will check we're OK with her, I know she will. She won't have to worry; I'll pass some sort of message through Jackie. We'll just have to figure out how to get back in touch properly later. But I really feel like we need to leave while we have the chance.'

Arthur paused, looking at the chaos around them. Leslie had a point. They weren't safe here right now. 'I'm due some annual leave anyway. Let's get out of here.'

CHAPTER FORTY-SEVEN

The following morning Anna stepped off the train onto the platform in Woking, stiff after her journey and a sleepless night of worry and guilt. She had picked this place the same way she picked the bank for her large deposit – at random. Somewhere nowhere near where she lived and which would leave no trail. She had no doubt he would eventually track Jackie down and check her phone records. It was better to be safe than sorry. Her tired, red-rimmed eyes gave away the time she'd spent crying after destroying the phone, her only link back to her parents.

She had risen above Tony's systematic abuse of her body and mind. But to threaten her parents was the one thing she couldn't handle. She clasped on to the one piece of information her mother had given her. The letter. It had been Anna's idea, something to use if the worst came to the worst. Hopefully it had worked and he had left them alone.

She made her way out of the station and peered up and down the road. There. Two phone boxes just to the left, down the road. She walked into one, her breath turning white in the cold air as she fumbled with the change in her pocket. She dialled the number she knew by heart and waited for Jackie to pick up.

'Hello?'

'Hi, Jackie? It's Anna, Leslie's daughter.'

'Oh, hello, love. Your mum said you might call this morning.'

Anna melted forward, pressing her head against the plastic walls as fresh hope set in. 'She's called you then?'

'Yes, of course. Every Sunday morning without fail.' Jackie paused. 'Are you OK?'

'Yes, yes, I'm fine.' Anna wiped away her tears of relief and tried to steady her voice. 'Sorry, I've got a cold.'

'Ah, I see.'

'Did she give you any message for me at all?'

'Yes, she did. She said you'd call, said you'd be worried because she didn't phone you today. She said to tell you that she and your dad have finally gone on that long holiday they've been talking about and that in her excitement she forgot her phone. Apparently mine is the only number she can remember without it. The silly sod! She said to tell you not to worry and that all is well with them both.'

'That's brilliant, really good to hear. Thank you, Jackie.'

'Not to worry, love. She said that she'll be away a while but if you have anything you need to let her know, just call me and I'll pass the message along.'

'OK, thank you.'

'Any time, love. Bye.'

Anna put the handset down and breathed a huge sigh of relief. She opened the door and left the tiny phone box and its stench of urine and stale cigarettes. Burying her head in the thick scarf wrapped around her neck, she made her way back into the station.

Her parents were safe for now. But she knew Tony wouldn't forgive. He stored resentment up and always took revenge on anyone who crossed him. Her parents would be on his shit list now. She needed to figure out a way to keep them safe. But how?

*

Bill knocked on Freddie's door. It was barely past the crack of dawn, but this couldn't wait. Thea opened the door, still in her thick dressing gown.

'Alright, Bill. What you doing here so early?' she asked, opening the door wider and giving him a friendly smile.

He walked in and stamped the frost off his shoes on the welcome mat. It was toasty and warm inside, which Bill was glad of having been out all night following one of the Greeks.

'Sorry, Thea, didn't mean to interrupt your breakfast but this couldn't wait. Is he about?'

'Sure, yeah. Come through to the kitchen. Mum will get you some breakfast while I go get him.'

'Thanks, love.' Bill gave her a tired smile. He had known Thea since she was a tot. He had known the whole family pretty much all his life actually.

He ambled through to the kitchen where Mollie was piling up a mountain of food on the table, and his mouth started to water.

'Billy Hanlon, I ain't seen you in ages. Where have you been hiding? Come for breakfast, have you? Go on – take a seat. The others will be down in a minute.' She ushered him into a seat and immediately began piling eggs onto a plate. 'There you go, love. Get some of that bacon too. Dig in. You look like you need it. Let me get you a coffee.'

'Thanks, Mollie; you're a star.' He tucked in as instructed and wolfed down his breakfast as fast as good manners would allow.

He was mopping up the juices left on the plate with a slice of toast as Freddie entered.

'Alright, mate. How's things?' He sat next to Bill and began to fill his own plate.

'They're OK, Fred. Just need to talk to you about something.' His eyes flickered to Mollie. He knew Freddie preferred not to discuss the details of his work in front of his mother.

Putting Freddie's coffee in front of him Mollie smiled and removed her pinny. She could take the hint.

'Right. I'll leave you boys to it then,' she said, leaving the room.

'See you later, Mollie. Thanks for the breakfast,' he called after her. They waited until they heard her begin to climb the stairs then began.

'What's going on? You alright?' Freddie asked, his first concern for his friend.

'I'm fine, but you might not be.' Bill twisted so that he was face on to Freddie. 'Dev – you know, the Greek that Paul put me on to tail? I've been watching him these last few weeks. He's been all over our turf, specifically going to places that we have prominent, but not documented, hands in. At first he was just moving around, spending time there. Then he started coming back at night, checking the joints over for access points.' Freddie frowned at this information. 'Then I followed him to a guy called Tony's house. Tony is Cos's cousin. He has an interlinked firm up there. Cos doesn't work closely with him, says he's too much of a loose cannon, but he has to keep him on side as it's all family. You know what the Greeks are like with family. I've had a touch with Tony before; he's paid for my services on a couple of bank jobs.' Freddie nodded. This wasn't unusual. Bill's area of expertise was much sought after in their world. He tended to freelance when he wasn't busy with Freddie.

'There was a meeting, loads of them there. I couldn't get anywhere to hear what was going on but I figured it was big. I've been following him since, closer than ever. I finally heard what I needed last night.'

Bill took a deep breath. 'Dev met up with his brother for a drink last night. I got the table behind them. Apparently Tony Christou, their boss, told them that they're taking over Central London. And get this, it was Angel Face that took out Big Dom on his order, and now he reckons he's going to take you out. Thinks you're all that's standing between him and the East and West End. He's planning to invite you for a friendly meet and do it then.'

'That jumped-up cunt,' Freddie spat, furious. 'He orders a hit on Big Dom, face fucking royalty, and then thinks he can roll in here and take our turf? He thinks he can get away with this?' Freddie's blood boiled. He would love to go over there now, burst in all guns blazing and take the fucker out. But aside from the fact that it would start up World War III, Freddie would need to be sensitive to Cos in all of this.

Tony Christou was his cousin. If this was handled correctly, their relationship would not be affected. If Freddie gave him a courtesy visit to explain what Tony had done, Cos would understand. It might hurt him personally, but that was the life. There were rules. He would accept that Freddie had the right to dole out the appropriate punishment.

'OK.' Freddie sat up, his face sober. 'We need to set up a meeting with Cos. We have too many dealings with him to do things the wrong way here. Soon as we've shown him that respect, I want Tony brought to me at the warehouse by the docks. I need you to prepare it for the clean down after. He's signed his own death warrant. Do we know when they mean to move?'

'No, they didn't say.'

'OK. Keep a twenty-four-hour detail on Tony and his closest men going forward, and keep me up to date. Find out as much about Tony's routine as possible.'

'Yep, I'll get onto it straight away.'

'Great.' Freddie stood up and Bill followed suit.

'Fred, you good?' he asked gruffly. He wasn't a man who particularly showed sentiment, even to old friends.

Freddie smirked. 'I'm fine. Takes more than a badly planned death threat to get to me, mate.'

CHAPTER FORTY-EIGHT

It was a bright day as Freddie and Paul walked together down the busy London street. They were off to see Estelle, a tough old bird who ran one of their massage parlours. They were thinking of moving her to larger premises as she was bringing in so much business.

Freddie's phone rang shrilly in his pocket. He picked it up and listened for a minute.

'On our way.' He ended the call and halted in his tracks, grabbing Paul's arm to stop him too. 'Forget this, we need to get home.'

'Why? What's happened?'

'Not quite sure, but Thea said it's urgent. Something to do with Michael. Come on.'

'Shit,' Paul said, trying to keep up with Freddie's fast pace.

Half an hour later Freddie's car screeched to a halt outside the house and the pair rushed inside. Thea opened the door the second the car came into view. She had been waiting for them.

'What's happened?' Freddie demanded.

'He's in there.' She pointed to the living room and stepped back, crossed her arms across her chest and said nothing more. Freddie entered the lounge and looked around. Mollie stood in the doorway leading through to the kitchen, crying softly.

Michael sat nonchalantly sprawled in one of the armchairs. His expression was relaxed, unaffected by his mother's tears. What the fuck was this? Paul went straight to his mother and hugged her.

'What's going on?' Freddie demanded. 'Michael? What are you doing here? And why is Mum crying? And why,' he asked incredulously, 'do you not seem fucking bothered by that?'

'I'm back,' Michael replied in a lazy tone.

'You're back? What do you mean you're back?'

'I don't go to school anymore.'

'What do you mean you don't go to school?' Freddie was beginning to lose his temper at the rude and careless attitude his youngest brother was displaying. 'What happened?'

'They chucked me out. Didn't you get a call? Oh, you must have given them one of your burner numbers by mistake,' Michael said mockingly, turning to look at Freddie for the first time. Freddie took a step back, shocked by the hatred he saw in Michael's eyes.

'What?' he asked, not quite believing that his brother could have been expelled. Michael had always been a nice kid, a clever kid.

Michael shrugged theatrically. 'Apparently they didn't like how well my business was going.'

'Your business?' Paul asked, confused.

'Yeah, my business. I was doing pretty well with all those stupid, rich bastards. I was cleaning up. Made loads of money. Should make you proud,' he said to Freddie sarcastically.

Freddie went cold. He was beginning to understand what Michael was dancing around. Surely not. This was why he had sent him away to that school in the first place. It was far enough out of London that Michael would have nothing to do with this kind of life, but close enough that he could visit whenever he wanted on the train. Michael was so bright; he had so much potential. Freddie had sent him there and paid the extortionate fees so that he would have the best start possible in life. So that he could sleep safe in the knowledge that he had managed to get at least one of them out of this game.

'You were dealing drugs,' he said flatly.

'Bingo!' Michael said and stood up, clapping. 'You got it in one.'

'But why? I gave you a decent allowance each month. If you needed more all you had to do was ask.' Freddie was devastated. His family were everything to him. And right now he felt like he'd failed them.

'Not everything's about money,' Michael shouted as he shook with pent-up emotion. 'That's all you care about, isn't it? Money,' he spat.

'That is not true—'

'Shut up!' Michael shouted. Paul stepped forward defensively, but Freddie held his hand out.

'Let him speak.'

Michael looked around the room at them all resentfully, then back to Freddie. 'You sent me to that stupid school to show off your money, to show that you could. You didn't stop to think about what I might want, or whether I could be happy there, did you?' he yelled. 'You sent a fucking East Ender into a school full of toffs! At what point did you really think that was going to work out? At first I put up with it.

Told myself the jokes would stop eventually. I figured they would get tired of it, start to just put up with me, if nothing else. I tried to distance myself from my life here. I stayed up nights, trying to change the way I spoke and learn their ways. Thought if I could start sounding and looking more like them, that it would help.' He laughed bitterly. 'I kept my nose clean, tried to make friends, but nothing changed. Then one day while they were all around me, taking it in turns to hit me, one of them asked if I was related to the big London criminal, Freddie Tyler. Apparently his dad works for the Department of Justice and he had overheard a few stories about you.' He paused. Freddie closed his eyes and groaned internally. 'Once they knew you were my brother, it just got worse. I couldn't hide – they sought me out. The kid brother of the big bad criminal,' he cried. 'So eventually I thought, fuck it. If I couldn't escape you, then I might as well be like you. So I started fighting back. And I fought dirty. Just like I learned growing up here.'

'I never let you fight as a child,' Mollie cried.

'No, you didn't,' he snapped back, 'but that don't mean I didn't pick it up from watching those who did. So I fought back and blacked a few eyes. But then, you see—' he paced back and forth in front of them all '—then I was the feared one. No one would come near me. I still had no friends, no one would even talk to me.' His face darkened. 'So I made myself useful. I got some new contacts in town and began supplying those toff-nosed little weasels with things to help pass the time. They had more money than sense, and no one else in the school had the balls to deal, so I took advantage of that gap in the market. That was my business. That is, until that bitch of a headmistress ordered a spot locker check. And mine was on the list.' He stepped back and opened his arms wide. 'So there you go.'

A heavy silence fell over the room. Freddie's mind whirled with the horror of it all. All this time his baby brother had been in pain, unhappy and bullied, made to feel like an outsider. And it was his fault.

'I'm so sorry,' he said helplessly. 'Michael, I had no idea you were struggling.'

'Of course you didn't. You were too tied up in your empire to notice anything about those closest to you. You know, I used to really look up to you. But not anymore. I've learned a good lesson. You can only rely on yourself and what you know. And I know a fair amount now. So watch this space, big brother.' He leaned towards Freddie, venom in his voice. 'One day I'm going to overtake you. And the day that happens, I want you to remember one thing.' He came right up to Freddie and finished in a deadly calm voice. 'You made me who I am.'

Staring Freddie in the eye for a moment more, he walked out of the room and disappeared upstairs. The only sounds in the room were the ticking of the clock and Mollie's subdued sobs. Eventually Freddie seemed to break out of his trance and turned to her.

'Mum? Mum, it's going to be OK. I'll sort it, alright? He's sixteen years old; he's just an unhappy kid acting out. We won't press it with the school. Sending him there was obviously a mistake. My mistake.' The guilt settled heavily onto Freddie's chest. 'From now on he stays here, around his own. We'll give

him some space to calm down and then help him get back
to the boy we all know and love.' He rubbed his temples. 'I'll
stay out of his way for a while. It's me he's angry at.'

He watched as Thea took Mollie through to the kitchen
and waited for the door to close.

'What are we going to do?' Paul asked.

'I don't know. I wanted him out of all this and it turns out
I've just pushed him right into it.' He sighed. 'We'll need to
talk the local school into accepting him with an expulsion
on his record. That won't be easy. We'll probably have to buy
them a new science lab or something.'

'It ain't your fault, you know. You did the best you could.
He was always too clever for his own good, even when he was
a tyke. He could have just told you he was unhappy in the
first place and we could have avoided all of this.'

Freddie looked at Paul and smiled sadly. 'Thanks, mate.
Guess you just can't win 'em all, eh? I'll work something out.
Come on, we need to get back out. Time stops for no one.'

CHAPTER FORTY-NINE

Anna picked up her phone and smiled as she read the text message she'd just received. It was Freddie. He was outside. She had invited him here to meet her, but all she had given him was an address. He still didn't know that the club was hers. She glanced over to Tanya, who was busy arguing with one of their suppliers.

'It's not our fault if you're too cheap to use a reliable delivery company. I'm only paying you for the orders that have turned up in usable condition. Oh, hang on a minute, will ya?' She put her hand over the speaking end of the phone and turned her attention to Anna. 'Is he here? I'll deal with this joker and be straight out, yeah? Get some drinks going.' She turned her attention back to the phone. 'Right. What? No, I'm not talking to you. Why would I be having a drink with you? Anyway, as I was saying…'

Skipping through the club, Anna slipped out of the side door. She glanced up and down the street and spotted Freddie standing a few feet away, his back to her. She grinned and crept up on him.

'Got you!' She pinched his sides and he jumped, startled.

'Jesus, didn't no one ever tell you not to sneak up on people?' he said, laughing.

'Nope.' She laughed. 'How are you? It's good to see you.'

Freddie looked down at her soft face and into her deep blue eyes. If only she knew how good it felt to see her too.

'I'm good. How's tricks with you? You going to tell me what we're doing here then?'

'Well… I was thinking that we could check out this new club. This one here. What do you think?' Anna hid her smile.

'In the middle of the day?' he answered, bemused. He looked up at the front and frowned. 'Um, I don't think this is the sort of club you would enjoy, even if it were open.' He shifted his weight from one foot to the other. 'It's, er… well, it's not, like, a dance club…' His voice was stilted as he awkwardly tried to avoid explaining the nature of her club. Anna couldn't help laughing. 'What's so funny?' Freddie narrowed his eyes, smiling.

'Come with me. I want to show you something.' She grabbed his arm and pulled him to the side door she had just come out of.

'Hang on, what are you doing?' he protested as she dragged him through to the inside of the main club. She turned round and stretched both arms out to the side.

'Ta-da! This non-dance club is actually mine.' She clasped her hands behind her back and waited nervously for Freddie's reaction.

Freddie looked around, putting the pieces together. This was her club? He'd heard about this place, knew that the new owner had a deal with Vince. But he had told him that the woman in question was an old hand in this game, a flirty little minx. There was no way he could have been talking about Anna.

'This is yours?' he questioned.

'Yes! Well, half mine. I'm actually more on the paperwork side of things. My business partner Tanya runs the front of house.'

Ah. That made more sense.

'Wow. I did not see that one coming. You're full of surprises, aren't you?' he said with a laugh. 'Well, congratulations. This place has turned into a real hit from what I hear. I had heard about the opening, just didn't realise that it was anything to do with you.' He shook his head in admiration. 'Right, this is cause for celebration. We must toast to your good fortune. How can I buy a drink?'

'No need, it's on me. I have some bubbles in the fridge. If you fancy popping the cork, we can have a toast.' Anna nipped round to the back of the bar and pulled a bottle from the champagne fridge. She handed it to Freddie and fiddled around on the shelves until she had hold of three flutes. Freddie unwrapped the cork and popped it.

'Who's the third one for?'

'Tanya. She's just on the phone but she'll be through in a minute. She's my business partner as well as my flatmate. I've probably mentioned her a few times. Can I get you anything else?'

'No, no, this is more than enough. Thank you.'

*

Tanya finally ended her phone call having got the result she wanted. Feeling smug, she flicked her hair back and tousled it to add some more volume before checking her face in the mirror and opening the door to the club. Stepping forward she put a big, welcoming smile on her face, ready to meet Anna's secret crush. She looked over to where the voices were coming from and focused in on the scene in front of her. In that split second, time seemed to slow down and she somehow forgot how to breathe.

She heard the laughter, saw the champagne glasses and the happiness on her friend's face. But the part of the picture that almost stopped her heart dead in her chest was the man seated on the bar stool, looking at Anna as if she were the only girl in the world.

It was Freddie Tyler. The only man that she'd ever loved. The one man who had totally, and utterly, broken her heart.

*

Anna stared at the television, not really watching it. Instead she went over the events of the afternoon in her head. Something wasn't right, but she couldn't put her finger on why. Freddie had come in and seemed excited and happy for her, which was exactly what she had been hoping for. Tanya had been eager to meet Freddie for ages and had been upbeat most of the morning. Then when Tanya had come out, the atmosphere had changed. Tanya had politely greeted Freddie but then hardly said a word. Freddie had closed down and become quieter too. Not that she was surprised after he received such a frosty reception. He had stayed long enough to drink his glass of champagne, then made his excuses and left. It had been a disaster, and before she'd had a chance to even properly question Tanya on what was wrong, she had disappeared.

Bemused and disappointed, Anna went home, poured herself a glass of wine and treated herself to a long bubble bath. Even that didn't shake off this feeling though. What was going on with Tanya?

Pouring another glass of white wine, Anna stared out of the lounge window, over the bright lights of the busy East End. It was almost 10 p.m. She was just considering an early night when her phone rang.

'Hello? Yes, it's me. What's up?' It was Carl, one of the barmen on this evening.

'It's Tanya. She's... well, she needs picking up.'

'Picking up? I've had a couple of drinks. Tell her to get a taxi,' Anna replied, frowning. Why was she getting Carl to phone her for a lift?

'Er, I don't think she's in any state to get a taxi. She's pretty much passed out blind drunk on the bar.'

'What?' Anna's eyebrows shot up in disbelief. It was Tanya's turn to manage the club tonight, what on earth was she doing?

'I tried to cut her off a while back, but she kept threatening me with the sack if I didn't serve her. She told me not to call you, but she's starting to get a bit lairy, and I know you wouldn't want the customers to see that.'

'Don't worry, Carl, you've done the right thing. And I promise you that no one will be getting the sack.' She rolled her eyes, pissed off at Tanya. 'I'll be there soon. Just try to manage her as best you can.'

Anna closed the call off and swore loudly. What the hell was Tanya thinking? It was one thing being moody and rude to her, but it was another to be so reckless when in charge of the club. She stormed into her bedroom and pulled on a pair of jeans and a jumper. Grabbing her keys, she left to collect her drunken friend.

CHAPTER FIFTY

Tanya stared at the empty glass in front of her. She couldn't stop her mind playing over the image of Freddie, standing there in her club. The way he looked at Anna, so adoringly…

'Carl, get me another one. And a shot of tequila.'

Carl pursed his lips, but he did as she asked. Good, Tanya thought. She was his boss, the owner of this place. He should know his place.

'Damn right,' she muttered to herself.

The fresh double vodka, soda and lime was put in front of her along with the shot. She downed the tequila immediately, not bothering with the salt and lime. She relished the burn as it slipped down her throat. She knew at some point that if she kept drinking she would reach oblivion. That was what she was aiming for.

How could this be happening? Of all the people in the world that Anna could have met, how could it be Freddie? She rested her head in her hands for a second. Of course she would fall for him. Who wouldn't? He was Freddie Tyler. Smart, handsome, fun, charismatic. When he looked at you that way, you felt like you were the only girl in the world. She squeezed her eyes shut at the memories.

It had been a few years since she'd met him in a club and they had hooked up. He would see her casually over the next few months, and she would live for those moments when he would give her his time and attention. She started falling in love with him, tried to move their relationship onto more serious ground. The more she tried to do that though, the more he'd pulled away. In a desperate attempt to make him see how perfect they were together, she had opened up to him one night and told him of her feelings. He had gently but firmly told her he didn't feel the same. From that point on, Freddie had distanced himself from her, made excuses not to see her and eventually stopped talking to her altogether. She had been crushed.

She knew why he didn't see her as worthy girlfriend material. It didn't take a rocket scientist to work out that a decent man would never have any real respect for a stripper. She had nothing to offer him. It was then that she had realised what she needed to do. She'd picked herself up and set about making plans to do something worthy with her life. She'd focused all of her energies on doing what she had to so she could move up in the world and had sworn to herself that one day she would be worthy of a man like Freddie Tyler.

Now, though, he was in love with Anna. The lovely, beautiful, perfect Anna. Her best friend. She knew he was in love with her. Freddie Tyler never usually bothered with a woman he actually had to work for. He just accepted the best of those who threw themselves at him. Anna hadn't even slept with him and yet here he was, going out of his way to make plans with her, inviting her to meet his family, even taking a genuine interest in her life. He was in love with her. And Anna was in love with him.

'Carl, another shot.' She waved her hand at him and closed her eyes again, trying to squeeze the image out of her head. She felt a tap on her shoulder and looked round, bleary-eyed. It was a middle-aged man she hadn't seen before.

'Do I know you?' she asked.

'How much for a private dance?' he asked, pulling out his wallet.

'What?' She shook her head slightly, trying to understand what he was asking.

'A dance. How much?' he asked again, smiling at her.

Tanya finally caught on to what he was asking. She rounded on him angrily.

'How dare you? Who the fuck do you think you are? I'm not one of the girls; I fucking own this place,' she slurred loudly.

The man backed off, his cheeks reddening as people turned to look at what was going on. 'S-sorry, I didn't realise. You looked, well…'

'I looked what?' Tanya screeched at him, the alcohol making her louder than she had meant to be. 'I looked like a stripper?' She looked down at herself. She was wearing a knee-length pencil dress, but it had ridden halfway up her thigh while she had been sitting drowning her sorrows. 'Really?' she demanded sarcastically, pulling her skirt back down into place.

'I'm sorry, my mistake.' The guy put his hands up in surrender and hurried back to his table. Tanya glared around her at the people still looking at her. 'And what are you lot looking at? Can a girl not just have a fucking drink in peace?' she yelled.

The people around her quickly looked away, though some continued to laugh at her under their breath. Maybe that guy was right. Maybe underneath these nice clothes, she would always be just a low-life tom. She lowered her head and rested her forehead on the bar. At last the tears came, silently falling.

*

Anna jumped out of the taxi and her doormen cleared a path to the club.

'Glad you're here,' one of them remarked. 'She's been causing right hag in there. She ain't herself at all.'

'Sorry, Mick. I'll get her out of your hair,' Anna replied. She rushed over to the bar and looked around as Carl came over to her.

'I put her in the back room. She's out cold.'

'OK. Can you ask Mick to get me a taxi, and can you get Ron to come and carry her out for me?'

'Sure thing.' Carl disappeared and came back with Ron a minute later. 'There's a taxi outside ready for you.'

'Brilliant, thanks. Ron, could you put her in and tell them to wait for me?'

'Yep. She in the back?'

'Yes, thanks. OK, Carl.' She turned her attention to the club. 'Do you think you could make sure that clean down is done properly, mark down everyone's leaving times and lock up? I need someone to manage things with us both gone.'

'That's fine.'

'Great. I appreciate that, Carl. I'll pop a little something extra in your pay this week. Thanks for calling me.'

'Of course.'

Anna squeezed his arm and headed out towards the waiting taxi. She knew she could trust Carl. She made a mental note to promote him soon. It would be a good idea to have someone on hand to look after the club in case there were times that neither of them could be there.

About to step inside the cab, she looked in and realised it was still empty. She turned back to the front door.

'Mick? Where's Ron?'

Mick frowned. 'I don't know, he should be out by now...'

The door opened and a flustered Ron stepped out. 'She's gone.' He shrugged, flummoxed. 'She must have sneaked out the side door while we weren't looking. She ain't nowhere to be seen. Sorry, Anna.'

'What?' Anna said, alarmed. 'I thought she was in a state! Why would she have left?'

'Who knows. She was acting real funny tonight.'

Anna looked up and down the busy street. There was no sight of Tanya, though she hadn't really expected there to be by now. She ran her hand up through her hair and held it on her head, unsure what to do next.

'Maybe she's making her way home,' Mick offered gently. 'She probably just wants her bed now, the amount she's drunk tonight. I'd put money on you getting in and finding her passed out on the sofa with a doner kebab,' he joked.

'Yes, probably,' Anna said, still a bit unsure. But it was the most logical answer, she reasoned. 'OK, I'll head off then.' She gave them a tight smile as she got into the waiting cab. Mick gave the cabby her address and then tapped the door to send them off. Anna crossed her arms and looked out of the window. She was already annoyed at Tanya's rudeness earlier in the day and now she was fully pissed off at having to travel halfway across London to pick up a drunken drama queen who wasn't even there. What was she playing at?

*

Tanya stared out of the window of the cab, her sight still slightly blurry.

'And this is the best Greek club in north London, you say?' she asked. 'This is where everyone goes at the weekends, yeah?'

'From what I've heard, yes, love.' The cabby paused. 'You sure that's where you want to go?'

'Yeah. I'm sure.' She paid the man and stepped out onto the pavement. Steadying herself she ran her hands through her hair and puckered her lips together.

When she'd woken on the sofa in the back office, Tanya had mulled over the situation again. In her drunken state, everything suddenly became crystal clear. Anna had done this on purpose. She was the one who had been asking all the questions about love and relationships and heartbreak. Tanya had told her all about Freddie. Sure, she hadn't told her his name, she didn't think, but clearly Anna had worked it out somehow along the way. All of this pretending to be her friend was total bollocks.

She had muscled her way into being part of the club – Tanya's club. And now she had muscled in on the man Tanya loved too. It was jealousy. That was what it was. Anna was clearly jealous of Tanya and wanted to steal everything that was hers. Yes, suddenly it all made total sense. It certainly explained all the secrecy; explained why Anna had never wanted her to meet him. All this time she had been making out her wariness was because of Tony.

As she had sat there in the back office, swaying back and forth, lost in her thoughts, she had come to an idea. She would play Anna at her own game. She would get her back. If she couldn't have anything worthwhile in her life, then she might as well go and bag herself a decent shag. But this time it would be with a nice North London Greek. Someone who worked in the business, who was part of their small, small world. It wouldn't be that hard to find – she could spot someone in the life a mile off. It was just a case of figuring out where they would be on a Friday night.

She would bring him back home, maybe a mate of his for Anna too. She would make damn sure they saw her and then if luck was on her side, Tony would come and take Anna off her hands for good.

She had grabbed her bag and sneaked out, making sure Carl didn't see her go. She didn't need anyone stopping her tonight. Because now she finally saw Anna for the snake she was, and she was on a mission to wreak revenge on her so-called friend.

Standing tall and sticking her chest out, Tanya preened at the bouncers. 'Evening, boys,' she purred. They removed the rope and let her pass. Full of drunken determination, Tanya stepped into a throng of Greeks.

CHAPTER FIFTY-ONE

Anna had tried Tanya's phone a million times but after a while it stopped even ringing, the calls going straight to voicemail. Her phone must have died. She was really worried about her friend and had no idea what to do. Tanya had no boyfriend to check with, no other really close friends, not even any local family. If she wasn't here or at the club, Anna had no idea where she might be.

Suddenly there was a noise outside the door. A muffled giggle. Anna sat upright, relieved that she was back.

'Shhh,' she heard Tanya laugh. 'You'll wake the building.'

There was a deeper murmur and Anna paused. Tanya had brought someone back with her. She pulled a face, unsure what to do. Should she go shut herself in her room, stay out of the way? She heard Tanya swear and the key scratch the door in circles around the actual keyhole. Rolling her eyes she walked over and opened it up for her drunken friend.

As the door opened she caught sight of the two men accompanying Tanya and froze. She recognised one of them instantly. One of them was Dev; he worked for Tony. She slammed the door, fear and horror replacing her earlier relief. Why were they there?

They hadn't seen her; she had been lucky. When the door had pulled back, they were both focused on helping Tanya up from the floor. They hadn't noticed the woman they had been searching for all this time opening the door. It was the slam that had caught their attention.

'Anna?' Tanya asked, her voice slurring. 'Oh Anna!' she sang, ending in a giggle. 'Anna, open the door. I have a surprise for you.' Anna stepped backward, her hands beginning to shake.

What was Tanya doing? How had she met Dev? If he caught sight of her now, that would be the end. Even if she got away, she would never be able to come back here, to the life she had built, to Tanya, to Freddie. Anna felt the walls of her new life come crashing down as the key finally made contact with the hole. Turning, she fled to her room and shut the door. She leaned against in, slipping down to the floor, her eyes wide. She kept the lights off and listened.

The front door opened and she heard Tanya's heels clacking on the wooden floor of the hallway. Heavier footsteps made their way through behind her.

'Where's she gone? An-*hic*-Anna?' Tanya called, cackling a devilish laugh.

Why did she keep laughing like that? Anna thought.

'Where are you, ya little minx?' Her tone was mocking and Anna's fear grew. What had got into her friend? 'You boysssss... juss take a seat in there, yeah? And I'll go bring – *hic* – out my friend.' Anna moved and opened the door just enough to peer out. Seeing that Tanya was alone she reached out and yanked her inside, closing the door tightly behind them again.

'Oi!' Tanya squeaked at the unexpected movement. 'Easy, yeah? No need to goooo all like... *hic*, pulling me about...'

She drunkenly brushed herself down and Anna winced at the strength of the alcohol on her breath.

'Tanya, what the hell are you doing?' she hissed. 'Do you know who they are?'

Tanya stopped what she was doing and focused her gaze with some difficulty on Anna. A slow, nasty smile spread across her face.

'Do I know who they are? Yeah, I think I've got… a – *hic* – an inkling. Friends of your ex, right?' she asked.

Anna's frown grew more serious, and she studied the woman in front of her.

'Yes, they are, Tanya,' she stressed. 'Which means if they see me, I'm dead.' Her voice wobbled slightly at the end but she kept her cool.

'Really?' Tanya gasped dramatically and put her hands to her mouth. 'Oh dear.' Sarcasm dripped from her words and Anna backed away.

'What are you doing?' she asked in disbelief.

'What am *I* doing? What… what about what *you're* doing, eh?'

'What are you talking about?'

'Yeah, whatever,' Tanya sneered, the smile gone from her face. 'Poor little innocent Anna. Poor little privy… privileged girl with her nice family and her fat bank balance… and her sad little sob story.'

Anna blinked and her mouth fell open in shock.

'Weren't enough for you though, was it?' Tanya continued. 'Nah, you had to take my toys too. Well…' She slipped sideways as she tried to walk forward and ended up sprawled on the bed. She leaned up on one arm and squinted up at Anna.

'You can't play with my toys anymore. Go back to your old boyfriend and leave mine alone.'

'What?' Tanya wasn't even making sense. She would have to figure everything out later though. The threat that the men in the other room posed was at the forefront of her mind – she needed them out of her home before they saw her. 'Tanya, please. I don't know what I've done to you, but right now I need you to ask those men to leave. This is serious. If they see me, they'll tell Tony. I'm not messing around; I really need your help, Tanya. Please,' she beseeched her.

Tanya frowned slowly and shook her head. 'No, they… they're here to play. So let's play. Oh boys!' she sang out.

'Tanya, no!' Anna cried.

'Come through; we're in here.' She lay back on the bed, laughing with her eyes closed. Anna heard the creak of the men standing up from the sofa and went into panic.

Oh God, she thought, *how do I get out of this*? Her eyes shot across the room swiftly, trying to assess if there was anywhere she could hide. There wasn't, and there was definitely no time to get to another room. They were already beginning to make their way along the hall.

She darted to the window and flung it open. She looked down. It was a sheer drop and way too many levels to survive the fall. She glanced to the side. The old fire escape – it wasn't under her window but under one of the lounge windows that was next to hers. It was a risky play, but it was her only option. There was a knock at the door and she jumped.

'Er, just a minute,' she called, trying to sound like Tanya. She pulled herself up onto the windowsill and pushed the window open as far as she could. She leaned out and tried to gauge the distance. It wasn't far. She could almost reach it; it was about a foot out of reach. As long as she pushed herself forward with her legs she shouldn't have any problem. Looking down again, her head swam, and she squeezed her eyes shut. There were murmurings at the door. Her eyes shot to Tanya, who had passed out.

With a deep breath, Anna counted to three and then pushed out with her legs with all her might. She shot forward and held her hand out to grasp the railings. Her hands made contact and she squeezed tight. Her arms pulled taut as her body dropped against the rails.

'Argh,' she let out one terrified cry and then forced herself into silence. There was a second knock on the door. Using all her upper-body strength and her knees on the ledge of the fire escape, she pulled herself up and over the rail. Panting, she didn't allow herself time to stop. If they saw the open window, they would look outside. She reached back over from the safety of the rail and with the tips of her fingers pushed the window back in, so that it was only open a crack.

As her hand drew back, the bedroom door opened. Anna crouched down and pressed back against the outer wall. Biting her lip, she forced herself to stop panting, ignoring the searing pain in her chest. She strained to hear what was going on. Looked around, she saw there was nowhere to go but back inside. This escape hadn't been used for years, half of the rungs on the ladder going down had come away and there were none at all going upwards.

Looking up to the cloudless sky, she prayed harder than she had ever prayed before. *Please, God, don't let them see me.*

Visions of Tony's triumphant face played through her mind. The memory of Karen Holmes's body made her clench her shaking fists.

It was bitingly cold. The wind whipped around the building and shook the already hazardous fire escape from side to side. Anna tried not to look down.

The men began talking between themselves, puzzled.

'I thought she was in here with her mate?'

'Yeah, I'm sure she said there was someone here.'

'I didn't see anyone in the other bedroom when we passed. Bathroom either. Where's she gone?'

'I dunno. Did you actually see anyone?'

'Well, she opened the door, didn't she?'

'I thought so, but I didn't actually see her. Is this one 'aving us on, d'ya think?'

There was a pause.

'Maybe.' The second speaker didn't sound convinced. 'Have a look around.'

Anna held her breath and stared sideways at the open window. She could see shadows moving about in the light, and as she watched one grew larger and darker. Someone was at the window. A hand came up to the glass and a sliver of forehead appeared, leaning into the hand. He was looking out. Anna's heart felt like it was going to explode. This was it. All he had to do was push the window and look to his left and he would see her.

Time seemed to slow down, as if the weight of her whole world rested in that one moment. The head moved and the hand slipped away. She breathed a sigh of relief but didn't relax.

There was still the lounge window, the one she was almost directly underneath.

'What do you want to do?' one of them asked. 'She's passed right out,' he tutted. 'Slag. Dragged us out here for fuck all. You still want to have some fun with her anyway?' he asked.

There was a silence as the other man thought about it. Anna felt her heart jump up into her throat. She couldn't sit by and allow Tanya to be taken advantage of, but she couldn't reveal herself either. Her phone was in the kitchen, so she couldn't even call the police.

'Nah... I've got an early meeting with Tony tomorrow. Let's just go home.'

'Alright then.'

She breathed a sigh of relief.

Anna waited as she heard them move back through the house, joking about their night. When the front door clicked closed, she finally allowed herself to break into loud, emotional sobs.

She had no idea how the events of the night had come to this, but it had been far too close for comfort. The harrowing possibility of being caught by Tony had almost become reality tonight. And it was all down to Tanya.

Anna put her head in her hands as she cried it out. She had never felt so alone. Tanya was her best friend. She was like a sister to her. Why would Tanya betray her like that? Surely her best friend wouldn't want her dead?

CHAPTER FIFTY-TWO

Anna managed to jimmy the lounge window open, which wasn't very well fitted in the first place, and got back inside that way. She didn't fancy another death-defying leap back to her bedroom. Falling from the windowsill into the lounge, she hit her hip on the side of the TV stand.

'Ouch.' She stood up and quickly checked that they definitely were alone before making her way to the bedroom. Before she entered she took a deep breath and closed her eyes. Innocent until proven guilty. She would hold on to her faith in her friend until they were able to have a sober conversation and get to the bottom of what had happened here tonight. Nodding to herself, she stepped inside.

Anna wrapped her arms around her friend and picked her up awkwardly. Lurching forward one big step at a time, she finally managed, after some struggle, to get Tanya into her own bedroom. She dropped her onto the bed and stepped back to catch her breath, hands on her hips.

'Jesus Christ, Tanya,' she complained loudly. 'You could at least bloody wake up.'

'I am awake,' came a barely audible slur. Anna opened her eyes wide in disbelief.

'Are you serious?' she demanded. 'And you let me carry you all the way through here?'

'What?' Tanya moaned. 'What are you talking about?'

'Oh you are just ridiculous,' Anna snapped. She set about undressing her, trying to get her ready for bed. 'What were you thinking tonight? Aside from the fact you very nearly signed my death warrant, you were supposed to be working!'

'Working, ha!' came the slow reply. 'Yeah, that's it, just a working gal, me. All the work never goes away. Bring on the cocks, that's all I am.'

'What?' Anna frowned. 'You've had more than I thought.' She pulled Tanya into a sitting position so that she could unzip her dress.

'Yeah, haven't I just? More cocks. That's what you see…'

'What the hell are you talking about?' Anna frowned. 'You run the club, with me. That's your job. Or at least it's fucking supposed to be, except you didn't bother with that tonight, did you!' she said. 'I had to come all the way across London to get you, because you were so incapable, only to find you'd fucked off by the time I got there. To go chat up some fucking Greeks, of all things!' Anna's voice began to rise in anger. 'And on top of all that, I've had to leave Carl in charge. All because you decided to get bloody wasted.'

'You're so pretty,' Tanya said sadly, looking at Anna through her glazed eyes for the first time. 'You don't look like a tom. You're perfect. Proper. That's why he wants you. That's why…' She swayed and Anna steadied her. Tanya began to laugh; a long, sad, heart-wrenching laugh.

'Tanya?' The laughing went on. 'Tanya?' Anna shook her by the shoulders and she quieted down to a strange, drunken smile.

'He never loved me, you know. Never.'

'Who never loved you? What are you talking about?' Anna was concerned. Tanya sounded like she had lost the plot.

Tanya lurched forward and brought her face close to Anna's. 'Freddie. *My* Freddie. *Your* Freddie…'

'What?' Anna's blood ran cold as she started to piece together Tanya's ramblings.

'He broke my heart. He didn't want me. I'm not good enough, just a tom.' She shook her head sadly. 'Never good enough. Not even now. Now he has… he has you. He found a diamond.' She stabbed Anna's chest with her finger. 'You're a real diamond. Rare. The best. I'm just a bit of pretty, broken glass. Cheap. Not worth nothing. Never will be.' She fell back on the bed as Anna let go of her. 'Never ever…' she trailed off and began to snore quietly.

Anna was stunned. It couldn't be. It couldn't be him. Her heart painfully skipped a beat as she realised the implications of this. No wonder Tanya had gone off the rails tonight. Seeing Freddie, realising that this was the man Anna had spent all this time with, the man she was falling for.

'It was Freddie. The one who hurt you,' she whispered to the sleeping form in front of her. 'And I've bought it all back. I've hurt you.'

Tears formed in her eyes as she realised what she'd done to her friend. Those tears began to swell and fall as she realised that after this, she could never see Freddie again.

*

Tanya gingerly opened her eyes the next morning and immediately regretted it.

'Oh God,' she groaned as she held her aching head between her hands. She felt as though there were a hundred midgets inside her head, hacking away at the sides with pickaxes. She gingerly checked where she was. She was in bed, in her own room. Well, that was a small relief. But how did she get there? She fought through the fuzz enveloping her brain and thought back to the night before.

She had decided to take the edge off the shock of seeing Freddie and Anna. She'd sat down at the bar and let herself have a couple of drinks. Except those couple of drinks had turned into a lot of drinks. She groaned as she remembered battering Carl verbally. Then there was that punter – she'd made such a spectacle of herself. Then, like a frozen brick to the face, Tanya suddenly remembered the rest. She had drunkenly turned on her friend and nearly cost her her life.

'Oh God, what have I done?'

She curled into a ball and wished the ground would swallow her up. How was she going to show her face today? She needed to try to put things right. Would Anna ever forgive her? Her heart sank like a stone and she felt sick. Anna didn't know yet that her choice of one-night stand wasn't a coincidence. She couldn't tell Anna what she had done. She would lie and feign ignorance and pray that Anna believed her. Because if she knew the truth, she would never speak to her again.

She slowly pushed herself up onto her elbow and was about to swing her legs round when she saw the pint of water and two pills on her bedside table. Thank God for Anna, she thought, downing the pills and taking a deep drink from the glass. What a good friend she was. She broke into huge sobs. Even if Anna did accept her story and forgive her, she knew that she would never forgive herself.

Suddenly she remembered Anna dragging her through the flat. She replayed it in her head and groaned loudly when she remembered their conversation. She couldn't remember exactly what she'd said, but she knew that she'd told her about Freddie. She could remember Anna's face draining of colour and filling with horror. Shit. She kicked herself mentally. If she had just stayed bloody sober, this wouldn't have happened. She should never have told her. She should have just quietly sought Freddie out today and agreed with him that there was no need for Anna to know.

Their short affair was years ago, and as much as it had hurt her and left its scars on her heart, it was something that meant nothing to anyone else. She had fallen for Freddie back then, but she loved Anna so much more.

'Fuck sake, Tanya,' she berated herself. 'What have you done?' She rubbed her hands up and down her face, trying to sort herself out. 'Right.' She hoisted herself up and swung her legs over the side of the bed. Gingerly, she stood up, swaying slightly. Each step was more painful than the last. She took a few deep, slow breaths and silently promised herself that she was never drinking again.

'Anna?' she called out in a cracked, throaty voice. She listened, but there was no reply. She made her way down the hallway to the open lounge and kitchen. There was a note on the table.

Gone to cash up and sort out the club. There's a sandwich in the fridge for you and more painkillers in the cupboard. Anna x

Tanya sat down and began to cry again; deep racking sobs. How could Anna be so sweet to her after everything she had done?

CHAPTER FIFTY-THREE

Anna finished logging the last receipt and closed the laptop. She rubbed her eyes, red and sore from the crying and lack of sleep she had endured last night. Her phone went off and she stared at the screen. It was Freddie, asking if she was still on for meeting up for a drink later that day. She breathed out heavily as she picked up the phone and typed out her response.

I've got to work tonight. Things are getting busier here these days. No rest for the wicked. Sorry.

She hovered her thumb over the send button for a few seconds, then, with a sad expression on her face, sent the message. She couldn't quite bring herself to tell Freddie outright that she couldn't see him anymore. She would just keep herself busy with work and use that as an excuse to not make plans. It was easier that way. He would eventually tail off, and anyway, he would be fine. It wasn't as if he harboured any feelings for her deeper than friendship. Really, this was a good thing for her too. Without Freddie around, maybe she could fall out of love with him again. Unrequited love wasn't healthy for her anyway.

There was a soft knock on the door.

'Come in.'

Tanya walked in with a serious expression on her face. For once she was wearing casual clothes and only had the most basic amount of make-up on. Anna raised her eyebrows. Tanya really must be hungover to have left the house like this. She wouldn't usually even open the door unless she was sporting a full face and a show-stopping outfit.

'How are you feeling?' Anna asked gently. The guilt she felt at finding out about Freddie was still raw, even despite everything else.

'Oh, I've felt better.' Tanya chuckled wanly. She sat down in the chair opposite Anna. 'Anna,' she started, 'I'm so sorry. For everything. For the way I acted yesterday in the bar, for—'

'No, stop. Please. Tanya, you don't have to apologise. It's my own fault. If I hadn't been so secretive then I would have known from the beginning, and I would have never started spending time with Freddie.'

'It's not your fault at all,' Tanya replied. 'And as far as Freddie goes…' She took a deep breath. 'I acted awfully yesterday. It was a shock, yes, but that's no excuse for going off the rails. I never should have told you.'

'Of course you had to tell me, Tan. Freddie is the man you love, and I'm your best friend. There was never an option not to tell me.'

'Loved,' Tanya corrected. 'Anna, all that was a long time ago. I reacted badly yesterday. Unfairly, actually. And I am really sorry for that.'

'Well, we'll just agree to disagree then. You don't owe me an apology on that front – I understand. And it doesn't matter now anyway, because I'm not going to see Freddie again.' Anna tilted her head down to cement her statement. It hurt saying it, but it had hurt more seeing Tanya in such distress the night before.

'What? No! You need to see Freddie again. That's what I came down here to tell you. Oh God, I've messed things right up now,' she tutted, angry with herself. 'Listen, I saw the way he looked at you yesterday. He's in love with you, Anna. I've known Freddie Tyler for years and I can tell you now, he has never looked at a woman the way he does you. Never. You must tell him how you feel,' she beseeched. 'I won't get in the way. I'll be happy to see you happy. It was just the shock; it brought it all back. But it really *is* in the past, and I don't have any feelings for him anymore. I promise you. Please, Anna,' she begged, 'don't give up a chance of real love and happiness because of me.'

Anna looked at her friend's strained, open face. Of course Tanya would say that to her. Maybe there was some truth in her words. But if Tanya's past with Freddie had taught her anything, it was that loving Freddie Tyler only brought you heartache. She didn't want to end up like Tanya, devastated, suffering in the prison of unrequited love. And that was where she was heading. Because no matter what Tanya said, she knew Freddie didn't love her back. He couldn't. No. She needed to close the door on Freddie for her own good. This had just cemented her decision.

'You're wrong. The only thing Freddie feels towards me is friendship. That's it. And that's just not healthy to be around when you feel something more. So thank you, but I'm still not going to see him again. For my own sake.' She half smiled again and shoved the pile of papers she'd been collecting up into the wire tray to her left. 'But moving on to another subject, Tanya, what were you doing with those guys last night? I have to ask... did you know who they were?'

Anna's face was tense as she waited for Tanya's response. Tanya licked her dry lips and forced herself to maintain eye contact as she lied to her friend.

'No. Not until you said to me in the bedroom. But even then, in my drunk head I thought you was just joking, you know? I didn't think you were serious.' She looked down at her hands. 'I'm sorry, Anna. I wouldn't ever purposely endanger you. Last night was just—' she blew air out of her mouth and shook her head '—a total fuck-up. A total fuck-up from start to finish. I never usually get like that. It isn't me.' She looked back up with genuine honesty this time. 'It won't ever happen again. You mean the world to me, Anna.'

Tears threatened to spill over but she blinked them away. Anna swallowed the lump in her throat and nodded.

'OK,' she said quietly. 'I know I can trust you, Tanya. And in a world where I can't trust many people, that means a lot to me.'

'I know,' Tanya replied, her heart breaking. She would never forgive herself for what she'd done last night, but at least Anna had accepted the lie. She would take her sins to the grave and spend the rest of her days making up for it. She would never let her friend down again.

'Let's move on. And how about we go for lunch. Because you look like you need it. In fact, I don't think I've ever seen you look like such a tramp!'

The tension was lifted and they both laughed.

'Yeah, I've never felt so awful in my entire life.' She groaned and slipped down further into her seat.

'You should have stayed in bed,' Anna said.

'I was tempted, but I needed to get over here and put things right. Which reminds me, I need to apologise to Carl.'

Anna raised one eyebrow at her. 'Yes, you do! Come on, let's go.' She grabbed her coat and ushered Tanya back out the door, closing her mind to the whole thing.

Walking down the street, she thought about how much things had changed for her. She wasn't shaking in a corner somewhere; she wasn't hiding away in tears. She had walked straight back out into the world, holding her head high, running her business and living her life to the full.

A sense of pride ran through her. She may have been broken when she got here, but she certainly wasn't now. *It really is true what they say,* she thought. *What doesn't kill you makes you stronger.*

CHAPTER FIFTY-FOUR

Freddie stared out of the window of the car as Paul drove. Taking his phone out of his pocket, Freddie read Anna's last text again.

Sorry, I can't. I'm busy.

It had been nearly two weeks since the last time he had seen Anna. Since that game-changing meeting in her club. He had never pushed her into giving him more detail about her life than she wanted to give. When she had talked about her housemate she'd never used her name. He wished now that he had asked a few more questions.

The second he had seen Tanya, his heart had dropped. He watched the recognition, then confusion, then jealousy play across her face. Years before, he had been distracted by her obvious charms. He'd enjoyed some good times with her, had a bit of fun whenever he found himself at a loose end. But then one day she'd started getting ideas and he'd had to stop seeing her. He'd steered clear and given her the space to move on. Clearly, though, seeing her reaction as she spotted him in her club, she hadn't quite moved on completely.

He knew it would come out between Anna and Tanya eventually. They were so close. And from the following day,

Anna had made excuses not to see him. She hadn't outright told him she didn't want to meet up anymore, but her texts became shorter and she no longer suggested alternative times when she might be available. He knew what this meant. Friends stuck together, no matter what. Tanya would always come first.

He wasn't angry with Anna, or even Tanya. He was angry with himself. He was angry because he'd let someone mess with his head. He was Freddie Tyler. He was one of the heads of the largest and most prominent firm in London. But no matter how much he tried to put it to the back of his mind, he was still in a dark mood.

'You alright, Fred?' Paul asked, glancing sideways at his brother. Freddie had been unusually quiet for the last few days. Paul had just put it down to the growing tension in the household now that Michael was home, but he didn't seem able to shake it off while they were out either.

'I'm fine. Come on.' Freddie said curtly, as Paul parked the car.

The brothers walked down to Damien's Portakabin and entered without knocking.

'Freddie, Paul – good to see you,' Damien greeted them warmly. 'Here you go. Saw you coming so I poured you a coffee.' He handed them each a mug. They sat down in two of the vacant chairs laid out ready for the meeting.

'Thanks, Damien. Don't know how you stand the freeze down here all day,' Freddie said. He blew on his hands to try to warm them up a little. It was nearing the end of January and it had been the coldest week they'd seen all winter.

'Oh, I got used to it years ago.'

'Freddie, hi. I'm Tom.' The lanky youth leaning against the wall interrupted and stepped forward, holding his hand out, a confident smirk on his face. Freddie turned towards him and stared at him steadily with a cold gaze. Tom's hand hovered in the air for a few seconds before he pulled it back.

'Alright then,' he said sarcastically. 'Friendly chap, aren't you?' He laughed, amused. Freddie lifted an eyebrow, his eyes glinting dangerously. Paul caught the look on his brother's face and took a deep breath in, getting ready for whatever happened next. No one mugged off Freddie Tyler and got away with it. Tom looked around at the three sober faces in front of him. Damien tried to warn him by shaking his head slightly, but Tom didn't pick up on the subtle hint.

'OK, well, if you don't want to talk to me there are plenty of other people who will,' he said indignantly. Freddie frowned.

'You come in here asking for an audience with me,' he said, his voice dangerously quiet, 'you make the effort to lug your wares across the border—' he pointed at the box on the sideboard next to Tom '—and then you stand there with the attitude of someone meeting the local fucking grocer. Do you know who I am?' he questioned.

'Of course I know who you are,' the boy answered, snorting as though this was a ridiculous question.

'Right then.' Freddie nodded at this confirmation. He marched over to Tom, grabbed a handful of his thick, wavy hair and slammed his face down onto his knee with force. Tom's nose split open upon impact and blood spurted everywhere. Freddie released him and waited with his hands back in his pockets for Tom to regain his balance.

'My nose, my nose, oh my God! Look at what he's done,' he beseeched, looking helplessly from Damien to Paul and back to Damien. They didn't react. 'Look!' he yelled. He held his hands out. They were shaking and red from holding his nose.

Freddie came forward again, this time grasping his neck and slamming the man back against the wall. He lifted him a few inches, so that Tom's feet were barely able to reach the floor. Tom grasped at Freddie's wrist, trying and failing to fend off the much stronger man. Gone was his earlier swagger and bravado.

A lazy bum of a man, he had come from money but never liked to do anything that cost him actual effort. He had flitted from job to job until his father had given him seed money to invest in his own venture. Not knowing anything himself, he had followed his cousin into the illegal-spirits business. This was the first time that he'd actually met a potential new client. Never having dealt with the real world, he had no idea how to conduct himself.

'Right, you jumped-up little shit,' Freddie yelled in his face. 'Now if you hadn't known who I am, I might have let you off with a warning. Might. But you know who I am and you still came in here, mugging me off. Well, that don't sit too well with me. You understand me, boy?' Tom made gagging sounds; Freddie's vice-like grip was still crushing his windpipe. 'You ain't selling your shit to the local fucking barmaid. I'm Freddie Tyler,' he spat. 'I run this city. In more ways than your tiny little brain could possibly comprehend,' he snarled. 'The hardest men in this city wouldn't have the balls to come into a meeting with me and talk to me the way you just have. The only reason you haven't just signed your own death warrant is because I think you are genuinely just that stupid. Am I right?'

Tom made more gargling sounds, the veins in his temples sticking out and his face turning purple. Freddie relaxed his grip just a little.

'Yes,' he choked with difficulty. 'Yes, I am. I'm stupid.'

'Yes, you are fucking stupid,' Freddie said, releasing him and curling his lip in disgust. Tom fell to the floor, grabbing his neck and gulping deep breaths in. Freddie wiped the blood from Tom's nose off his hand with the old rag Damien passed to him before turning back to face Tom again. 'Now. You are going to take your box and go back to your little factory. You won't be supplying me, or any of the other big firms here in London, ever. I don't want to hear your name again. If I so much as hear a whisper of it, your cousin can kiss goodbye to his contracts too. Understood?'

'Yes,' Tom said shakily, still sitting in a pile on the floor.

'Good. Now fuck off.'

The young man got to his feet and ran out of the door immediately, leaving his box of booze behind. Freddie reached into his pocket and pulled out a thick pile of notes. Counting nearly half of them out, he put them onto Damien's desk.

'Sorry about your carpet. Get yourself a new one.'

'Thanks, Freddie,' Damien said in a normal tone as if nothing untoward had just occurred. 'We still OK dealing with his cousin? There's another shipment due to arrive this week.'

'Yeah, that's fine. He's a good supplier, no need to rock the boat there,' he said. 'We'll be off now. Catch you later.'

'Bye, mate.' The door closed behind the two brothers and Damien sat down in his chair, looking thoughtfully at the bloodstain on the carpet. There was definitely something up with Freddie. He shrugged. Oh well, wasn't any of his business.

CHAPTER FIFTY-FIVE

Anna stared at her computer, not really taking in the bright lines of figures. She had been there for over an hour without much to show for it. She rubbed her eyes, feeling drowsy. She hadn't been sleeping well since she'd found out about Freddie and Tanya. His invites to meet up were getting further and further apart. It tore her apart, every time she had to bluntly decline, but she knew it was the right thing to do.

Tanya kept on at her, trying to get her to reconsider, but Anna knew this was the only way. Seeing what Freddie had done to Tanya had made her realise that that could easily be her, if she didn't curb her addiction to Freddie now. He didn't feel the same way. It was time to move on and let her heart heal.

She picked up her coffee and took a sip, grimacing. It was stone cold. She'd been sitting here self-indulgently thinking about Freddie for far too long. She tutted, annoyed with herself. Picking up the next invoice, she began typing in the details.

Tanya's head popped round the door. 'You OK then, if I head off? Carl can lock up if you fancy coming home early. You've been here all day again,' she said. 'We could watch a girly film, crack open a bottle? I'll cook us something nice.' Then she screwed up her face. 'Actually maybe you should cook. We both know all I'm good for is an oven pizza.'

Anna laughed. 'As much as I do love your oven pizza, I really do need to get this finished. I'll probably be here late anyway, so I might as well stay until lock-up tonight.'

'OK,' Tanya said. 'If you change your mind, that's what I'll be doing. And Carl's on until finish anyway.' She waved goodbye and left.

After another hour of ploughing through paperwork, Anna glanced up at the clock. It was 7 p.m. The new act they'd hired would be debuting right about now. Sure enough, she heard the music go quiet and the dull drone of a deep voice making their introduction. These two had trained with a touring circus and were looking for a home in London where they didn't have to keep moving around. Tanya had given them a week-long trial, starting tonight, and Anna had promised her she would watch them perform.

Picking up her mug of cold coffee, Anna headed for the bar. She stood at the end, out of the way of the paying customers, and waited for one of her staff to become free. The new act was in position and the spotlights suddenly turned on them. In perfect synchronicity they began whirling and dancing around the stage, then jumped high up into the air and landed together in a perfect split. Anna nodded, impressed. The audience cheered as they picked up batons and began twirling them in their hands, faster and faster, until they burst into flames at each end. The audience gasped in awe at the edgy, exciting fire show, and Anna grinned, pleased with their latest choice.

One of her barmaids came over to exchange her empty cup for a fresh coffee. She smiled her thanks and disappeared back into her office. She didn't spot the man across the room at one of the smaller tables, watching her through narrowed eyes. She didn't see him reach into his pocket and pull out his phone.

*

Tony looked up from his card game, cursing in annoyance at being interrupted by a phone call.

'Stavros. What?'

'I've found her, boss. Anna. I've just seen her.'

'What?' Tony jumped up from the table. Remembering where he was, he turned back for a second and threw his cards in. 'All yours, I fold.' He grabbed his jacket and left the room. 'You're sure this time? Where?'

'Yeah, it's definitely her. In a club on Greek Street. Looks like she works here. She's in an office through the back. Just came out to the bar, got herself a drink and went back in.'

Tony wet his lips with his tongue, excited. His heart began to race. He had found the bitch.

'Who's with you?' he demanded.

'No one. I'm only here by chance,' Stavros admitted.

'Are you pieced up?'

'I've got a knife.'

'Good. Do you have your car?'

'Yes, just down the street.' He had been on his way through from another job when he'd decided to stop and take in some entertainment on the way home. He'd heard of this club and wanted to see it for himself. He hadn't realised at the time, of course, that he would strike gold in finding Anna.

'Do you think you can get her into your car on your own?'

Stavros paused, thinking about where he had left his vehicle. It was down a dark side street where there were no cameras. Something he always made sure of.

'Should be fine.'

'I'm going to text you an address. It's a warehouse of my cousin's, just outside of London, down the river. Get her there. I'm on my way.'

'Got it.' Stavros put the phone down.

Tony began to laugh – a deep, sadistic laugh. Her time was up. Tonight was the night he would finally kill that ungrateful, scheming bitch. But not straight away. He had some very special plans for her. He had spent months planning all the ways he was going to torture her, and he was going to make sure he savoured every second of it.

Oh yes, Anna Davis would die tonight. But not before he made her wish she'd never been born.

CHAPTER FIFTY-SIX

Stavros stood at the bar, pretending to watch the show in front of him. Being the one to find Anna would boost him right up the ladder. He would be greatly rewarded and be in Tony's good books for months to come.

He swirled his drink around in its glass. It had been an hour and a half since he'd seen her come out of that office. There was no back door; he had checked. She must still be in there.

The music changed and the limber fire-swinging girls from earlier came back on. He saw the door open out of the corner of his eye.

Anna walked out, her attention trained on the two girls on stage. She wandered near to him, like a mouse unaware that it was walking into the jaws of a snake, and Stavros stepped sideways so that he was right behind her. He moved forward and pressed the tip of the knife he was holding against her back, grasping her arm at the same time so that she couldn't move.

'Make a sound and I'll stab this knife right through you.'

Anna froze. Feeling the sharp blade pushing against her skin, she didn't try to pull away. Her eyes filled up and her body started to shake. This couldn't be happening. He couldn't have found her – not now. She squeezed the tears out of her eyes so that she could see again. Twisting her neck slowly to the side, she glanced at the man holding her. It was Stavros. Shit. She kicked herself for not seeing him before he had seen her. She tried to think quickly. Thoughts raced through her head as she desperately searched for a good idea. There wasn't one. If she didn't do exactly as she was told, she knew that the knife in her back would slip through her ribs faster than she could blink.

'OK, we're going for a little walk. You're not going to look at any of your staff on the way out, or anyone else. You got that?' She nodded, tears dripping off her chin. 'Don't even think about trying to make a run for it.' He shoved her forward, hiding the knife with his own body and holding her close.

They were out of the club in seconds, slipping out of the door to the side of the main entrance. Anna had hoped the bouncers would notice how she was being held, but it was a busy night on the door and they didn't even notice her as they left. She swallowed back a desperate sob. That had been her only hope.

'Where are we going?' she asked shakily, through terrified tears.

'You'll see,' Stavros answered gruffly. He didn't particularly care what happened to Anna. He was uncomfortable with being in such close proximity to her, having been used to avoiding her in the past. Tony was extremely possessive and didn't take kindly to anyone interacting with her. It was putting Stavros on edge, now that he had to talk to and touch her. It was probably safer to put her in the boot, he thought.

He hurried her across the busy London street and down the small, dead-end side road. It was dark and dank with only the reflected light from the main street reaching it. Anna's breathing spiked into fast, panicky breaths when she saw his car. She knew that if she got in that car, that would be the end of it.

'Please, Stavros, please, I'm begging you – let me go,' she pleaded. 'Let me go, say I got away. Say my bouncers saw you and saved me, anything. I'll make it worth your while. I have money. You saw my club. I'll give you anything you want.'

'Stop it,' he growled, pushing her against the car with the knife while he fumbled for his keys.

'Stavros, please,' she sobbed. 'He'll kill me, you know he will.' Stavros hesitated, something that resembled guilt flashing across his features just for a millisecond. Anna saw it and pushed forward. 'He'll torture me. He won't kill me quickly.' Her voice cracked. 'I saw that girl. I saw what he did to her. It will be so much worse for me.'

This seemed to remind Stavros of the lengths his boss had gone to in order to get this girl. He snarled and opened the boot, grabbing a pair of handcuffs. 'Put your hands behind your back,' he barked.

'Please, Stavros. You have to help me. Just let me go, please.' Her panicked cries became whispers as he pushed the blade harder into her back. 'OK, OK, I'm sorry. I'll be quiet, I'll be quiet,' she pleaded softly, wincing as the blade pierced her skin. Tears streamed unchecked now down her face.

Stavros cuffed her wrists behind her back roughly, then grabbed her hair and shoved her head into the boot. Her face scuffed along the rough carpet on the floor of the open boot as he lifted the bottom half of her body and dumped it unceremoniously inside. She bit her lip to stop herself crying out in pain as her face took the brunt of her weight and her neck twisted awkwardly. She tasted blood and realised she'd bitten through the skin. The boot slammed on top of her and she was enveloped in total darkness.

The car began to move, jolting her around. It backed out of the side street slowly, then jerked forward as Stavros began his journey. The action sent Anna flying back against the back of the boot. The back of her head connected with the metal door of the boot and this time she couldn't help but cry out.

She narrowed her eyes, trying to make out anything at all in the dark. There must be something she could do. She had read somewhere once that a woman had been saved from a kidnapping when she'd kicked out a tail light and waved out of the hole. The person in the car following her had called the police, alarmed. She clearly hadn't been restrained in handcuffs though, Anna thought. It was a long shot, but it was all she had. She had to do something.

She wriggled, trying to turn herself over so that she could face the back of the boot, but after several attempts she gave up. She couldn't turn over her twisted arms and the boot wasn't high enough for her cramped legs to move properly anyway. She caught her breath and felt the edges of the cramped space with her foot. She gauged where she thought the tail lights would be and kicked out as hard as she could. As her foot connected, her body rocked forward and she struggled not to end up on her face. Pulling her left knee up and forward to spread out her balance, she tried again. That was better. She pushed her right leg forward, then kicked with all her strength, not stopping until she physically couldn't keep kicking anymore. Nothing happened. Nothing gave way.

She laid her now aching leg down and sighed, squeezing her eyes shut. The tears began to fall again, scalding the graze on her cheek from the rough carpet. There was no escape. She'd tried everything she could think of and there was no chance of Stavros showing pity on her. If he let her go, *he* would be the one to suffer the fate that Tony had in store for her. He knew that as well as she did. She shivered as she thought of what lay ahead of her. She squeezed her eyes shut and sobbed, defeated. The only thing she could wish for now was a quick death.

CHAPTER FIFTY-SEVEN

Freddie leaned against the tiled wall of the shower, letting the water cascade over his neck and down his broad, muscular back. It had been a long day. He ran his hands up and down his face, trying to shake off the heavy mood that seemed to follow him around lately. Turning off the water, he stepped out and wrapped a thick, soft towel around his waist.

As he got back to his bedroom, he picked up his phone to see he'd had eighteen missed calls from Bill Hanlon. What was going on?

Before he had a chance to dial back, the phone rang again. He picked it up on the first ring.

'Bill, what's happening?'

'Freddie!' Freddie had never heard Bill sound so urgently relieved. 'It's Anna. The Greeks have taken her.'

'What?' Freddie exclaimed in disbelief.

'I'm following them now; I'm on the A13 heading east. Just get in your car and call me from there. I'll direct you and tell you the rest when you're en route. Bring guns.'

Freddie didn't bother to waste time answering. He put the phone down and grabbed his clothes.

'Paul! Paul!' he yelled at the top of his voice as he shoved his legs into his trousers.

Paul appeared in the hallway almost immediately, concerned at the urgency in Freddie's voice.

'What?'

'Tool up, now!' Freddie demanded. 'Get the keys and be in the car in two minutes.'

Paul disappeared and Freddie heard the clunks as Paul grabbed the gun from under his mattress. Freddie lifted his mattress to collect his own. Shrugging on a jumper and coat, he shoved the gun into the inside pocket, then ran downstairs, Paul already ahead of him with the front door open.

'Freddie?' Thea questioned as she saw her brothers running past. He didn't answer. He was already in the car. He revved the engine as Paul slammed the passenger door shut and the wheels screeched as he raced down the street. He dialled a number from the car phone.

'Sammy, can you be outside the front of your place with two guns in exactly five minutes?'

'Yes,' came the immediate answer. No questions, as Freddie had known there wouldn't be.

'Good. Be ready.' He clicked the button to end the call and rang Bill, who answered straight away.

'What happened?'

'Right,' he started. 'I had one of my boys on Tony tonight. I was following another one of his guys, Stavros. He's been getting a little too close to your whereabouts the last few days and I wanted to be sure there wasn't a change of plan. He stopped off this evening at Club Anya on Greek Street. He just seemed to be watching the show, but the next thing

I know, Anna comes out from the back somewhere, and he puts a knife against her back. Forced her to walk out quietly.' He still didn't know whether or not Freddie was aware of her connection to Tony. 'I didn't even know she worked there.' If he'd known, if he'd spotted her earlier, when Stavros first had, he would've tried to warn her. He liked Anna.

'She owns it,' Freddie said, sighing heavily. 'Fuck!' he shouted, hitting the steering wheel. He breathed deeply, trying to calm down. 'What then, Bill?' he said, back to business. He indicated to turn left towards Sammy's place.

'He took her outside. I followed them but couldn't grab her; he had the knife right up against her ribs. He cuffed her and put her in the boot. I jumped in my car and I'm following them now. Just gone past Dagenham, still going east. Not sure where he's taking her yet. Where are you?'

'Maybe fifteen minutes behind you. I'm going for Sammy now.' As he said this, he pulled over to the side of the road and Sammy jumped in the back. Freddie sped off again.

'Put your foot down, Fred, because I have no idea what to expect. I haven't seen any of them out this way before.'

'On it.' He put the phone down.

'What the fuck is he doing?' Sammy asked Paul. Paul had just filled him in.

'I have no idea, but he won't be breathing for long after this.' Freddie's lips formed a thin line and he focused on the road. He couldn't understand it either. It wasn't in keeping with the rest of Tony's game. Going after big players was one thing; going after civilians or family members of your enemy was another thing entirely. No matter how dirty or vengeful things got in their dealings, people in these categories were totally off limits.

Clearly the reason they had taken Anna was to get to him, Freddie surmised. Tony must think that Anna was his girlfriend. When he finally had Tony in front of him he was going to give him the kicking of his life before he sent him back to his maker. He had better find Anna totally unharmed or not only would he kill Tony, but he would rain hell down on North London for years to come.

He put his foot down on the accelerator. He hoped and prayed that he wouldn't get there too late.

*

The car came to a stop and Anna's ears pricked up, trying to make out what was going on around her by the muffled sounds. Suddenly the boot swung open. Anna looked up fearfully, expecting to see Tony's face. She almost felt relief when she saw that it was still only Stavros. Not that it would be for long, she thought.

Stavros grabbed her awkwardly by her upper arms and yanked her up over the lip of the boot. She teetered there for a moment while he tried to shift her weight, then she fell onto the ground, face down in the dirt. She spat out some grit that had made its way into her mouth. Stavros picked her back up and left her on her feet. She stretched out, her muscles complaining from the cramped-up position they had just been in.

'Can you take these off me please?' she asked, shaking her wrists behind her back.

'No,' Stavros grunted. 'Move. That way.' He shoved her in the direction of a small warehouse. Anna looked around as she walked, slowly. She couldn't see any other cars. There was a wire fence surrounding the immediate area and the warehouse, with large grass-covered verges surrounding most of that. They appeared to be somewhere remote, but that was all she could tell about her location. She wished she'd put her phone in her back pocket, but unfortunately it was sitting on the desk in her office.

The stars were bright in the clear night sky. It would have been beautiful, Anna thought, if she wasn't walking towards the scene of her own murder.

They entered the metal-sheet-covered building. It was dark in there. Stavros turned on the one solitary light bulb that hung low from the high ceiling. It swayed slightly in the breeze coming in from the open door. Picking up a wooden chair from the side of the room, he put it down under the light, dragging Anna by the arm as he did so.

'Sit. Stay there or I'll cut you. Got it?' She nodded. He didn't go far, only to the corner to grab some rope and a hessian sack, keeping one eye on her the whole time. Hurrying back, he tied the rope around her middle, securing her to the chair. He tied her legs to the thin wooden feet of the chair and then, without warning, shoved the large hessian sack over her head and shoulders.

'No! Get this off me!' She struggled but immediately stopped when a large hand grabbed her throat through the sack. She nearly passed out with terror. Was it Tony? Was he here? She couldn't see. Stavros's voice came from near her ear.

'Shut up or it'll be worse for you. Be silent.' Anna trembled as he backed away.

Please let me die now, she prayed silently.

*

Freddie parked where Bill had instructed, around the back of the building, off the track where no one would be able to see them. The three men ran over to where Bill was waiting for them in some bushes.

'Bill.' Freddie nodded in greeting.

'Freddie, Paul, Sam,' Bill greeted them grimly. 'They're in there. It's just the two at the moment, but I caught a phone call. Tony's on his way. I don't know how many will be with him.'

'OK, good. That's good,' Freddie replied, nodding. His eyes were bright and hard. 'Sammy brought you a gun. I figured you wouldn't be carrying.'

Sammy handed the gun over and Bill thanked him. He hadn't been carrying anything. None of them did unless there was a reason. It wasn't worth the risk of getting caught.

'Can we get in?'

'Yes, the door's open, and from what I can tell, all he has is a knife.'

'OK, then that's what we do. We go in there now, get her out and knock that fucker out. Then we wait for Tony.' His eyes glinted coldly in the moonlight. 'He ain't leaving this place alive.'

'Lead the way,' said Sammy. Freddie looked at Bill.

'You OK to come in with us? I wouldn't blame you if you want to leave now. You've done more than your share tonight.'

Freddie patted Bill's shoulder to let him know he meant it. But Bill shook his head.

'No, I'm all in. I wouldn't forgive myself if something went wrong and I'd clocked off like a wanker. And anyway, I like Anna. And Amy would have my balls for earrings if I left now,' he joked. They all laughed.

Paul looked back at the road. 'We should hurry if we want to be a step ahead,' he said.

'Yeah, let's go.' Freddie ran ahead silently, the others following.

Freddie stared through the crack of the partly open door. Anna was tied up in the middle of the room with her back to him. She wasn't making any noise. Freddie began to worry, then noticed her nervously clenching and unclenching her bound hands. He closed his eyes in relief. She was alive. For now at least.

CHAPTER FIFTY-EIGHT

They barged in and marched over to Stavros, Freddie in the lead. He gasped in shock at the sight of the four men coming towards him with their guns pointed in his direction. He blinked and his head darted back and forth between the four very angry faces as they approached. Stavros held his knife out in front of him, but he already knew this was pointless. He was outmanned and outgunned. The men reached him and Freddie immediately took the knife off him.

'Get on the floor,' he yelled in Stavros's paling face. 'Get on the fucking floor now!' His face turned red with rage as he spat the words at the other man.

Stavros got on his knees. Freddie took a step back and kicked him in the face with all his might. Stavros fell back on the floor, out cold. Freddie wiped the spit off his chin with the back of his hand. He put his gun back in his pocket and straightened his hair. He breathed in deeply, trying to dispel the worst of his rage before Anna saw his face.

'Tie him up. Quickly,' he ordered.

Paul went in search of some rope, while Bill and Sammy began to drag Stavros from the floor to one of the metal support beams. Freddie walked over to Anna's shaking form.

He made to lift the hessian sack, but as his shadow fell across it she began to scream.

'No, no! Get off me, no!' Her screams began to turn hysterical, and she struggled against her restraints.

'Anna! Anna, stop! It's OK.' Freddie stopped her chair from going over and pulled the hessian sack off. She was still screaming uncontrollably, convinced it was Tony. As her face came into view he could see her eyes were squeezed shut. She was still sobbing and screaming, not having taken in his words. 'Anna!' he yelled, grabbing her face between his hands. 'It's me – it's Freddie.' Anna stopped struggling. Slowly, not quite believing it, she opened her eyes.

'Freddie? What… what are you doing here?'

He knelt down in front of her, grasping her head between his hands and turning it gently from side to side.

'What has he done to you?' he said, his voice full of emotional anger. He took in the grazes down her cheek, the cut on her swollen lip and the mud smeared across her face. Her eyes were swollen and her face blotchy from crying for so long.

'Nothing, I'm fine,' she croaked. Her voice was hoarse from all the screaming. She cleared her throat as he set about untying her. 'Freddie, what are you doing here?' she repeated.

She had no idea how he had known she was here, but he'd put himself in grave danger by saving her. He had no idea what he was really dealing with. Tony would arrive at any minute.

Freddie still hadn't answered. He was trying to work out how to break it to her that it was his fault that she had been kidnapped. He finished untying her and pulled her up from the chair.

'That can wait. Are you OK? Nothing broken?'

'No, I'm fine, but, Freddie, we need to go,' she urged, her eyes darting towards the door. 'Please, we have to leave right now.' She grabbed his arm and tried to pull him towards the door but he stopped her.

'Not quite yet. There's something I've got to do. But you're going to be OK, I promise. I'll explain everything later.'

'*You'll* explain everything?' Anna questioned, frowning. 'Don't you need me to explain things?'

'What?' Freddie stepped back and looked her in the eye as though she was mad. They both paused, unsure what was going on.

Bill stepped forward and cleared his throat. 'Um, I don't mean to interrupt, but Tony's going to be here any second. If we're going to take him, we need to get in position. Preferably outside, so if there's too many we can disappear.'

Anna shook her head, trying to understand. What was Bill talking about? 'Wait, how do you know about Tony?'

'What do *you* know about Tony?' Freddie asked, totally confused.

Bill groaned internally. He hadn't wanted to get involved; it wasn't his business. He stepped forward.

'OK, look… Freddie, she's Tony's ex. She ran away and has been hiding from him ever since she arrived over this way. He's had a small army out looking for her on the quiet – that's why she was taken.'

Anna's eyebrows shot up, and she felt her cheeks grow hot. How had Bill known all of this? He looked away towards Freddie.

'It wasn't my business, Fred. I kept out of it.'

Paul sighed and walked over to the door to keep watch.

Freddie studied the other man's face, his brain working ten to the dozen. He didn't blame Bill for not bringing this to light sooner. You kept your mouth shut in this game as far as other people's business was concerned. Still, it pissed him off that he was only finding this out now. What had she been doing with someone like Tony Christou?

'You were with Tony?' he asked.

She nodded. 'Yes. Or rather I was kept by Tony. I wasn't there by choice.' She held her head up and felt a stab of anger at the disappointment she saw on Freddie's face.

'Don't you dare judge me,' she said heatedly. 'You don't know anything of my life back then. I was naïve, an idiot, and I fell into his trap. He turned on the charm, used my vulnerabilities to get me right where he wanted. Then he beat me and threatened me for three years. Told me if I ever left that he would hunt me and kill me. That was the only reason I stayed.' She blinked away the tears, not wishing to break down in front of him.

'I hated him. I was a prisoner. Our local hospital became my second home.' She laughed bitterly. 'Broken bones, cuts, bruises, concussions – you name it, it's on my file. The authorities asked me time and time again if I wanted to tell them anything, but how could I? I was too afraid. The only reason I worked up enough guts to run away was because I finally just gave up on life. I realised I would rather die trying to leave than exist another day there.'

There was silence as everyone took in this new information. She looked around at them. 'How did you know, Bill?' she asked.

'I met you a couple of years ago at a meeting Tony held at your house.'

Anna frowned; she didn't remember Bill's face. If she had recognised him, she would have run, months ago.

'You should have said something to me when we met,' she said accusingly.

'Perhaps. But you seemed to be happier thinking no one knew you.'

Freddie suddenly snapped out of his silent daze.

'That fucking bastard. That absolute fucking bastard.' His anger and horror was mounting as exactly what Anna had been through hit him. No wonder she had always been so secretive and reserved. She was on the run from a monster. 'So that's why you were taken tonight? Not because of me?'

Anna turned back to Freddie. 'You? Why would I have been taken because of you?'

Freddie narrowed his eyes and bit his lip. This was the last scenario in the world that he could have imagined being in with Anna when he told her who he really was. Perhaps this was the worst one too, because once she knew that he had the same background as the man who had tortured her for years, she would run away as fast as her legs could carry her.

'Do you know what Tony did for a living?' he asked carefully, studying her face.

'Of course I knew,' she replied. 'Like Bill said, they had meetings in the house—' She stopped and frowned. Bill had been in one of the meetings. Which meant that Bill was involved in that sort of work. She suddenly looked down at the guns that Bill and Sammy still held in their hands.

'We're in a similar line of business,' Freddie said gently. 'The life is — well, I'm in that life. It's who I am,' he admitted.

Anna nodded, turning away and pacing the floor slowly. It was a lot to take in. Freddie's words echoed in her head. He was a face. Freddie was a face, like Tony. Was Freddie like Tony? Had she really been that stupid all over again? Freddie seemed to pick up her line of thought.

'I'm not like Tony, Anna. I don't treat people I care about the way that Tony treated you. I may be in the same line of work, but that's it.'

She studied his face. Was he really the person she thought he was? His greeny-blue eyes pierced into her and she thought back to that day on the beach. Her heart softened at the memory of his face close to hers, both of them in a heap on the sand, laughing. Freddie wasn't Tony. He wasn't anything like Tony.

'I know,' she answered softly. 'I know you aren't.' She smiled, then grimaced at the pain that shot through her cut, swollen lip as she did so.

'Freddie, I see lights,' Paul said, raising the alarm. He jogged back over. 'We don't have time to get outside. Get to either side of the door in the shadows. Cut him off at least, once he's in.'

Freddie looked at Anna. 'It's OK. I won't let him hurt you again.'

He pulled her up from the chair. 'He will never, *ever* touch you again. I won't let it happen. I'm going to finish this once and for all. For both of us,' he stated vehemently, his eyes boring seriously into hers. He searched her face. He needed her to be on board with this.

Anna nodded. She still wasn't quite sure what Tony had done to Freddie, but she figured she was about to find out. Suddenly she felt invigorated. Tony was here, expecting to find her tied up and scared and instead he was going to find Freddie.

'I'll sit in the chair. Draw him into the middle of the room. Go.' She pushed Freddie towards the shadows where the others were already in place. She could hear the car doors closing now. One, she counted, then two. Two people. OK.

'Are you sure?' Freddie asked, concerned.

'Yes – now go,' she ordered.

Freddie crept off to the side and Anna sat down again, her back to the door. Her nerves jangled now that she could no longer see what was going on behind her. She squeezed her eyes shut. It was going to be OK. She wasn't alone this time.

CHAPTER FIFTY-NINE

Seconds later she heard the sound of the door being banged open and fast, heavy footsteps coming towards her. As they got closer, she stood up and turned around. Tony stopped, surprised to see her stand, but Anna's new-found strength seemed to sap out of her the moment she laid eyes on him. There he was – her own personal demon.

She looked at him properly as they stood there, facing each other. He wasn't a particularly tall man, nor muscular. His strength had always come from packing his weight into each punch. A few stone overweight these days and broad, he had plenty to throw at her. His black hair was beginning to speckle with grey and his swarthy face was starting to puff out. He had been handsome once, Anna remembered. He still was in a way, though she could no longer see it through her hatred for the man. All she could see now when she looked at him was his rotten, evil core. His large brown eyes, which she had once thought looked warm and passionate, were glinting dangerously. His madness shone through them as he grinned wickedly at her. She shuddered as the sight of him brought back a flood of horrific memories.

'There you are, you slippery little bitch. Happy to see me?' He laughed at the disgust on her face. 'Oh, you look at me that way now. I'll wipe that off your smug, ugly face soon enough.'

Tony looked her up and down slowly, his words becoming more and more excited as he stepped forward. 'Did you see your twin on the news? She was perfect to practise on. Her heart gave out a little too soon for my liking though. I won't let that happen with you. I'll make sure to keep yours beating well beyond the point you beg me to kill you. And you will beg…'

Anna stepped back, her eyes shooting to the men who were now creeping up behind Tony and Angelo.

'I don't fucking think so, mate,' Sammy said.

Tony turned just in time to see the gun handle being smashed down on his temple. Angelo turned but before he knew what was happening, he got knocked out too.

*

Tony groaned as he came around. He tried to put his hands to his head but his wrists were bound tight. What had happened? He blinked his eyes open and looked around as his focus cleared. He was tied to a chair. Stavros was tied similarly on one side and Angelo on the other. Angelo was cursing. Stavros was just hanging his head, looking terrified. Tony honed in on Anna. She was perched sideways on the edge of a fold-down table that had been dragged over, one foot on the floor. She was studying her nails, seemingly unfazed. Tony's blood boiled. *How dare she look so comfortable?* To one side of her leaned a well-built man wearing a dark expression. Three more men lurked around them. All of them were carrying guns. He recognised one of them as Bill Hanlon. Licking his dry lips, he honed in on this one piece of information that he had.

'Billy the Banker… Or should I say Billy the Wanker, seeing as I'm currently tied to a fucking chair for some reason.'

Bill didn't rise to the comment, staying silent as they all stared hard at him. Tony narrowed his eyes and, picking another one of them, tried a different approach.

'She's alright in bed, I'll give you that. But a bird ain't worth causing hag with the likes of me over. Especially one that's been mine for so long. She tell you how many years she's been leeching off me, did she?' He aimed this at Freddie, seeing as he looked like the main man, but not a flicker crossed the man's cold face. His fury began to bubble over.

'Do you know who I fucking am?' he raged. 'You might think you're some knight-in-fucking-armour crew here, but you haven't got a clue who you're dealing with. Except you,' he aimed at Bill. 'You should know better. If you lot don't let me and my men out right now, you're gonna wish you'd never been born, you jumped-up little cunts.' He seethed with anger and strained hard against his restraints.

Freddie stepped forward and stopped in front of him. 'Do *you* know who *I* am?' he questioned, curiously.

'No I fucking don't, you no-mark,' Tony spat back.

'In that case, your plan was doomed from the start really. It's never a good idea to plan to take someone out when you don't even know what they look like.'

Tony didn't answer. Freddie could see the cogs turning slowly in his head. 'I believe that you were planning to take me out over a friendly meet up. Was that how it went down with Big Dom?'

'Freddie Tyler,' Tony hissed, the penny finally dropping.

'Ahh, you've caught up. Good.' Freddie scratched his chin, pacing up and down in front of the three men. 'So how *did* it go down with Big Dom then? Which brainless lackey did you get to pull the trigger? I'm curious to know what made you think you'd get away with it.'

'I'm the one who put that bullet in his head, you asshole,' Angelo spat. 'And I'm no fucking lackey. When we get out of here we're taking you down,' he spewed, puffing out his small chest.

Freddie shook his head, dismissing the ridiculous statement. He turned to Tony and raised his eyebrows.

'He really is stupid, isn't he? I can see why you picked him. He even thinks he still has a chance of walking out of here.' He stopped and leaned in nearer to Angelo's face. 'The minute you walked through that door your chances of leaving here alive were zero. Is that clear enough for your little brain?'

He left the young man with his mouth flapping open, unsure what to say. Tony glared at Angelo.

Freddie looked at Tony, overcome with the urge to rip him apart. He pulled his fist back and smashed it into his face without warning.

'You took out Big Dom.' He hit him again. 'You planned to take me out and steal my businesses.' He punched his face twice more. 'And now I find out that you repeatedly hurt someone I care about.' He grabbed Tony's bloodied face and shoved the end of his gun into his mouth.

'No, wait!' Anna cried out. She stepped forward.

'Anna?'

Tony started laughing; a deep, mocking laugh. 'She won't let you kill me. She would never forgive you – she's too fucking soft. You're screwed, mate.' His laugh grew louder. Anna took Paul's gun from him and, cocking it, pointed it at him. He stopped laughing.

'You're wrong, Tony,' she said, her voice unsteady. 'You were wrong about a lot of things.' She stepped in front of him and her voice grew stronger. 'You know nothing about the person I really am, because you never allowed me to *be* a person. I was your servant. I was a punchbag. But I was never allowed to be a person. I *will* let Freddie kill you today. I might even watch. And you know something?' She cocked one eyebrow, coldly. 'I'll be glad.'

Anna stared down at the man who had ruined her life for so long, the man who had haunted her dreams and who had nearly managed to kill her. His nose was bleeding where Freddie had hit him. He was staring at her with unbridled hatred.

'You beat me. You used me. You tried to destroy me in every way possible. But I escaped you, didn't I? You never truly broke me. I've flourished out here in this world. *My* world. I have friends, and I have a good business that I built with my own two hands. Mine,' she yelled. 'I'm not stupid. I'm not worthless.'

Angry tears began to spill down her face. Tony sneered at her and laughed. She saw red. Stepping forward, she smacked the handle of the gun across his face. She put all of her force into the blow and his head shot to the side, silencing him.

'Yeah, I'd be quiet too if I were you,' she spat.

He looked up at her with a smirk on his face.

She stared at him bitterly and began to tremble under the weight of her emotions. She handed the gun back to Paul.

'You took so much from me for so long. You will never take anything from me again.' She turned and walked away, her energy spent.

'No matter what you do, you'll always be worthless,' Tony called after her.

She turned back and a half smile crept over her face.

'You can say whatever you want. It means nothing now. At the end of the day, Tony, I've won.' She paused, looking him up and down, her face hard. 'I'm off to live my life, exactly how I want to.' She gave Freddie the nod and walked out of the warehouse.

'Anna. Anna! You fucking slag, get back here!' Tony yelled. How dare she leave him to die like this? How dare she? He turned back to face the barrel of Freddie's gun.

'You're lucky,' Freddie said quietly. 'If she hadn't been here I'd have beaten you until you begged me for death. It's funny the form that small mercies take.'

He pressed the gun against the other man's forehead and pulled the trigger.

CHAPTER SIXTY

Outside Anna heard the sharp crack of the gunshot. Looking up at the stars, she ran her hands through her long, dark hair and breathed a heavy sigh of relief. Her body relaxed for the first time in as long as she could remember, as she finally let go of all the fear and anger that had been weighing her down for so long. She was free. He had succeeded in killing some parts of her, but he hadn't won. Perhaps if he hadn't put her through all that he did, she would still be soft. Perhaps she would have asked Freddie to spare him. Now, though, he was finally gone, and she would never have to hide again. She smiled – a slow, elated smile. She felt so weightless. She could live freely again. And she could finally reunite with her parents.

*

Freddie wiped the end of his gun with his top and put it back into his pocket. The other two men started begging for their lives.

Sammy approached Freddie. 'What do you want done with these two?'

'That one signed Anna's death warrant.' He pointed to Stavros. 'And that one put the bullet in Big Dom.' He moved his finger to point at Angelo. 'They both need disposing of.

And that,' he addressed the two tied-up, snivelling men, 'is me being fucking kind.'

Paul tapped him on the shoulder. 'You take her back to London; we can finish this and sort the clean-up here.'

Sammy and Bill nodded their agreement.

'OK. Come by the club tomorrow evening all of you, when you get a chance. And thank you. For everything.' He patted all of them on the shoulder as he passed. Nothing more needed to be said.

He stepped outside into the cold and made his way over to Anna. She was standing a few feet ahead of him, staring up at the sky, her arms crossed over the thin jumper that she was wearing. His heart leaped when he saw her. He had come close to losing her forever tonight. It had scared him, and there was very little in this world that could scare a man like Freddie.

Everything that had just taken place had put things in stark perspective. They would go back to London and she would thank him, before going back to distancing herself. He was going to lose her anyway. Now was the time to tell her how he felt. At least that way, when she disappeared from his life, he'd know he'd done everything he could.

'Freddie, I—'

'No, Anna, please listen to me. I'm sorry you had to find out who I am this way. I shouldn't have hidden it from you. But it is what it is. I know that you've always seen me as just a friend and that now, considering my past with Tanya, you don't want to see me anymore. I get that. I do. But—' He lifted his hand to her face, pushing back a loose strand of hair from her forehead, and stared into her eyes. 'I need you to know something. I love you, Anna. And if you never talk to me again, that's fine. At least now I know you're safe. But I had to do this, just once.'

Freddie grasped Anna's head with both hands and pulled her lips to his. He kissed her deeply, with a passion he had never felt before. To his surprise, after initially tensing, Anna pulled him close and kissed him back with just as much fervour.

Eventually Freddie pulled back and looked into Anna's face. It shone with happiness.

'I—' She laughed in disbelief. 'I thought that it was just me. I didn't think you felt the same way.'

Freddie shook his head. 'What have we been doing, for fuck's sake?' He bent his head and put his forehead to hers. 'We've wasted so much time.'

He looked at her soberly. 'Anna…' He stepped back slightly, giving her room. 'You know who I am now. That's never going to change. This is me. Can you accept that?'

He waited for her answer, not sure what it would be. She had suffered badly over the years with Tony. He wouldn't blame her for wanting to start afresh, out of that world completely.

But she stepped forward and grabbed his hand, squeezing it and pulling him back to her.

'I accept you, Freddie Tyler. Not in spite of who you are, but because of it. I know exactly who you are. And I love you too. That's all that matters.' She pulled his face back down to hers and kissed him again as though it was their last minute on earth. Freddie wrapped his arms around her and picked her up, never losing contact with her lips.

Carrying Anna off towards the car, Freddie felt invincible. Tonight he had neutralised his biggest threat, saved the woman he loved and was finally holding her in his arms for the first time. Their world would go on. There would always be another fight, another problem. He still had to watch his back and keep people in line. He would always have to keep one step ahead of the law. But right now, he had the woman he loved in his arms. And that, as she had said herself, was all that mattered.

A LETTER FROM EMMA

Dear readers,

Firstly, thank you so much for choosing my book and entering into my little world for a while. I hope you enjoyed the story and the journey it took you on.

This book has taken me many years and personal experiences to create. I started writing the first draft back in 2012, in my old home in North London. Initially, writing this story was a way for me to vent some of my emotions after leaving a very abusive relationship. As I grew stronger, I left the book behind me and moved on to a new chapter of my life.

Later in 2015, I rediscovered the manuscript and decided to carry on. Over time, my characters developed into really interesting people, and they truly came to life. This really excited me. Suddenly it became so much more than just a little story for myself.

In March 2017 I self-published the book, and towards the end of the year, I was approached by my publisher and together we edited it and developed it even further before re-releasing it as *Runaway Girl* in May 2018.

I'm so proud of what this book has become and of the strong, colourful characters within it. I hope you loved Anna,

Freddie, Tanya and the rest of them as much as I do. Except Tony, of course – no one loves Tony!

If you enjoyed *Runaway Girl*, I would really appreciate you leaving a review. I love to read all the comments from my readers, seeing what you enjoyed or what you hope to see next.

And to keep up with what I'm doing and where I am with things, please come follow me on my Facebook page.

Finally, thank you so much again for all of your support and keep your eyes peeled for the next instalment in the series!

Best wishes,
Emma x

f emmatallonofficial
🐦 EmmaEsj
🖥 www.emmatallon.com

ACKNOWLEDGEMENTS

I want to thank all the friends and family around me who have supported me through writing, rewriting, editing and finishing this book. It has been an amazing journey and it would not have been the same without such valuable support and help along the way.

I want to thank my amazing editor Helen for seeing something in here worth taking on and for working so dedicatedly with me to make this the best book it could be.

And finally I want to say a special thank you to my partner Richard, who probably still won't actually read my book (he's waiting for the film apparently), but whose belief has been unwavering.

Here is to us all journeying together through the next one!